A publication of Lone Wolf Press Ltd.

Amy Wolf

Table of Contents

"Yin and yang, male and female, strong and weak, rigid and tender, heaven and earth, light and darkness, thunder and lightning, cold and warmth, good and evil... the interplay of opposite principles constitutes the universe."

- Confucius.

Acknowledgments

Tim Whittome, Proofreader
Jenn T., Proofreader

Dedication:

This book is dedicated to the memory of my mom, Sylvia Faith Wolf (1938–2020),

our beloved "Did"

And Ted E. Bear, my sweet dog

DRAGONS OF LIGHT AND CHAOS
Copyright: Amy Wolf 2022
Published: May 15, 2022
Paperback edition
ISBN: XX

Find out more about the author and upcoming books online at:

https://amy-wolf.com & @AmyWolf_Author on Twitter

Find out more about this book at https://www.facebook.com/amywolfauthor/

To download a FREE FANTASY BOOK, go to:

https://amy-wolf.com

TikTok: https://www.tiktok.com/@amywolf_author

NAMES

Abarōz – 17-year-old Dardan girl who rebels
Shāhpuhr – boy of the forest
Rastag – Abarōz's father
Adrina – Abarōz's mother
S̄āh Al-razi – ruler of Dardan
Bükrek – a dragon of creation
Sangal – dragon of chaos
Şahmeran – snake queen
Kavad – Dardan escapee
Husrav – evil vizier
Manuchehr – a Peril
Berislav – werewolf leader
Catanes – Shāhpuhr's dragon
Mihrab – Abarōz's dragon
Iatopa – Abarōz's dragon
Az – Abarōz's dragon Iotapa
Baba Yaga – a witch
Pabag – an Ōšmurdan
Tengri – god of creation
The new god – Jesus

PLACES

Dardan – an underground city
Šahr – adjoining city to Dardan
Razūr – forest
Rōd – river in Razūr
Gehān – world / name of country
Paristan – land of the Perils
Belarod – the near North
The North – land of bad dragons
The South – land of good dragons
Abaxtar – far Northern land

CREATURES

Erbörü – werewolves
Yaryond – centaurs

Gurg Kamāl – wolf-headed dragons
Maran – Şahmeran's snakes
Xūg – wolverine

OTHER

Mihr – the sun
Māh – the moon
axtar – star
ebren – a dragon
Bērūn – the outside
Azēr – underground
zarr – gold mine
Zarran – miner
dahigān – farmer
Axwaš – The Discarded
Aswār of Ebrens – a dragonrider
Ōšmurdan – a Tallyman
dēnārs – money
zand – tribe
Zeh̬n̥ Xɑn – a mind reader
dahigān – farmer
Hamwar – Level of Dardan
father – Pid
mother – Mād
Hrōmāyīg – the Greeks
Nārig – lady of the house

GEHĀN
Abaxtar
The North
Razūr
River Rōd
The Bērūn
The South
Šahr
Dardan
Catheral
Šāh
Zarr
The Azēr
2022

The Azēr

The light of the candle, though dim, hurt Abarōz's eyes. She rose from her bed of rock, tossing back straw which served as a mattress.

"Abarōz, you overslept!"

Her mother Adrina slammed down stone bowls filled with their morning meal. Her father, Rastag, dragged himself to a seat at their rough stone table.

"Daughter," he said, accepting his portion of oats, "you must help your mother today and not go running off."

"Yes, father," said Abarōz, digging a spoon into her pebbled bowl.

She sighed. Every morning, it seemed like she got the same lecture: "Abarōz do this—don't do that—and be sure not to do *this*.

Her father, an Ōšmurdan or Tallyman who worked just outside the mines, smiled into his breakfast.

"We are doing well," he announced, and though the news was good, he spoke in a soft whisper.

"I am glad," said Adrina, clapping her hands. "With luck, the Šāh will reward us."

"It can only be hoped," Rastag said, his voice even lower. "If Al-razi takes notice, it will mean more dēnārs."

Abarōz tried to stop herself from snorting.

Dēnārs, dēnārs . . . didn't anyone in Dardan think about anything else?

Her father rose abruptly, the scrape of rock upon rock unsettling her nerves.

"Time to go," he said, straightening his cloak as he headed out their archway. "I mean it, Abarōz," he frowned. "Try to stay out of trouble."

She nodded, suppressing a feeling of anger which swelled and threatened to burst. *In Tengri's name!* She was so tired of being told what to do: help Mother cook and clean, stitch up holes in wool, and lower her eyes if she happened to meet a boy. She felt her life was stifling . . . not to mention boring. But what could you expect in a city carved underground?

She helped her mother wash up, then crept from their cave, hoping to find something new. Not a chance: there were the same rock walls; long, bending tunnels; and narrow stone stairs leading to other Hamwars. She already knew almost each one by heart: livestock on the first, the new god's temple below; and the mines, or zarrs, buried so deep that few would dare to visit—if they were allowed.

As she walked down the torch-lit hallway, she saw the back of a dahigān, rock hoe gripped in one hand. He was one of the few allowed to leave Dardan and set foot in the Bērūn. Fortunate, or not? Having your tongue cut out so you couldn't tell what you saw was a too-steep price for freedom. The same was true of the zarran who toiled below in the mines. No, Abarōz thought, better to live like a mole than undergo such torment.

She smoothed down her dress of wool (stifling in the constant heat) and frowned as she noticed Kavad coming around a bend. She knew him only vaguely as a friend of her father's who'd earned many dēnārs and from her received a stiff bow. There were whispers on every Hamwar that he was in the pay of the Šāh, and, as one of the inner circle, held the power of life or death.

Abarōz was relieved she hadn't seen any boys. She'd just turned seventeen and was now of marriageable age, though the thought of a husband filled her with creeping nausea. She wouldn't even know him and he would marry her for her dowry: three pigs, a goat, and twenty-five dēnārs. She wasn't ready for this, unable look at a boy without blushing. She didn't know how to flirt, though Mother had lectured her on how to lower her eyes. Well, she could talk herself into the next Hamwar. Abarōz would *not* be bullied into following mindless custom.

As she walked deeper into the tunnel, Abarōz wondered if anyone else felt the same. Did they chafe under constraints left over from Tengri knows when? Did they hate being trapped in Dardan, a place so far underground that even the fish were eyeless?

If they shared her sentiments, she knew, they couldn't say a word. The S̄āh cut out dissent as surely as zarran tongues. "Detention" meant prolonged torture, followed by a slow death.

No, Abarōz thought, *as bad as life here could be, it wasn't worth speaking out.*

The Bērūn

Shāhpuhr rolled his eyes in frustration, mangling another word in a language he knew fairly well. Still, it was so foreign he stumbled and made mistakes. Happily, his teacher—his adoptive mother, Bükrek—as always had the patience of Tengri as she repeated the lesson.

He loved her with a deep feeling: She was the one, after all, who'd rescued him after Dardan had cast him out. It was still hard to grasp he'd been sacrificed at birth, given over to the enemy due to his jutting foot. Yet, to prevent his demise, Bükrek had swooped in, just halfway through her tenure of recreating the world. Incredibly kind by nature, the dragon had taken him in, sheltered him in the forest, and raised him for seventeen years.

"Ōšmurd-dan," Shāhpuhr stuttered, though, after all this time, he should be conversing with ease. "Mād," he asked Bükrek, "May I question again why we bother? After all, it's not likely I'll meet a human."

"My son," she said, in the same dragon tongue, "knowledge can never be useless. Those who think so align themselves with Sangal."

"Very well," Shāhpuhr sighed, nestling into the grass of their clearing. "If I happen to meet some person crouched behind a tree, I'll be sure to greet them."

Bükrek laughed, her green dragon throat producing more of a rumble.

"The chances are slim," she said, exposing sharp, jagged teeth. "But in my experience, which has lasted well . . . forever . . . simply talking may smooth over unpleasantness."

"If you say so," nodded Shāhpuhr.

As the only being he'd known besides animals in the forest, Shāhpuhr believed all she said.

"Ōšmurdan," he spoke again, emphasizing each syllable. Even if he never used the word, the pride beaming from his mother's face was worth every effort.

Kavad

Kavad was up to something: of that, Abarōz was sure. She kept seeing him on her Hamwar, heavy packs of leather dragging him down. It wasn't like him to be here since, per her father, he spent his time in the zarr or upstairs flattering the S̃āh. But Abarōz, who fled from her cave often, had come to notice the Ōšmurdan and the strange burden he bore.

On his fifth appearance, she decided to follow him even though her curiosity might well get her killed. Treading lightly over stone floor, she hung back and trailed him up six winding stairways.

Whatever was in his pack made a metallic clink. Abarōz knew enough to realize it could only be one thing—gold from the zarr.

She shook her head, willing her mind to stay on her quarry. When they finally reached the first Hamwar, she was breathing so hard from the climb she clapped a hand to her mouth. Kavad kept up his swift pace, though there was nowhere for him to go: he either wanted to check on the livestock, or, incredibly, venture out to the Bērūn.

She hid behind a fat sheep, peeking over its back. What she saw made her gasp: Kavad *climbing* a small rope ladder which led to a rock hatch? Surely, he knew the penalty for thwarting his master the S̃āh, and, if that wasn't bad enough, the enemy stationed outside would soon rip him to pieces. Either way, it would be a terrible death.

Though Kavad seemed to hesitate, he raised an arm, yanking the hatch's handle to reveal a square empty space. Abarōz ducked even lower. She saw him brace his arms on opposite sides of the opening, lifting his body until it jerked free. From wherever he was, he shut the hatch with a bang.

Abarōz couldn't believe it. Kavad had . . . had left. As far as she knew, he'd been the first to work this miracle in all of Dardan's history. Now he was surely dead, like all the other sacrifices. *Those* poor souls, the Axwaš, were given no choice: imperfect at birth, or suffering from disease, they'd been shoved out to the enemy. Yet Kavad had gone willingly, something her swirling mind couldn't quite comprehend.

Perhaps he was tired of living—of scuttling underground like a groveling insect. Still, he'd been rich and privileged, but, she supposed, even that sort had troubles . . .

What Abarōz feared was what would happen next. The Šāh would be in a rage, revenging himself on Kavad's wife and children, but it wouldn't stop there. Al-razi would seek out others to punish and kill simply because he could.

By supper that night, word had spread through all fourteen Hamwars. Kavad had not only escaped, but had managed to do so with large sackfuls of gold.

In their cave, Rastag shot a wary glance at his family. He ignored the lamb stew set before him.

"This is very bad," he muttered, scanning every crevasse for spies who he clearly believed were hiding.

"How so?" Adrina asked, bored as ever with events that didn't affect her directly.

"If he stole gold," said Rastag, "we Ōšmurdans should have noticed at the daily weighings."

"But how?" Abarōz asked.

She took up a forkful of lamb, pretending to still have an appetite. As long as she stayed silent, not telling what she had seen, her father would be safe.

"Our Šāh is mighty," Rastag said in a low voice. "That doesn't mean he is rational: he will find someone to blame, and I fear it will be us Ōšmurdans."

"I suppose you mean *you,*" said Adrina, cheerfully lifting a spoonful. "Bah! You are not Chief Ōšmurdan, so why would they even bother?"

Abarōz heard her mother's bitterness at her father's lack of standing. Being chief would mean more dēnārs, perhaps twenty a month.

Rastag didn't answer: just sighed over his bowl. Now Abarōz had doubts. Should she tell him about what happened on Hamwar One, or would that just draw him in further? She decided to keep her own counsel before the one that would surely come—the S̆āh's.

Inside Sangal's Lair

Once Kavad emerged from the hatch, his body strewn over small gravel, he instantly flung one hand over his burning eyes. There was something above: something that shone with the light of at least a thousand torches. Though he had no idea what it was, he was convinced it must be a god. Peeking through fingers adorned with rings of gold, he prepared to confront the enemy who could often be heard from Dardan emitting their high-pitched shrieks But to his surprise, it was not armed warriors whom Kavad spied. No, it was—some kind of snake?—but enormous, spanning a full twenty feet, and, what was more, sported thin wings attached to its yellow back.

"Don't hurt me!" Kavad cried, hurling off his pack to spill out its contents. The dragon (for, according to legend, that's what it must be), seemed to be acquainted with gold. It even *smiled,* crawling forward on its front claws to seize the back of his cloak. Kavad felt himself climbing into a blue expanse, across that yellow orb which so assailed his eyes.

His captor, the yellow dragon, flapped on for some time, creating a wind until it slowed to a glide. It landed smoothly before a complex of stone openings, then skid to a halt upon a flat boulder. Never having been in the Bērūn before, Kavad had no idea what those openings were—he was just glad to be alive. The dragon put him down and began to nudge him toward the largest opening. Peering in, Kavad saw it fronted a cave. Well, at least this was familiar. But he felt sheer terror when he at last entered.

This cave was filled by dragons of every conceivable hue: some with scales of red, others gold, while a few had mixed swirl, stripes, and even circles. They were all about the size of Kavad's new yellow friend . . . except one. This red beast stood on a stone platform, three times the size of the others, its scales seeming to gleam as if with a sheen of gold. Its expression, though reptilian, seemed to Kavad to project haughtiness, and almost, he thought, a sneer.

As the dragon lifted a claw, black talons curved in the half-light, the beasts assembled before it ceased their quiet growls. The red one began to "speak," if you could call it that. From its mouth came a series of roars, hisses, and even a spout of flame. After what must have been its "introduction," the red dragon turned his head, one black pupil glaring at Kavad.

So used to obeisance, Kavad didn't hesitate before falling to his knees. He made a deep salaam, happy to stay like this forever.

"I see we have a guest," the red dragon roared, in words that Kavad understood. "I assume, human, that you are from Dardan or Šahr."

"Dardan," Kavad breathed, his nose bent against stone.

"I am Sangal," said the beast. "What brings the rat to the surface?"

Kavad took this to mean he could rise, and stood up on shaky legs.

"A–a proposition, great Sangal."

"From a rat? Very well, I am curious."

"Where I was found, great ebren, there are packs filled with gold coins. And this is just a glimpse of what exists in our zarr. The Šāh's mines are overflowing and he can certainly spare you more."

"Well spoken," said Sangal. "Fate must have brought us together, for I too have a plan." Kavad didn't move. "Your defection alone cannot produce more gold. But stemming the city's water supply—now *that* is the way to do it."

"But, excellent Sangal," Kavad said, forgetting for a moment whom he spoke to, "my zand holds massive aqueducts."

"That is a point," said the ebren, "though a decidedly poor one. Do you happen to know their ultimate source?"

Kavad shook his head.

"I beg you, Dragon King, please forgive my ignorance."

"I am much more than a king," huffed Sangal. "I appreciate that you Dardans never had a chance to get out, but know that my river feeds you every drop." Kavad started. This was news indeed. "And if my flight and I flap over it, we will raise an amount of debris that renders its waters useless." The dragon seemed to grow restless. "I planned to send an ebren to Dardan as a messenger of sorts, but you'll do even better. Inform the Šāh: Unless my tithe of gold is increased to seven-eighths of the zarr's treasure, with the number of sacrifices raised to thrice of what it is now, his zand and precious kingdom will shortly go extinct." Sangal smiled, revealing his vicious teeth. "As an immortal," he said, "I have seen many things. Whole cities devoured by sand when their water ceased flowing."

Before Kavad could answer, the yellow ebren who'd brought him nudged him out of the lair, grabbing his cloak to reverse their journey. Before long, it dropped Kavad at the Dardan main gate, where he adjusted his clothing, then knocked. As the dragon flew off, a small stone peephole flung open, revealing one dark pupil.

"Who goes there?" shouted the guard.

"It is I, Kavad, newly returned from the dead, and you will allow me to enter since I am the vassal of Sangal."

An Unseasonal Sacrifice

It didn't take long for the bells on each Hamwar to chime, summoning all of Dardan to yet another council meeting.

Great, Abarōz thought, forcing down a last spoonful of lamb. Trying to look dutiful, she trailed behind her parents, who in turn merged with a crowd all seeking Hamwar Two. The staircases overflowed with people, and in all the tumult, she could only hope that her father had been wrong.

After what seemed like hours, thousands of Dardans ascended to the Great Cathedral. Abarōz looked above the crowd's heads. The sheer size of this cave, coupled with the oddity of its new god, always made her wonder. What had those strange priests wanted, venturing out to their city some five hundred years prior, completely unafraid of the enemy just outside? Was it merely to preach some strange new gospel about the figure who hung on a wall, suspended on a rock cross? All her questions dissolved as her eyes sought the roof, its vastness shrouded in black. Who could not be impressed by the magnitude of this temple?

It seemed to be the S̄āh. Appearing from behind the altar, he was encircled by his large family and a host of viziers. Ironically, beneath him sat a gold idol—of himself—just as portly and sour as the original. Naturally, he was also surrounded by a phalanx of guards and lances, but this was nothing as Abarōz glimpsed the man who came out behind him.

Could it really be Kavad, his body still whole and his expression smug?

"My subjects!" the S̄āh began, his voice bouncing against all that rock, "as you may or may not know, We discovered a traitor, one so black of heart he defied Our rules and crept into the Bērūn." Most of the citizens gasped, though this was hardly a secret. "As you can see with your own eyes, he lives.

Much against Our wishes, he has met with the enemy, who in their endless avarice desire even more gold. And, I fear, an unseasonal sacrifice."

Craning her head toward the back, Abarōz felt a chill. As long as she could remember, sacrifices took place only at the start of a season.

Now the throng erupted in murmurs until the S̄āh raised a hand.

"I tell you we must comply. For ten centuries, Dardans have sheltered here, safe from the rampaging enemy. Yet now my vizier Kavad has defied all decency, breached Our law, and tightened upon our throats the enemy's grasp. Hence, I command that ten Ōšmurdan and fifteen zarran be made Axwaš tonight. It is *them* I hold responsible for Kavad's shameless theft. *Guards!*"

Abarōz stood on tiptoe as four of them lurched forward, steel helmets from a bygone age glinting in the light of candles. She watched, horrified, as they grabbed a woman and her three small children.

Kavad's family, she thought.

Then Kavad himself performed an act more worthy of a snake. He slithered beside the S̄āh, whispering into his ear. A command was shouted, and before Abarōz knew it, three metal-clad guards stomped over, seizing Rastag by the shoulders and binding his hands before him.

"NO!" Abarōz screamed, trying to force her way after them. But the guards shoved her aside as her father, joined by other prisoners, was marched up the stone stairway.

Abarōz turn to her mother who looked relieved she'd been spared. Trembling, she followed the grim procession up to Hamwar One.

There, the massive boulder at the Dardan gate was rolled aside via a system of pulleys. The Axwaš were pushed out before the boulder closed behind them. Abarōz could hear the sounds. Bloodcurdling screams, almost as if the Dardans were being devoured whole.

Revenge

When Abarōz, sweat-soaked and shaking, let herself be steered by Adrian down to their cave, she tried to ignore the woman. Her mother had made it clear that she couldn't care less about the death of her husband . . . as long as *she* stayed safe. Selfishness had been engrained in all the women of her family, but Abarōz swore to let it die out with her.

Rastag. She couldn't speak or think the name without a sob of anguish. On balance, he'd been a good father, though his desire for self-protection often overrode his courage. Still, he'd worked hard to support them in the crushing heat of the zarr. He'd tried to keep his head down, to be a shadow among shadows, but even that hadn't prevented his bloody end.

Once Abarōz calmed down a bit and took a draught of warm milk, she felt every part of her being crying out for revenge. Against the Šāh and the rotten Kavad, but her list didn't end there. There were the viziers of the city, keeping the people down while they bathed themselves in gold. There were the *rules* themselves, trapping thousands here like ants when they should be fighting the enemy.

All the grief and rage that Abarōz had held in check now exploded through her insides, kindling a deadly fire. It was then that she realized what she'd really known all her life: she had to follow Kavad, not in black deeds, but in freeing herself from Dardan.

Was there anyone here, she wondered, *she could persuade to go with her?* The answer came back in a second as a ringing no. She knew a few girls whom she might have thought of as friends, but they were so modest and dutiful they barely emerged from their caves. Besides, if they did, they might attract the S̄ah "finders" to see themselves hauled before him for the "honor" of spreading his seed.

All men are virtuous, Abarōz thought, *until* they *were put in charge . . .*

It was at that moment that she knew the bleak truth: she was on her own. Fine. She tossed her head. If that's the way it must be. She resolved to attempt her escape after a good night's sleep, and, once Adrina was snoring, she stole some basic provisions. She wished she had a weapon to fight the enemy, and, in desperation, seized a large kitchen knife.

Abarōz tiptoed to her bed, wrapping straw snugly around her. She wondered where she'd be sleeping the following night ... that is, if she weren't killed.

The candles outside in the hallway had barely begun to flicker before Abarōz eased herself out. She had no goodbyes for her mother—there was nothing to say. Stealthily, she retraced her steps of yesterday, throwing her hood over her face and nodding politely to those who bothered to stir at this hour. It wasn't easy ascending six levels on those narrow stairs. But, remembering her mission, she refused to halt, merely casting a glance at the new god as he hung over Hamwar Two.

At last, she reached the top, stumbling toward the livestock. Patting a goat on the head, she crept toward that rope ladder, mounting it with her flimsy shoes. Not much of a barrier between her soles and that rough twisted twine. Still, she didn't stop until the handle of the stone hatch was within her grasp. Though she wasn't as strong as Kavad, the raging fire within helped to thrust the stone aside. Scraping her fingers on rock, she groaned as she struggled upward onto a grainy surface. Abarōz grabbed a handful and looked: this stuff was brownish and poured from her palm.

Still lying on her stomach, she lifted her head to study the Bērūn. Such strange sights! Above was an orange circle, its head fighting to emerge from behind a towering mound. It emitted a feeble light, but one still strong enough to make her turn her head. She rolled over before standing, looking to every horizon for some sign of the enemy. But all she saw were those brown grains surrounded by a rich blue itself dotted with white things.

Abarōz brought out her pathetic knife, ready for a charge of warriors. If she couldn't make some kind of bargain to bring down the Sāh, she would quickly join her father.

Abarōz kept staring up as she heard a sound like whirring. Moving at great speed away from the orange orb, she saw a green-scaled snake ... one with wings . . .

Abarōz crouched, almost wishing to go back to Dardan before the dragon reached her. As it neared, she saw its fierce claws and a tale shaped like a spade flattened behind its scales. This was it. Surely, the end was near. At least she wouldn't die a coward like those human moles underground.

It was then that she noticed something: something quite out of place. In the middle of all this brown, there sat a small blade of green completely on its own. Since it grew from those tiny pebbles, Abarōz wondered how it could live without a drop of water. Was it cursed? A sign from the new god, or Tengri? She didn't have long to ponder as the blade began to sway, growing steadily larger with each passing second.

"Get away!" Abarōz shouted, wielding her stone kitchen knife.

But the blade of green didn't listen, coming even closer as it changed from a single sprout to a good-sized plant and then to a strange brown and green object.

"Who are you?" Abarōz yelled, looking for a place to run.

"Lower your voice," the thing insisted from an invisible mouth. "I am Archura in tree form and I'm here to help you. Şahmeran has sent me."

"I don't know who that is," said Abarōz, firming up her hold on the knife. "And what exactly are *you?*"

"For Şahmeran's sake!" cried the tree. "You're quite an ignorant girl."

"I beg your pardon," Abarōz answered, putting her hands on her hips. "I just so happen to be from Dardan, and we live in the Azēr."

Archura gave a shrug with two of his largest branches.

"Sorry," he said. "Şahmeran told me nothing except that I was to fetch you."

"I suggest you do it fast," said Abarōz, cowering as that dragon winged even faster, no doubt having spotted its target.

"We needn't fear her," said Archura, "but the other ebrens. We should go before we both become a sacrifice."

Abarōz grimaced, thinking of Rastag, but most of her sadness fell from her as the tree used his branches like arms to pop her onto his top.

"Hold on now!" Archura yelled, hopping away from the dragon at a surprising pace.

"Can you not bounce so much?" asked Abarōz, her entire body in motion. All that she could see was that blue shaking up and down.

"You're rather ungrateful," said the tree with a snort. "But I guess that's to be expected since you haven't met Şahmeran."

"A-rre you t-taking m-me to h-her?" Abarōz asked. Her head was shaking so much, she sounded like she was drowning.

"No," the tree said calmly, still hopping away like a child. "To Bükrek. Those are my orders."

Abarōz was tired of orders—she'd been following them her whole life. Still, her mind was taken off jolting as more trees came into view.

"W-what is t-this?" she asked, relieved to find that Archura had slowed down to a hobble.

"I see you really know nothing," he said sadly. "Of course, this is a forest, where only good things dwell."

"I take it that you're one of them?"

"That goes without saying," he huffed. "Otherwise, I could have stomped you to death or left you to the ebren."

"I suppose that's true," said Abarōz. The tree had a valid point. "Have we arrived to where we're going?"

"Impatient, I see," he answered. "A curious little thing too. Just take care that doesn't get you in trouble."

"Too late," Abarōz mumbled, her attention drawn by dense thickets.

"Do they all talk?" she asked.

"No, I'm afraid, just me," said Archura, sounding sad. "But the rest of the trees have their ways." Before Abarōz could inquire further, the tree slowed to a crawl, shuffling up to a ribbon of water surrounded by pleasant green. "Here we are," he exclaimed, all his tree cheer restored. "I'll just leave you to wait for Bükrek."

"No!"

But he was already off, perhaps to gossip with his tree friends.

Abarōz looked around her. She had never seen such sights: water that flowed free and not in a man-made basin; different kinds of trees, and even some plants with red blooms. Beneath her feet was a soft brown surface, not made of grains but solid.

Lost in this verdant landscape, she barely noticed as a scaly green head raised itself from tall green. Before she could scream, the dragon spoke.

"Welcome. I am Bükrek: one who helped create our world and hopes to restore it. Şahmeran said to expect you."

"Who is she?" Abarōz asked for the second time that day.

"She is everything."

"You mean . . . she's that blue above and all this green?"

Bükrek's face reflected a smile.

"That's right," she said. "She is closer than you think and you might meet her someday. But right now, I suggest we deal with the present."

"I'd like that," said Abarōz, "for I have always been practical."

The dragon nodded.

"You may soon be called upon to put that skill to use."

The Boy Who Rose from the Dead

After Abarōz recovered from the shock of speaking with a dragon, she realized just how kind this green one was. Bükrek made sure she was comfortable, clearing a place for Abarōz to sit by the water. She even took a roasted bird in her giant claws and offered it to her guest. As Abarōz started to eat, she smiled up at her host.

Bükrek did look like a snake, except for her delicate wings. She was as large—maybe half a Dardan hallway—her scales curled contentedly into a mound of wrapped coils. Her face, despite the presence of sharp teeth, was gentle, and the way her yellow eyes glowed told Abarōz that she had nothing to fear.

Once Abarōz finished her meal, she found herself, as always, bursting with curiosity.

"How," she asked Bükrek, "did you catch and roast a fowl? It seems your claws are too big, and your dragon fire too strong."

Bükrek gave a slight chuckle.

"Oh, I am not the source of your breakfast. For that, you must thank Shāhpuhr."

"Another dragon?" asked Abarōz, craning her neck in alarm.

"Oh no," laughed Bükrek "he is one of your own. A boy of I'd say just about the same age."

"A Dardan lives *here?*"

Abarōz's skin prickled: what if he were another Kavad?

"Yes, he's been with me nearly since birth. He was meant to be an Axwaš, but I couldn't abide such cruelty. I took him in, and here he's stayed."

"Can I meet him?" Abarōz asked, not knowing if this were wise. After all, her zand had cast him out, and wouldn't he despise her? Want to get his revenge just the way she wanted hers.

"He is out hunting," said Bükrek, nestling her head on the ground. "But he should return soon."

Abarōz nodded, deciding to explore. This part of the forest was not heavily wooded, its trees becoming more sparse the closer they came to the water. This natural marvel, flowing in its narrow channel, looked so clear and clean and inviting that Abarōz scampered down until her feet were submerged. Cupping her hands, she took a long thirsty drink, delighting in the coolness as the liquid soothed her throat. She never could have imagined water delivered naturally, as opposed to the huge aqueducts lying dormant in Dardan. She couldn't imagine most things: that now-yellowish orb above, sending such bright rays her way that she nearly cried out. She'd never known any plants besides the vegetables that dahigāns brought from above. But now, the variety of life around her—the sounds of the trickling water and strange chirps emerging from branches—almost made her dizzy as, for the first time, she saw life unshadowed by rock.

She even ran toward a thicket, spinning around with arms out as if she were finally free. Though this made her more dizzy, she couldn't be bothered to care.

"Gra-greetings," came a hesitant voice, accompanied by the sound of plants being crushed.

Abarōz whirled, flushing down to her chest as she spotted the form of a boy. But that's not what caused her discomfort: He was dressed in nothing but a loincloth, as the new god's book named it.

"Uh, greetings," Abarōz answered, remembering her manners. "I am Abarōz of Dardan."

As he approached, Abarōz saw that the boy was quite lanky, though his muscles looked hard and well-formed. She blushed even more when she saw his face was handsome, with the same olive skin as hers, though his hair, dark as her own, reached down to his shoulders. At the moment, his near-black eyes looked puzzled.

"Do you speak our language?" she asked, as he stopped six hands' breadths away. After all, he might know only the word for "greetings."

"On the whole," he said, giving a hesitant smile. "But I still jumble some things."

"Who taught you?"

"Oh. My mother, Bükrek."

Abarōz's mind began to turn like the tumbrils of a lock. *Of course!* Raised by a dragon, he would naturally call her "Mother."

She returned his smile.

"I think you speak it quite well."

"Thank you. That means a great deal coming from a Dardan."

"Really? You still have a fondness for people who sacrificed you to a dragon?"

"I don't so much blame our zand as the tyrant Al-razi."

Abarōz raised a brow.

"You must be very forgiving."

"My mother told me," he said, "that anger is pointless. You only injure yourself."

"Wise," Abarōz told him, unused to truths being spoken aloud. "For what it's worth, I find the custom of Axwaš barbaric."

"I could tell," he said thoughtfully, "just by looking at you."

Abarōz blinked, the top of her nose buzzing with a familiar ache. No. No tears. She was here to avenge her father, so the grieving must wait.

"I am Shāhpuhr, by the way."

"It is an honor to meet you."

Abarōz dropped her head in the usual bow. It seemed silly in the middle of a forest, but that was all she knew.

"I . . . er . . . l-likewise," said Shāhpuhr, trying to summon the word. He motioned for her to follow him into a green-filled clearing. "Tengri has blessed me today. I not only captured two pheasants, but found some mushrooms nearby."

"Bükrek must be happy to have you."

Shāhpuhr sighed and looked down.

"I hope so," he said. "Sometimes, I feel like a basket to her."

Abarōz suppressed a giggle.

"Did you mean to say 'burden'?"

"Yes!" he shouted, laughing openly at himself. "Now I'll have *two* fine teachers."

"In two very different forms."

"That does not matter to me."

From his standing position, he gracefully sat cross-legged while she needed three separate moves. Staring at him, she wasn't sure how to think about this boy of the forest. In her life, she'd barely *talked* to a boy, much less one in a loincloth.

"So," she began, trying to make small talk, "do you enjoy living here?"

"For the most part," he said. "Sometimes it gets a bit lonely."

Something dawned on her then.

"Have you–have you ever met a human before?"

"No, so please forgive me if I seem awkward."

She gave him a warm smile.

"You're doing fine."

"How–how did you escape from Dardan?" he asked. "I believe you are the first."

"The second. Someone called Şahmeran helped me."

He let out a low whistle.

"You must be very special."

"Why?"

"She rarely interferes in our lives."

"Oh."

Abarōz didn't know what else to say. She looked at him hopefully.

"Are you hungry?" he asked.

"Starved! Escape took all my strength."

He smiled and rose to his feet. Limping over to a mound of tree parts, he pulled out several, then stacked them crossways. Retrieving two small rocks, he repeatedly rubbed them together, at creating a spark which he applied to his creation. Like a master, he plucked and cleaned his two birds, spitted them neatly, and dangled them over the fire.

"You seem to do very well on your own," Abarōz told him, impressed.

He grinned, crossing his arms. She tried not to notice the swell of muscle.

"I had no choice in the matter."

She grinned, watching him turn the birds. Then, he threw a handful of mushrooms into a hard clay pot.

"Do you . . . wish they had let you stay?" Abarōz bit her tongue, regretting her words almost instantly.

"I couldn't say." He handed her a generous plate, to which she applied her stone knife. "I can't miss what I never had."

"True." Abarōz thought. "I don't wish to be rude, but in the city, they take care of your needs. Mostly."

"I'm sure that would be easier. Yet . . . there is also the S̃āh, controlling your every move."

"And word," she added.

"I daresay," he smiled, "I like it better here."

Abarōz looked around the placid clearing.

"I can certainly see why."

They finished their meal in silence, the boiled mushrooms perfect along with the smoky meat. Shāhpuhr reached behind him, passing Abarōz a skin of water from which she took a deep draught.

"Thank you," she said, averting her eyes from his chest. "You are truly a good provider."

As she realized her words' import, she blushed down to her neck. *Stupid, Abarōz, stupid!*

He saved her from further embarrassment by leaning back and asking, "Are you an Axwaš too?"

"Oh no," she answered, not knowing what to reveal. But Shāhpuhr seemed so simple: so incapable of deceit. "My father. I have come to seek revenge."

"He was a good father then?"

"Yes. He always worked so hard and put up with my mother. As for me: He often turned a blind eye whenever I got into trouble. I—" She sniffed. "I miss him."

"I see," Shāhpuhr said at last, and she wondered if he saw more: her refusal to back down. "Well. What is your plan?"

Abarōz plucked at some green blades, sifting them through her fingers.

"I–I really don't know."

"You must devise one."

"Yes," she said, "I think that's fairly obvious." He blushed beneath his dark skin. "I–I'm sorry. I'm not usually this ill-mannered. It's just . . . I lost my father last night."

She could see the pain in his eyes.

"Yet you enjoy the gods' favor."

"What makes you say that?" she asked.

"Şahmeran herself helped you."

"Yes, but I don't know who she is . . . besides everything."

Shāhpuhr steepled his long fingers.

"In light of your being a fool, perhaps she can aid you again."

"I beg your pardon!" huffed Abarōz, leaping to her feet. "At least I don't live in a forest with a dragon for a mother!"

He looked stricken, touching his forehead to the ground. Abarōz took a deep breath.

"I am sorry again," she said, resisting the urge to reach out and touch him. "I believe what you meant to say was, 'in light of my being *alone.*'"

Shāhpuhr brought up his head.

"Yes!"

Staring down at his shaggy head, Abarōz wondered what she should do. In her short life, she hadn't had reason to think: just what to serve for supper and how to ensnare a husband. Her poor mind, as pebbled as Dardan, struggled with simple strategy.

"All right," she said, "if this Şahmeran is everything, it follows she must be everywhere. What if I call for her now?"

Shāhpuhr look slightly abashed.

"I fear it's not that easy. Though she is mother to all, she herself lives in a cave."

"Can you tell me where?" asked Abarōz. Caves at least were familiar.

"Only with Mother's help. And it's likely you'll end up close to the place you left."

"You mean Dardan?" She snorted. "You more than anyone know why I can't go back."

"Not openly," he answered, "but with Bükrek on our side, we might frighten away Sangal's ebrens."

"'We'?" she asked. "I can hardly ask you to join me, since this is my quest alone."

"You will fail," he said calmly, "without an–an accomplice . . . is that what they're called?"

"Yes. But please understand the danger—for you as well as for me."

"Happily, we don't have to enter Dardan: just the adjoining city."

"You mean Šahr?"

"Yes."

"I've never been there," Abarōz said, "and I don't know where the gate is. I think we should start with what we know, and for me that means Dardan."

Shāhpuhr stood, getting a little too close.

"And how," he asked, "do we avoid the Šāh and his men?"

Abarōz let out a breath, feeling herself deflate.

"We can't. Not with his network of spies." She paced in a circle around him, her mind lit with visions of every Hamwar. "Wait." She felt a tingle. "What about the miners?"

"They suffer a terrible fate. What more?"

"The Šāh punished my father because he was an Ōšmurdan." Shāhpuhr looked uncomprehending. "It's rather a long story, but he was made Axwaš along with fifteen zarran. Which leads me to believe . . . they thoroughly hate the man who sent their friends to their deaths."

"And cut out their own tongues."

Abarōz shivered.

"Which means," she said, "we need to get to the Fourteenth Hamwar—that is, the lowest."

"My mother says no one may enter: it is reserved for the zarran—"

"—And the guards who whip them."

Shāhpuhr shook his head.

"How to descend so deep?"

"In Dardan," Abarōz told him, "we have worktime and sleeptime. For the latter, most torches are unlit."

"Night," he nodded.

"That's when we must go."

"Very well. We must travel to the city by the light of the moon."

"Is that what you mean?" asked Abarōz, pointing up to that yellow orb.

"No," Shāhpuhr said, "that is Mihr, mother of Māh. When she rests every night, her daughter comes out to play."

To Abarōz, this sounded strange, part of the old religion which the new god would frown on. Yet, she wasn't concerned. They needed *all* the gods on their side for what would be a perilous journey.

"Very well," Abarōz said. "But you must ask your mother Bükrek to fly us during the night. Once there, we implore the zarran to join us. They might know the way into Šahr."

Shāhpuhr grinned, his eyes sparking with light.

And, for the first time, Abarōz no longer felt alone.

A Perilous Journey

For the rest of the day, Abarōz couldn't keep still. Her thoughts turned to Shāhpuhr and why he'd agreed to go with her. Certainly, he had little to gain, and everything to lose. Once the Šāh found out that a long-ago Axwaš still lived, he'd be more than happy to remedy the error. Still, Abarōz was relieved at having someone else join her: especially in Dardan's treacherous halls.

While they waited for his mother, Abarōz asked Shāhpuhr for the names of the things around them: she learned that the brown stuff was *dirt*; the blue expanse overhead *sky*; and the channel with water was called the *River Rōd*. Its sides were known as *banks*, while the green they sat on was *grass*.

Shāhpuhr seemed eager to help, and for that she was grateful. She could only wish that his clothing was . . . more expansive. Despite her mother's lectures, it was hard for her not to glance at his muscular thighs; smooth, olive skin; and even the slant of his nose. Was this what Adrina meant by temptation? Abarōz shook her head, distracting herself with the notions of grass and sky. At last, Bükrek appeared, slithering up to their side.

"My son," she greeted Shāhpuhr, "and our welcome guest. How goes it?"

"Well, mother," he said with excitement. "Abarōz has devised a plan to unseat the Šāh!"

"We both—" Abarōz started, not wanting to take all the credit.

"It was mainly her," said Shāhpuhr, then described to his mother what they intended to do.

"Bold," Bükrek nodded, her yellow eyes gleaming. "This will require much skill and a fair amount of luck. I confess I am concerned, but will not attempt to stop you. It is high time for Al-razi to lose his hold on Dardan."

"Thank you," Abarōz told her, struck again by the dragon's kindness. "You're able to take us then?"

"Yes, at the first sign of Māh."

Abarōz studied Shāhpuhr for the rest of the day while pretending not to. She knew she shouldn't—after all, they weren't betrothed. But something about his simple nature brought fresh air into her life.

At last, to her relief, Mihr dipped below sight and Bükrek found them again. She slithered across the long grass, green scales reflecting moonlight. The dragon gently lifted Abarōz in one claw, then Shāhpuhr in the other, winging across the sky—*now black!*—with a whoosh of wings. From her dangling position, Abarōz sensed, rather than saw, other ebrens around them. Yet they remained at a distance, clearly cowed by Bükrek. If she hadn't been so frightened, Abarōz would have laughed. These other dragons of Sangal must be as scared as she was. She realized now why they didn't attack when she'd first emerged from Dardan: Bükrek, soaring above, had acted as her shield.

Abarōz felt almost weightless in her dangling state. There was a freedom in flight so different from her stifling cave. She had the sensation of being one with the Bērūn; a part of its moon, sky, sands. There were even dots of light nestled against the black, and she wished she could rise and touch them.

Thankfully, it didn't take long to reach Dardan, and, when Abarōz looked down, she spotted the gate. Māh hung over that dirt-covered mound behind the city as Bükrek landed noiselessly, a massive shape on the sand. She set down her passengers, lowering her head to speak.

"Children," she said, "the bravery—or foolishness—of what you're about to attempt is admirable. If you do find indeed Şahmeran, please give her my greetings. As for you two—" She looked at her son sadly, "—never let down your guard since ears are always listening. The S̃āh is even rumored to be a Zeh̬n̥ Xɑn—a reader of minds. Though this is a lie, he is still cunning and vicious. I wish you both a safe journey, but more important, is a safe return."

Shāhpuhr did not change his expression. But Abarōz felt moisture creeping from her eyes.

What right do I have, she wondered, *to wrench this poor boy from the only mother he's had?* To put him in deathly peril, and all for the sake of her father, who was, after all, gone.

Her face, even in shadow, must have reflected her thoughts, since Shāhpuhr patted her arm.

"Do not fear," he whispered, "that you forced me into this task. There is so much at stake: the future of our zand, the truth of its past, and the remaking of the present." He looked up at Bükrek. "Goodbye, mother," he said. "I promise to return to you bearing only good tidings."

The green dragon nodded, extending her thin wings before heading into the sky. As Abarōz watched, her form seemed to grow smaller, resolving into a dot.

They had to get moving. She turned to Shāhpuhr.

"Follow me," she whispered, resisting that urge to grab his wrist.

He stood without moving before the Dardan gate.

"How do you propose," he asked, "that we move that boulder?"

"We don't have to," Abarōz told him, sinking down to a crawl. The last thing she wanted was to be spotted by guards.

"Another entrance?" Shāhpuhr asked, dropping down behind her.

Abarōz nodded, leading him to the ceiling with its barely visible hatch.

"Escape route?" he asked, looking down at the etched stone.

"I would assume," said Abarōz, "but only for Al-razi."

Shāhpuhr gave a small laugh, the first she'd ever heard from him. Abarōz rose to her knees to grab the small rope hanging from the hatch, then wrenched it open with one determined pull.

"By Tengri!" he exclaimed.

Abarōz gave a tense smile as she eased her way in, catching hold of the rope ladder before landing on solid rock.

"Your turn," she whispered up.

Despite his left foot, Shāhpuhr scurried down like a goat. One even greeted him with a sleepy "baa."

"We made it!" he exulted, landing beside her.

Abarōz gave him a stern look.

"We've barely started," she told him.

"I am amazed," he said, "that our careful S̄āh does not post a guard here."

"Well," answered Abarōz, "who's coming in or out? He made a pact with the enemy, who were supposed to be warriors, and no one besides me and Kavad has ever escaped. So, in the S̄āh's mind, Hamwar One is perfectly safe."

"Then he's a fool," Shāhpuhr hissed. "So much the better for us."

Abarōz shook her head, unwilling to discount the ruler. But knowing each moment they spent here could well mean life or death, she gestured for him to follow as she approached the first set of stairs.

So unlike her last venture here, the stairwell was plunged in darkness, no servants of the Šāh at the ready to light his torches. Abarōz thrust out one arm, trying to find a smooth wall. Since there were no rails, this was her only means to check the steps' position. Under these conditions, the descent from One to Two was frightening, but Shāhpuhr's light touch on her back steadied her. She had just begun to relax when her toe scuffed a sharp step.

"Ouch!" she cried, her voice ringing against the rock.

"Shhh!" Shāhpuhr cautioned, pressing his chest against her as he wrapped a hand over her mouth.

Abarōz stiffened. Prior to her escape, her response would have been, "*How dare you touch me?!*" But now, she held back the words. Even though Shāhpuhr was a Dardan, he didn't know all their customs, or why boys shouldn't touch girls. She gently removed his hand, vowing to be more careful as they wound their way down through each Hamwar.

So many stairs and so many levels: Abarōz had lost count of which they were on. To make matters worse, there were at least three sets of stairs assigned to each Hamwar, and after awhile, Abarōz felt dizzy from having to look down.

In the sticky darkness, she found herself sweating thanks to her wool. She almost envied Shāhpuhr who must be cool as the Rōd. At such an immodest thought, a blush overtook her cheeks and she nearly stumbled again.

Down, down, down . . .was there no such thing as up? Abarōz pinched herself, trying to stay alert. You never knew when some Dardan, unable to sleep, might decide to take a stroll.

How many more Hamwar? She wasn't fatigued since their path led downhill, but her calf muscles tightened. If only she could tell which Hamwar was home, she'd have some idea where they were. As it was, each Hamwar merged into sameness. She and Shāhpuhr continued their trek for what felt like a full sleeptime. As they came to a sharp-angled staircase, Abarōz felt heat assault her cheek.

"We're close," she whispered. "My father always said his time spent in the zarr was like being inside a dragon."

Shāhpuhr grunted, wiping the sweat from his face. They came to a set of stairs much shorter than all the rest, and, once they hit level ground, Abarōz stopped so abruptly that Shāhpuhr ran into her back.

"Sorry."

The two of them moved forward, then stared up at a looming obstacle: a door of gold so wide it spanned the entire cave.

"The zarr," said Abarōz. "It must lie behind."

"How do we enter?"

Abarōz started to search for a handle. She really had no idea. Maybe find an Ōšmurdan and hope he knew her father? Or, since he was an Axwaš, was his name now forbidden? She put a hand up to the gold: it was cool, despite the temperature, and felt more solid than stone. But its smoothness seemed unmarred by any lever or lock. Abarōz stamped her foot, angry in defeat. Then, she felt something veil-like settle over her mind. Unable to stop herself, she lurched at Shāhpuhr, scraping all her nails roughly across his back roughly.

"Ow!" he cried. "What are you doing?"

He turned and tried to grab her, but she was gripped by a panic like a giant's fist.

"Don't touch me!" she shouted. "You are the very devil who tempted Our Lord in the desert!"

"Wha—?" her companion began, but was stilled by her fist which struck him full on the nose.

A thin trail of blood made its way toward his mouth.

"Why did you do that?" he asked, putting a hand to his face.

"I HATE YOU! I wish you were dead!"

He looked amazed as she began to cackle. Hitting him had been fun—she wanted to do it again! As she swung back her arm, he grabbed it, and in his eyes she thought she saw a new light.

"A Çor," he said. "Abarōz, I don't know how to tell you, but I think you've been possessed."

Her mad laughter rose and she found she couldn't stop. Between bursts, she panted, "LIAR! There's no one with me but you!"

"I am no Çor," he told her. "They are invisible spirits who never leave one place." In frustration, he bent down, trying to hold back her kicking. *"This one* must be bound to the door."

Abarōz didn't care—she only wanted to bite. To commence, she bared her teeth, but was stopped by an unseen voice.

"You have guessed right," it said, emerging from the door. "None shall enter," it sneered, "lest they are missing a tongue."

"I don't have one!" Abarōz shrieked, throwing out her arms and spinning. She felt so unbearably light.

"Let her go," said that near-naked boy, "or I'll send you back to Çoristan."

The door seemed to laugh. Abarōz broke into a dance, which was odd since she didn't know any. She stuck out her tongue at that horrible boy. Who was *he* to spoil her fun?

"I must think," he said. "What did my mother tell me?"

"Of what use is a mother?" she asked. "Only to torture and scold!"

"Er," said the boy, no longer looking at her. "The Çor—what are they afraid of?"

Abarōz continued her dance.

"Mihr, the moon, and those dots in the sky!" she crowed.

"No." The boy looked alert. "it is iron and citrons and salt." He turned to Abarōz, gripping her firmly by the shoulders. "Abarōz," he said, bringing his face close to hers. "Do you have any salt?"

Abarōz widened her eyes as she began to chant: "It is not really my fault/ That I neglected to bring the salt." The olive-skinned boy looked pained. Though he was a devil, he might make a decent bed partner. *"Don't look!"* she screeched, gripping her pack tightly. "GET AWAY!"

The boy's dark eyes blazed as he reached for the pack, tearing it from her back. When he started to rifle through it, she let out a wail.

"NO!" she cried, "you will be the death of me!"

He didn't seem to mind as he brought out something in triumph. It was a leather pouch which contained that hateful substance.

"DON'T!" she pleaded, wresting herself from his grasp. But she was too late as he undid a rope knot, creating a rain of salt.

"NO!" shrieked the Çor, *"now the door will have no guardian!"*

Abarōz heard a hiss as the veil left her mind. She felt rather silly to find her arms outstretched.

"Abarōz?" Shāhpuhr asked. He seemed unsure.

"Shāhpuhr," she breathed, "what–what happened?"

"The Çor has left and you are back to yourself. Though I must confess: You *are* an excellent dancer."

She felt her face heat up as she turned away.

What *else* had she done while under the spirit's power? She was too afraid to ask.

Among the Zarran

Abarōz hung back in shame, watching Shāhpuhr's fingers trace the door as he looked for some kind of handle. When she recalled her recent behavior, her checks flamed like dragon fire.

"I–I'm sorry," she told her friend's back, pulling her cloak around her face. "I'm sorry I attacked you, and, as far as the dance ... I'm not sure there are words ..."

"You needn't apologize," he told her, craning his neck to give her a smile. "No human can resist a Çor, and you did better than most."

"Thank you," Abarōz whispered, feeling the heat leave her face. Bükrek's kindness had clearly passed onto her son.

Feeling useless, she began to explore the door, starting at the opposite end.

"I wonder . . . " said Abarōz, pursing her lips.

"What?"

"How long has that spirit been here?"

"I imagine as long as there's been gold to mine."

Abarōz shook her head.

"I knew the Šāh was corrupt," she said. "But to deal with spirits?"

"From what my mother told me, he won't turn away anyone who promises him more riches."

"Like dragons?" she asked.

"That's a different matter. Sangal takes gold *from* him in return for not attacking."

"Yet we were told they were warriors."

"To hide the unpleasant truth."

"So . . . Al-razi's an all-around briber and liar."

'I think," said Shāhpuhr, "that captures him well."

"That's why," Abarōz said with passion, "we must end his reign now! I beg you: keep trying to find a way in."

He nodded as they both continued their search until her fingertips ached.

"Any luck?" called Shāhpuhr. "Did you feel a handle, lock—anything?"

"No." The oppressive heat was stifling, not helped by her clothes. Her faith began to flicker. "I hope," she said, "we don't have to give up . . . before we've really begun."

There was silence, then an excited, *"Wait!"*

Now Shāhpuhr did a dance as he pounded his fist on gold. Abarōz ran over, leaning in at his side to see a tumbler with ten random numbers.

"Great." Abarōz wiped away sweat as she stared at the squat gold box. "How," she asked, "will we ever find the true combination?"

"That is an excellent question. There must be thousands of choices."

"Probably more," said Abarōz. "I'm not sure what to do."

Neither did Shāhpuhr, who paced in a small circle. He shut his eyes and sighed. "Do you know," he asked, "when Dardan was first founded?"

"By the new god, no! And if I did, it would probably just be a lie."

"Come to think of it," he said, "ten digits would be too many. Such a number would be before the zands—perhaps even Gehān itself."

"I can't imagine such a time."

"Hmm." Shāhpuhr gazed at the lock, thoughtful. "My mother said she helped Tengri when he created the world. She even told me the year: 4,543,000,000."

"What?" exclaimed Abarōz. "Does such a number even exist?"

Shāhpuhr nodded, using his index finger to slowly revolve the tumbler's digit. It gave a loud click after he'd reached the last zero, causing the giant door to move.

"Careful!" Shāhpuhr yelled, pushing Abarōz back. But the door swung inward, coming to a smooth halt.

As the two of them stood there, neither was able to speak. What Abarōz saw before her was an enormous quartz tunnel, lit almost as brightly as Mihr to support the work of its zarran. These looked a sorry lot, dressed in filthy robes, with what looked like gold helmets affixed to dripping candles. Overseeing them were glowering guards, a steel lance in each of their hands and a long whip in the other.

Abarōz cringed at the crack of leather as a poor zarran's back was struck. His flesh was already striped with the scars of old wounds.

"You there!" cried a guard, whirling as the door shut. "No one is allowed to enter if they have the power of speech!"

"You must be an exception," Abarōz said fearlessly.

"Hold your tongue, girl, lest you lose it!" Abarōz crossed her arms. "Who sent you here? Or are you just another traitor looking to steal the Š̄āh's gold?" Abarōz held firm. "Daughter of a dog!" yelled the guard, lowering his lance to charge her. "You won't live to see another worktime!"

"You may be describing yourself," said Shāhpuhr, rushing not away but *toward* the guard. In one swift motion, he relieved the man of his weapon. "I think," he said, "you should apologize to my friend."

The guard nodded to Abarōz, his face contorted in a smile.

This act of defiance—perhaps the first one down here—seemed to embolden the zarran, who lifted their stone axes at the heads of their oppressors.

"That's the way!" cheered Abarōz, clasping her hands together. "For too long, you've been silenced. Now is the time to strike back!"

One too-thin zarran, his arms made burly by mining, raised his ax in a sort of salute. Taking advantage of the rebellion, Abarōz ran down the tunnel, motioning for Shāhpuhr and the zarran to follow. She finally halted, panting, to a far section that wasn't blazing with light.

She put her hands on her knees, trying to recover.

"I know," she told the zarran, "they've taken your power of speech. But I think you've seen things—know things—that those above you don't."

He nodded, giving a gritty smile as he reached up to his helmet, setting its candle down.

"How," Abarōz asked, "do we get to the city of Šahr? I've heard rumors there is a passageway, but of course the Š̄āh keeps it secret."

The zarran nodded, dropping the head of his ax to etch crisscrossed lines on the floor.

"What's he telling us?" Abarōz said to Shāhpuhr.

Her friend smiled.

"He's making us a map."

He and Abarōz crouched over the complex drawing. She saw what the zarran was doing: piling Hamwar on Hamwar until he came to Four—just one up from the Šāh. There, he drew a dirt arrow.

"Oh no," Abarōz groaned. "Do you know what this means?"

Shāhpuhr groaned.

"We have to go back almost to where we started."

Abarōz tried to buoy their spirits.

"If we made the trip once," she said, "then we can do it again."

"Let's hope so."

"You know the old Dardan saying? 'A person does not seek luck: luck must seek the person.'"

"I've never heard that," said Abarōz, "but if it's a Dardan belief, it probably isn't true."

She looked at his face, the zarran's candle plying it with shadow. That's when she made a decision.

"Shāhpuhr," she told him, "this was never your fight. Finding Šahr seems far too dangerous. I must insist you must return to Bükrek."

Shāhpuhr just stood up straighter.

"Just because," he said, "I was considered imperfect does *not* make me a coward. I am with you until the end—wherever that may lead."

Abarōz blinked back tears.

"Right now, it leads ten Hamwars up."

He nodded, then whirled to face the door. They could all hear sounds getting louder.

"Ayār," he said to the zarran, using the Dardan word for "friend," "we can't thank you enough. But I must ask a last favor: is there any way out besides that massive gold door?"

The zarran gave a wink, pointing down the dark tunnel. He spread his hands wide to indicate distance, then traced a small square on the wall.

"Thank you, Ayār!" cried Abarōz.

Shāhpuhr bent and seized the candle before she, foregoing all modesty, grabbed his hand to drag him along.

"Not so fast," he groaned, his cheeks flushing, Abarōz slowed to a walk. But something strange came over her as they passed gold-streaked quartz.

"Wait," she hissed, standing on tiptoe to grab a palm-sized white stone whose top sprouted a nugget. Shāhpuhr stared at her find. "You never know," she said, "but in a city that worships gold, this might well proof useful."

He nodded as they resumed their trek. The voices behind became faint, dwindling into silence. After striding for what seemed hours, Abarōz let out a sigh as their candle did the same. They were now enveloped in darkness.

The two of them locked arms as they not so much walked as stumbled into the depths of the mine. If Dardans only knew how deep these gold veins stretched, they might have wondered why there was none for them.

"How much longer," panted Abarōz, as the heat became stifling, "do you think we need to go?"

"I'm not sure," Shāhpuhr said. "But if that map was to scale, at least another half level."

"This is daft," muttered Abarōz, Shāhpuhr keeping her from falling—again. "I should have thought my plan through. And asked the zarran to join us. I should have brought more candles—"

"Should have, would have, could have," Shāhpuhr intoned from her side. "And if I had wings, I could fly like my mother."

Abarōz laughed. He was right. On a mission like this, there was no room for regret.

They faltered on in silence through what seemed the endless mine. It was only Shāhpuhr's fingers tracing the tunnel wall which kept them both from sprawling.

Weary from this taxing trip, Abarōz turned her thoughts to her mother. What would she say to see her daughter creeping along in the dark, holding onto a near-naked boy? Abarōz could commit murder and not be so reviled . . .

"Ouch!" Shāhpuhr yelled, unlocking his hand from hers and lifting it up to his face. "Is that where 'being nosy' comes from?"

"What?"

"I just hit my nose on a wall. Thanks to the Çor, it already hurt. But I think this means we've reached the end of the mine."

"Thank Tengri!" cried Abarōz. "Let's look for the zarran's door."

They both sank to their knees, running palms over warm rock. Abarōz's fingers searched for a groove, one that was perfectly straight. She was starting to get annoyed when her hand found a narrow gash.

"This might be it," she called. Shāhpuhr scooted closer, using his whole body to press against that stone. Abarōz did the same, her shoulder brushing his lightly. "Sorry," she whispered, glad he couldn't see her red face.

"Push!" Shāhpuhr ordered, his taut muscles straining. With a final groan, he dislodged what looked like a door.

"Good work," Abarōz smiled, crawling through the small opening. "Does this mean we've reached—" She saw a cave without quartz. "—Šahr?" Shāhpuhr crawled out to her side. "But if they don't have gold," she asked, "then how do they bribe the 'enemy'?"

"With silver," he said. "That's why so many more are sacrificed."

Abarōz shivered, stepping away from the torches lined in their sconces.

"It must be worktime," she said. "We'll have to wait for their night to find Shāhpuhr."

"Where should we hide in the meantime?" Shāhpuhr asked.

She jerked her head to a corner that wasn't blazing with light.

"You stay here," she whispered. "I'll try to find you some clothes. If someone sees you, there might be screaming—and not just from the women."

He gave her a grin as she slunk off, worry filling her mind. After all, she knew *nothing* about this city. Were the people friendly or hostile? And did they despise their neighbors? She felt as afraid as she had when she'd first stepped on the Bērūn.

Abarōz looked around. Instead of a scarred zarr, what she saw was a series of holes—cave entrances. Creeping forward, she stared into one to find a woman cleaning. Trying to find her courage, Abarōz went up to her.

The woman gasped at the sight of this strangely clothed stranger. Her own garb wasn't as drab: it looked comfortable, thin, and awash with color.

Maybe, Abarōz thought, *they grow more outside than just vegetables . . .*

She smiled at the woman who was stalking toward her, raising her sweeper like a sword.

"It's all right," Abarōz said, putting up a friendly hand. "I swear by Tengri I won't hurt you."

A stream of angry words flowed from the woman's mouth: Abarōz was relieved to find she understood most of it. Now, how to strike a bargain?

She reached behind to her pack, pulling out her pilfered white quartz. From its top, she snapped off a piece of gold. The woman's demeanor changed: she but down her sweeper, running forward to give Abarōz a hug!

"Great," Abarōz mumbled, "it has that effect on everyone. To the woman she said, "What I need from you are some clothes: for me and a very tall man."

The woman displayed a wide grin, then ran deeper into her cave to return with an armful of fabric. Abarōz looked at the jumble. Though splotched with color, she'd happily swap it for her wool!

"Thank you," Abarōz said, handing the woman her nugget.

"Please," she implored, "feel free to return any time!"

Abarōz nodded as she went back into the hallway. Now wonder the Šāh loved this metal! It turned enemies into friends.

She hastened back to Shāhpuhr who was trying to look smaller by crouching.

"Here," she hissed, throwing him his new clothes. "Let's pray to Tengri they fit!"

She turned her back before hearing a gentle scrape. That must be his discarded loincloth. Then there was a rustling, followed by him clearing his throat.

"Ready," he said.

She slowly turned, then clapped her hands to her mouth. He looked like another person, green robes belted at the waist with a long cloak sweeping his back. Only his hair, now pulled back, betrayed his forest origin.

"You look . . . good!" Abarōz cried, though—new god help her—she missed the sight of his bare chest! Stepping back, she mumbled, "I am going straight to Hell."

"Is that nearby?" he asked. "I thought we were staying in Šahr."

"No, no" Abarōz put up a hand. "It's a place where bad people go."

"Then why would *you* go there?" he asked.

"I am guilty of . . . never mind. Let me get out of this wool."

She slunk away, making sure his back was turned. It wasn't long before her itchy dress was replaced with cool fabric.

"Ah," Abarōz sighed, walking back to her friend. "Two cities so close together and only one knows how to dress."

Shāhpuhr surveyed her.

"You look good, too," he said without embarrassment. "Bright colors suits you."

"Even this garish red?"

"I like it. It reminds me of sweet-smelling flowers."

Abarōz shut her eyes, willing herself not to blush. She needed to change the subject—quickly.

"We should stay here until sleeptime. Try not to draw notice."

Shāhpuhr nodded, slumping against a wall. Abarōz did the same, trying to keep her distance.

"So," she said, "for the first time, really, you've seen a city. How do you like it?"

"I haven't seen much: just some stairs, torches, and a mine."

"Right. Well, has it changed your opinion at all?"

Shāhpuhr sighed, sliding farther down the wall.

"I'm not sure. In the forest, I'm free to do as I like. I don't answer to anyone—except Bükrek, of course. But as I told you, it does get lonely. Not seeing other people. Sometimes, I wish I could stay here for just one season each year."

"I know what you mean. Even though Dardan is stifling, I'd miss having people to talk to."

"That's why I'm so glad you came." Abarōz watched him grow serious. "To the forest, I mean. It made me feel less alone."

"Hmm," she said, "maybe that's the answer. Life in the Bērūn, only shared with others."

"Yes," he agreed. "I think you'll achieve that."

"Me?"

"Of course. Is that not your goal? After the Šāh is deposed."

"It would be heaven," she sighed, "but let's not forget about Sangal."

He grimaced as they stood there, both smiling at all who passed. In their new clothes, they must make fine-looking Šahrians.

Abarōz's back was aching by the time two small boys came by. *Thank Tengri!* They were steadily quenching the torches, using buckets of water.

The only drawback was the white smoke wafting across the hall. She and Shāhpuhr coughed, eyes reddening, until they were left in the dark.

"Now what?" asked Abarōz. "Our candle is spent."

"Do not worry."

Shāhpuhr crouched, his hands scouring the floor. When he rose, he was holding two small rocks which he proceeded to rub together. Once a spark had formed, he held it to the tip of a torch. In an instant, they were surrounded by heat and light.

"Brilliant," Abarōz whispered, admiring his skill. This simple boy of the forest boy could outthink most Dardans.

She watched him grab the torch before they moved down the hall, followed by only their shadows. Based on the zarran's crude map, she knew they had to walk far—to the end of this level. She just hoped there would be no Šahrians who liked to walk in their sleep.

This journey was much more pleasant than the one in Dardan since they could see where they were going. This hallway was much like her city's with its smattering of small caves. Until they came to a large one.

Abarōz peeked around its opening to see a circle of men numbering perhaps fifty. They all sat cross-legged around an idol that was as tall as Shāhpuhr. This god (if that's what it was) had been struck from pure silver, but what was even more curious were the razor-sharp rays protruding from his head. What manner of cult was this? Did they feast on human flesh after capturing their prey? Worship Mihr and Māh? Abarōz was certain of one thing: She didn't want to find out.

She motioned to her companion and they both sunk on the floor, his large hand cupping the torch. Like two human snakes, they slipped across the entrance. Once they were clear, they rose, Abarōz shaky from holding her breath.

"That was odd," she whispered, thinking that Šahr might be very different from Dardan. After all, they had their own god, and for all she knew, could be in the thrall of Sangal. She tried to dismiss these thoughts as she and Shāhpuhr continued their torch-lit trek. Abarōz's instinct twitched, telling her they were getting close. It hadn't failed her since they now faced a grey blocking wall. For the third time in two days, Abarōz ran her fingers over its length. But this time, the door found her: A small circle of white materialized, tugging at her head before sucking in her whole body.

From the other side where she'd landed, Abarōz watched numbly as the circle closed.

In the Garden

Abarōz stared at the floor. It was all she could see since she'd landed on her stomach. Like most cave floors, it was nothing special: just smooth greyish rock with the occasional pebble.

She rolled over, examining the rest of this cavern. Disappointing. Just another Dardan. With a slight groan, she pulled herself upright.

"Hello?" she called, not sure if she *wanted* to be found. What was it, exactly, that had pulled her through the circle? And why had it barred Shāhpuhr?

No answers came, but she felt a weariness that dragged her into its arms. She lay back on the floor, falling into a dreamless sleep, hard stone her only bed. When she opened her eyes, she barely knew where she was, then looked down at her new clothes. It all came rushing back: Šahr, the circle, this place. But now as she looked around, the cave was no longer empty. The whole floor was laid end-to-end with off-white snakes, none of whom rose in menace. The cavern itself had become a garden filled with bright flowers that rested below gushing falls. As Abarōz rose, she turned, spotting in the cave's center a white spreading tree perched on the back of a . . . dragon. Its thin, leafless branches arced up to the ceiling.

If you discarded Bükrek and Archura, she'd never seen anything this strange. But this sensation heightened and she actually screamed when her gaze fell on a creature perched at the side of the tree. It sat on a throne of white, wearing a crown on its . . . top head. This was that of a woman, her dark hair luscious and flowing; but the rest of her body was *coils*—ending in the head of a snake.

The woman's face looked down, displaying a kindly smile.

"No need to be frightened," she said, "for I am the one you seek."

Abarōz tried not to stare.

"Şahmeran?" she croaked.

The human head nodded.

"Mother to all things in nature and queen of my Marans."

She arched her lower coils, causing her snake head to hiss.

"I see," said Abarōz. Those "Marans" must be her snakes. But why they were hidden here, along with their queen, was a question she feared to ask.

"The Imperfect One has suggested you see me. May I ask why?"

Abarōz slowed her breathing.

"His name is Shāhpuhr, and as for the rest . . ." She squared her shoulders, trying not to react as snakes lapped at her ankles. "My father—"

"—Made Axwaš," said Şahmeran. "I am very sorry."

"Thank you. It is my wish to avenge him and defeat the Šāh Al. He makes life in Dardan worse than a vicious snake pit."

Abarōz clapped a hand to her mouth.

"It is all right—you do not know," Şahmeran told her gently. "We are not evil; rather, we are healers. It is only since the one god that we have become despised."

"Oh."

A wave went through the Marans, almost as if they were laughing.

"Can . . . can you help me?" asked Abarōz. Now was not the time to flinch.

"What do you wish to achieve, apart from removing Al-razi ?"

Abarōz gulped. She tried not to stare at Şahmeran's coils. "Well, after that, we must defeat the enemy that lurks outside our walls."

"Hmm." Şahmeran closed her four eyes. "Abarōz, your name means 'great strength,' and you will surely need it."

"I promise to do my best."

Şahmeran reopened her eyes, gazing down at her guest with sympathy.

"I can tell you," she said, "that you and your zand have no chance against Sangal."

Abarōz felt her tears form. So this is what she'd come for after sneaking her way through two cities?

"Do not despair," said Şahmeran. "I meant only at present."

Abarōz perked up. What did the snake queen have in mind?

"To fight your greatest enemy, you must secure a magick which is not in my power to give. But . . ." Abarōz felt hope rush through her. "The Tree of Life at my side reaches into the heavens and is home to magickal creatures. I suggest you climb its branches and present your cause to the Perils."

"The–the what?"

"Some are good and some are not, but you will know the difference."

"How do I recognize them?"

"They will come to you."

Abarōz's mind was churning as she glanced at the Tree with fear. She'd come from a world where climbing—besides stairs—was all but was unknown. So how could *she* hope to scale those perilous white branches?

"You must," said Şahmeran calmly. "It is the only way."

Abarōz sighed. She had, after all, promised to do her best.

"Very well," she said. "But if I fall, I might tumble on top of your head."

Şahmeran's human head laughed while her snake one hissed. Abarōz took both as a sign of approval.

"I suppose I should go," she said, eyeing the Tree with distaste. "Any advice?"

"Trees have a mind of their own and can read your intentions. If they are pure, you'll be allowed to climb to the Perils. If not . . . you'll be shaken off to your death."

"I'll be nice to the tree," said Abarōz. "I just hope the Perils are nice to me."

"That remains to be seen."

"Thank you."

Abarōz bowed her head, turning from the snake queen.

"One last question. How do I climb?"

"Simple," Şahmeran answered. "Put one hand in front of the other."

Abarōz nodded, actually hearing her pulse as she approached the dragon.

"Greetings," she told it. "Would you . . . er . . . permit me to pass?"

The beast, white as any Maran, shook its head up and down. Hesitant, Abarōz put out a foot and stepped onto his back. Standing on tiptoes, she hoisted her way to low branches, gulping at their sharp points.

If this was the Tree of Life, then why did she feel that hers was about to end?

Paristan

Those branches really were sharp. As Abarōz grasped them, trying to avoid rough knots, she questioned her soundness of mind. Before long, her palms were scratched and bleeding; and her legs, shot through with pain, already trembled beneath her. She was a girl who had led a quiet life: one without much exertion. Now, she cursed herself as she struggled to find a perch, nearly losing her balance. By Tengri, she'd rather fight Sangal than continue this journey!

I suppose, she thought, *this wasn't meant to be easy,* a view reinforced by bodies hanging limp from low branches. Some were human and some were beasts, while others didn't look injured but simply sobbed to themselves. What kind of tree *was* this?

And just how high were these Perils? Was their home close to the ground or at the apex of heaven? Since there was no way to know, she worked her limbs in tandem, gaining a fair bit of height. Looking down, she saw a floor crawling with white and the top of Şahmeran's throne. After a brief rest, she grabbed the next branch up, but not roughly—whatever else, she needed the Tree to like her.

Though she'd had no experience except the flight with Bükrek, Abarōz found she wasn't afraid of heights. Just now, there was nothing to see anyway: merely a tangle of branches pressing into her skin. She wished that the Tree had leaves so she had something to smell. And that she weren't alone, but had Shāhpuhr at her side. He could be such a help, urging her up and ready to catch her if she started to fall. She missed, she confessed, his lanky form, his rich dark hair, and the intensity of his eyes.

Stop! she told herself. *You're going to fall to your death while sighing after a boy!*

She concentrated on her climb, taking it branch by branch. If she didn't think too far ahead, she didn't panic. But, as a knotty branch struck her head, she reserved the right to be cross.

Up, up, up . . . why was there never a down? She'd been doing this so long now, she had to take frequent breaks. But thank the new god, no bodies hung this high. At one point, Abarōz halted, wondering if she should sleep. Yet how would that work? Nestle in a perch and pray she wouldn't plunge to her death? Instead, she continued, moving her limbs like a confused camel: right hand and left foot together—then the reverse. As she started to sway from fatigue, her sense of time and place left her—she could have been in Dardan, the Bērūn, or nestled in Shāhpuhr's arms. But where was she, really? And what were those devilish sticks that spread endlessly up?

She lost the feel of her own body; she was made of mist and mist had no sensations. At least this way she wasn't aware of the pain in her arms and legs. Wherever she was glorious—she meant horrible; maybe somewhere in between. When her mind snapped back, she remembered it was Şahmeran who'd suggested this journey. And, she wondered, could this part-snake creature be trusted?

Her whole world became white branches as pain struck again. She almost welcomed falling if it meant she could stop. With such dismal thoughts, she went numb at the sight of a village. That must be what it was, since it held wood bridges fastened by rope and huts carved into the trunk of the Tree. There was light all around: not the dense blaze of a torch, but white dots spread out like a web.

Where in Gehān was she? Had she finally reached the Perils? And how would she know, as Şahmeran warned, the bad ones from the good?

With the last strength left in her arms, she crawled down a branch to a bridge, where she promptly collapsed. All she saw was blurred white rope until a pair of boots—pointed—came to a halt beside her.

"Greetings," said a bass voice, and Abarōz looked up to find a being of normal size clothed in a yellow robe, his hair quite long and dark, and his face obscured by a beard. But there was one feature which stood out above all—he had enormous white wings.

"An angel!" Abarōz cried. She'd heard all about them during the new god's services.

The being didn't smile; his mouth retained its tight line.

"No, I am a Peril. I know nothing of angels."

"At last!" breathed Abarōz. "You are the very creature I seek."

"Hardly a 'creature,'" the Peril huffed. "That's what I would call *you.*"

"Sorry," said Abarōz. "I did not mean to offend, but Şahmeran told me—"

"First things first."

The Peril offered an arm to help her to her feet, his wing brushing her shoulder. Its touch was smoother than stone: like being brushed by soft grass.

The Peril startled her by saying with resignation, "Let's get you watered and fed."

"Hmmp."

Abarōz wasn't too happy at being compared to a beast, but with little choice, she followed him over the bridge.

"My home." The Peril spread a wing over a large tree-hut. "By the way, my name is Manuchehr[1]."

"And I am Abarōz. Of Dardan."

"Well, at least you have manners." He folded in his wings. "Let's attend to your needs."

"Thank you," she said, then trailed him inside. The sweet smell of wood greeted her, along with mosses and plants spread across the floor.

"Beautiful," she exclaimed, thinking that her climb might have been worth it.

"Here."

Manuchehr[2] set a wood bowl before her, one filled with purplish grain. "Eat," he told her, "and drink." He poured a berry-red liquid into a goblet of pure gold.

"You–you have gold?" asked Abarōz, taking a tentative sip. She was no master of wine, but this one was delicious, tasting of . . . the forest. Flowers mixed with waterfalls.

---

1. https://www.behindthename.com/name/manuchehr/submitted

2. https://www.behindthename.com/name/manuchehr/submitted

"Yes," Manuchehr[3] answered, his face growing wistful. "There was a time we lived below, welcomed by every zand."

Abarōz couldn't help being curious.

"What happened?"

The Peril sighed leaning against one smooth wooden wall.

> "They grew suspicious of magick." He closed his eyes. "Sometimes, I can still hear their songs and see their merry dances."

> "They lived outside then?"

"Yes. All over Gehān."

Abarōz felt a deep longing.

"I wish I had been there," she said.

"And *I* wish," said the Peril, "that I still was." He gathered his yellow robes. "I must go. You'll assume my post as Guardian."

"Oh."

"I will not return until morning. You must be spent from your climb, so please, take that bed." He gestured to a small one made from intertwined leaves. "Be careful."

Before she could ask of what, he had floated out of his hut.

Well. She was stuck in a tree at the home of a stranger—one who gave new meaning to "strange."

Still, the Peril had been right: she was bone-tired from her journey. Grateful, she threw herself on the bed and immediately went to sleep.

When she awoke, groggy, she thought she heard a low growl. Forcing her lids open, she felt a presence around her: one shrouded in grey mist. At first, she refused to accept it, dismissing it as a dream, but dreams couldn't gather closely at the head and foot of her bed.

"WHAT DO YOU WANT?!" she screamed, digging into her pack for her only weapon. As she sat up, that pitiful knife in one hand, she heard the sound of laughter, and it was directed at her.

"This is Manuchehr[4]'s house!" she cried. "And I am his guest."

---

3. https://www.behindthename.com/name/manuchehr/submitted

"Well," said a voice, much rougher than her host's, "then we must show hospitality."

Based on his tone, Abarōz didn't believe him, which was reinforced when a head poked through the mist. Thank Tengri! Nothing scary: the face looked much like Manuchehr[5]'s, but with a cruel expression.

"What should we do with her?" the Peril asked.

Another voice came from the mist.

"She is a stranger and will tell her zand of Paristan. I say we kill her."

"Wait!" Abarōz cried, "have you no respect for a guest?"

"Yes," said the Peril bent over her. "And no." Abarōz shook her head. "We are, unlike the holy Manuchehr[6], neither all good nor all bad."

"Our kind," spoke another, "fall somewhere in the middle."

"Oh."

Abarōz tried to take this in, but it was an unknown concept. In Dardan, one was either fully bad (the Sāh) or good (her father). In the forest of Razūr, all those she'd met had been good.

"You struggle," said a grey-shrouded Peril, "as we are neither here nor there."

"I suppose," Abarōz said. "But, wait—doesn't that mean you don't have to hurt me?"

"Unfortunately," came a voice.

"Quiet, Adurnarseh[7]," snapped the closest Peril. He looked down at her with distaste. "Make your case," he ordered, "and please, try to be quick."

Abarōz nodded and told them everything: about the corruption of Dardan, the sacrifice of her father, and her discovery of Şahmeran.

When she'd finished, the closest Peril spoke.

"We don't give a firefly's tail about the affairs of men." Abarōz grimaced. "But the snake queen: she has our highest respect."

Abarōz let out a breath.

"Then you're willing to help me?"

"If Manuchehr[8] agrees, I'd say yes."

---

4. https://www.behindthename.com/name/manuchehr/submitted

5. https://www.behindthename.com/name/manuchehr/submitted

6. https://www.behindthename.com/name/manuchehr/submitted

7. https://www.behindthename.com/name/adurnarseh/submitted

Abarōz nearly flew from her bed, dispersing her nighttime guests. Once the grey mist drifted outside, she saw that they had gone. She stayed up until those white dots began to brighten the trees. When Manuchehr[9] returned, she tackled him, nearly dragging him down.

"Please tell me I'm mad," she begged.

He looked like he wanted to agree, then set her down beside him.

"Visitors?" he asked.

Abarōz crossed her arms.

"You knew?"

"I had a suspicion. I have talked to Adurnarseh[10]. His group's agreement seals mine: when you require our service, you need only call."

"Really?"

"Some of us may be questionable, but I assure you *I* do not lie."

Abarōz moved toward him, arms outstretched, but he tensed his wings and moved back.

"Oh. Well, thank you," she said. "Thank you very much."

"Know that our laws compel us to avoid the affairs of men." He smiled. "At least, not actively. However, we have skills that can . . . how shall I put it? . . . serve you best in secret."

Abarōz couldn't say she understood, but she really didn't care.

"Well, whatever you do, please know that I'm grateful." Her eyes met her host's piercing blue ones. "May I–may I ask just one more favor?"

The Peril stretched his wings.

"So like a human," he huffed. "What is it?"

"Er . . . is there a way you can return me to my friend? I know that down is better than up, but I'm a terrible cl—"

Those were her last words before she was flung into a tunnel: not one made of rock, but composed wholly of air.

---

8. https://www.behindthename.com/name/manuchehr/submitted
9. https://www.behindthename.com/name/manuchehr/submitted
10. https://www.behindthename.com/name/adurnarseh/submitted

The Perils of Mining

“*Shāhpuhr!*” Abarōz cried after smashing onto his lap. “I’m so sorry—did I hurt you?”

His face contorted in pain.

“N-no . . . not at all,” he groaned. She gave him a moment to recover. “Where have you been? “I was ill with worry!”

Abarōz related what had passed, from the Queen of Snakes to the Perils. His eyes grew steadily wider until it seemed they might burst.

“By Tengri!” he breathed. “Where does all this leave us?”

“I–I’m not really sure.” Abarōz rubbed her rear, still sore from her surprise landing. “We have two new sets of friends, but one cannot leave her cave.”

“And the other, from what you’ve said, cannot actively help us.”

“True,” she sighed, scrambling off his lap. She already missed him. “Come on!” she cried.

“What?”

“Er . . . I was just thinking: How best to use our new allies?”

“I am but a boy of the forest,” he said, “and know little of war. But I do know about hunting, which is why we must leave Šahr.”

Abarōz looked warily down the still-dark tunnel. How long had she been gone?

“I agree. We must head back to the zarr.”

“After our last visit, I assume they’ll have more guards to greet us?”

“That makes sense,” she said, glad that he was there. “I say we ask the zarran to rise against them. There are many, and they know how to swing an ax.”

Shāhpuhr nodded, leading her from the outside of Shāhpuhr's cave to the door between the two cities. Now that they knew where it was, they were able to scramble quickly into the heat-soaked mine. Like the Perils, it was both good and terrible: thin veins of gold glinting, trapped in magnificent quartz. How many lives had been lost to remove the precious stuff? To drape over the Šāh, but never the people below him.

This trip, at least, was slightly better than their first. They knew how long it would take and where the tunnel would twist. Small flickers in the near-distance, accompanied by loud cracks and groans, told them they were close.

Once the lights resolved into candles atop the zarran's helmets, Abarōz and Shāhpuhr slunk back against a wall.

"What's our strategy?" he whispered.

"We go in yelling, imploring the zarran." He gave her an odd look. "You'd be surprised: sometimes words are better than weapons."

He looked unconvinced, but readied to join her as she sprinted forward.

"ZARRAN!" she yelled, "I am the daughter of Rastag! I plead with you to join us—to cast off the chains of tyranny!"

Though their power to talk had been stripped, they could certainly hear. The zarran massed together, hefting their sharp rock axes. Then Abarōz heard a sound coming from hundreds of throats: the rallying cry of the speechless.

This terrified the guards, who looked like they were surrounded by wolves. And, in a sense, they were, since the zarran swung their hafts together like a pack on the hunt. No more would they be oppressed. No others would be savagely tortured. With every strike at one of the Šāh's hated men, their axes whistled *Enough*.

Soon there were no guards left: not those who were living, anyway. Abarōz faced the zarran whose faces glowed with pride.

"Today," she told them, "you have done something that future Dardans will write about. But, be warned—we cannot just sit on our victory. They will come for us, and we need to be ready." She walked out a bit and addressed the ceiling. Shāhpuhr looked concerned. "Manuchehr," she said, "and worthy Perils, now is the time to help us. I beg you to appear."

Nothing happened and some of the zarran looked sad. Then, there was the scrape of boots against rock as Manuchehr and six other Perils flew through the roof to land beside them.

"It's all right," Abarōz told everyone, including Shāhpuhr. "These Perils are our friends." She shot a look at Manuchehr. "I think."

He gave her a wry smile, looking out of place with his wings in a hot quartz tunnel.

"I did not bring," he said, "the Circle of Seven to harm you. Did I not have my chance in Paristan?"

"You did," agreed Abarōz, wiping her eyes, "and I can't thank you enough for coming."

"Pssh!" the Peril snorted. "Our first task here is to point you in the right direction." Abarōz opened her mouth, but before she could speak, he went on, "You think your 'enemy' is the Šāh? Did you even consider the ebrens who lurk outside your gate?" Abarōz dropped her head. In her haste for revenge, she'd almost forgotten Sangal. "For you to defeat your ruler, you must *first* defeat the dragons. Without their protection, he is nothing."

Abarōz looked at Shāhpuhr. The Peril's words rang true. Still . . .

"But Manuchehr," she protested, "how can mere men fight dragons? They're–they're *huge,* with enormous claws and teeth!"

"I am aware," he said tartly. "Do you think we Perils have never faced them?"

Abarōz blushed.

"Sorry."

"Hmmp. Now the worst thing about dragons isn't their claws or teeth. It's not even their size."

Abarōz knew the answer.

"Fire," she said.

"Right." Manuchehr faced her, blue eyes sweeping over the rest. "And . . . you Dardans cannot fight unless your plate is flameproof."

"But, that's impossible!" Abarōz cried. "Everyone knows there's no such thing."

"Not of your making," huffed the Peril. "But *we* have magick, correct?"

"Yes, but . . . how do you propose to do this?"

"The gold," he said, gesturing to the quartz. "It is all around you. It has sat so long in the mine, crying out to be free. Can't you hear it?" Abarōz shook her head. "You might consider gold a mere metal but it has feelings too. It doesn't like being used for greed. It would rather do something helpful."

"I see," said Abarōz, hoping that she did. "But what does that have to do with keeping us safe from fire?"

Manuchehr sighed.

"When we Perils lived on the surface, we witnessed mighty battles; horrible weapons of war. And men slain by the thousands."

Abarōz shuddered.

"That can't have been very pleasant."

"No," said Manuchehr, "but from this, we learned a lesson: the side with more and better armaments wins."

"I should think," Abarōz blurted, "that would be fairly obvious."

"Careful," the Peril warned. "If I turn against you, it could go badly." But his smile undercut his words. "What you need, child, is simple: plate that resists fire. And we are here to supply it."

"From the gold," she said slowly, starting to understand. *"But wait!* Doesn't gold burn?"

"Yes," he answered, "That's why we are required. Once the plate is forged, we instill it with our magick."

"Hmm." Abarōz thought, turning her gaze to the zarran. "And who will build this armor?"

"We will," said Manuchehr, "once these men provide the gold. Give us the materials, and we will do the rest."

Abarōz pursed her lips.

"Your presence here," she said, "must be kept a secret. If more guards come, imprison them, but that's all. Also, the miners must keep supplying the Ōšmurdan with their usual tally of gold."

The zarran who'd helped them by drawing the map walked up to her and smiled. He nodded, as did his fellow miners. They set off down the tunnel and began hacking away.

"Should we stay here with you?" Abarōz asked Manuchehr, gesturing to Shāhpuhr.

"You need not," he said. "I'll return you to a place that's safe . . . for now."

"Very—" Abarōz started, but before she got to "well," she was plopped into a forest which she recognized as Razūr. "Ouch!" She yelled, rubbing her bruised behind.

Couldn't the Perils with all their magick land her on her two feet?

"Are you all right?" asked Shāhpuhr from where he lay on the grass.

"Er . . . I think so."

He sprang up, then extended a hand. Once she rose, she was only a hand's breadth away.

"You look nice," she said, backing up, "in those new clothes. Though they're a bit much for the forest."

He smiled.

"Many thanks."

Abarōz turned her head. Just a week ago, she didn't dare *speak* to a boy—much less give him a compliment!

Shāhpuhr change his stance, trying to hide his crooked foot.

"Shāhpuhr," Abarōz said, "you know that I don't care."

He smiled.

"That's why I like you so much."

Abarōz retreated farther onto the dew-kissed grass.

"That's sweet," she said, "but how many other humans do you know?"

"Enough," he replied, "to know that you are special."

Abarōz felt that she should change the subject before it was too late.

"Don't you think we should find your mother?" she asked.

Shāhpuhr nodded, leading her through the woods to the riverbank. When Abarōz stared at the water, she thought she saw some green scales poking out.

"Bükrek!" she yelled, unable to hold back. "I was able to see Şahmeran!"

"Excellent," the dragon said calmly, raising her head.

"And–and I climbed the Tree of Life and the Perils agreed to help us! They're in the zarr right now."

Bükrek smiled, shaking water from her head.

"Their magick is ancient and powerful. We could not ask for better."

Abarōz felt a real pride: it was *her*, after all, who'd brought them here!

"Wonderful as this news is," said Bükrek, "we have a more pressing concern."

Abarōz felt her spirits fall.

"Sangal will tire of waiting. He will bring the war to our door. That is why we must prepare."

Abarōz had heard so much about this being, but she didn't know what he was.

"Is he some kind of ebren?" she asked.

"One of my kind who was there for the world's creation. We emerge every thousand years to appear on Gehān." She chuckled. "We once had a nine-year battle."

"By Tengri!"

"Yes, when I won, he plunged into a lake of fire." Abarōz stared at Shāhpuhr. He seemed to know this story. "He dwelt there for millennia, growing more bitter with each. It was he who called forth the ebrens who presently threaten Dardan. Of late, he has resurfaced with the aim of destroying our world."

"But why?"

"He is the very spirit of chaos. What has been made, he seeks to unmake."

Abarōz felt a chill.

"Can he?"

"He is both brutal and cunning."

Shāhpuhr crossed his arms.

"No one," he said, "has ever defeated Sangal." He gave his mother a pointed glance. "Except you. And you're not allowed to fight unless he attacks first. Where then does that leave us?"

Bükrek blinked her yellow eyes.

"We shall see," she said. "There might come a time when I ask you both to go on a journey."

Sangal Strikes

"I am most annoyed," I growl, staring down from my rock perch at the lone Dardan below. Kavad tries to look unshaken as I stretch my red neck, staring into his tiny eyes.

Such cowards. These men fancy themselves so clever but are hardly a match for me . . .

"Wh-what is wrong?" the Dardan asks, dropping his gaze from mine. As well he should.

"The gold," I roar back in his harsh, guttural language—speaking it hurts my throat. "The tithes are reduced," I say, my speech slow as if to an imbecile. "Your Šāh keeps my share for himself! Does he not think I know this?"

"Great Sangal," the dog says, stuttering, "I–I assure you it is not so. The Ōšmurdan tell him that the zarran work harder than ever."

"But . . . are they working for *me?*" I ask, blowing white smoke from both my nostrils. I know how this frightens these insects!

"Of course!" the mongrel assures me, shaking his head so hard it's in danger of flying from his body.

Perhaps a good future plan . . .

"My patience is at an end," I say. It is not something I'm known for. "If I am to crush Bükrek, I must lure the Gurg Kamāl with promises of treasure."

"I understand, Sangal," says the fool.

I pause to consider. A plan has been hatching for days.

"My ebrens and I will first cut off your water. If my tithe does not increase, I shall assail Dardan, underground or not!" The small man before me bows. "And one more thing," I say, giving him a view of my teeth. "If I don't get what I want, you'll be the first to die."

After I speak to my horde, I, of course, lead them from my lair. I am the first to unfurl my wings, flapping into the sky and shrieking a war cry. Behind me, I hear the whoosh of ebrens on the move; feel an unnatural wind as I guide them south.

It doesn't take long before desert gives way to a river. I lift my head, giving a call as I dive like a heron. I skirt close to the clear, placid water; my wings and those of my horde lifting huge chunks of dirt and thick branches.

"FASTER!" I yell. "I want to see those trees fall!"

To my delight, they do, unable to withstand me. One by one, they tumble, great trunks sliding down banks with splayed roots still attached. This was my aim. Before long, the Dardans will be starved of water, its source cut off at the head; before long, the parched and starving will beg on their knees before me, pleading for the great Sangal to please— oh please—relieve them.

Of course, I will make that promise—once I receive all the gold. But, like the river, I refuse to change my course, and those groveling moles will serve as meat for my horde. No more relying on traitors like Kangal. No more waiting for precious metal to be seized from the enemy's hands. Today marks a new beginning, and being immortal, I have seen many.

Once the river no longer runs, I summon my ebrens back home.

"Bring Kangal before me," I instruct my second-in-charge. "Tell him I have a message for his beloved Sāh."

The Stars

That night, while Shāhpuhr went off to find food, Abarōz lay in the soft grass. But she couldn't relax as she thought of Sangal. Where would he strike first? Here in Razūr, or Dardan? And when would her zand be ready to defend themselves in new plate? She almost wished she were back in the zarr so Manuchehr could update her.

Shāhpuhr returned just before supper with a rabbit, and, to Abarōz's puzzlement, a full sack of grain.

"Where did you get that?" she asked.

"Oh . . . I hide it in the forest." He gave her a wink. "For unexpected guests."

"I see." This must be the source of his bread. "Well . . . good," she said, pouring the grain in a bowl and mixing it with water. Then, using a branch as a pestle, she ground the grains, using small flat rocks to set out cakes of flat bread.

"You're better at this than I," said Shāhpuhr.

"I should be," Abarōz told him. "I've done it all my life."

He grinned, going off to gather sticks for a fire. Before long, he'd kindled a merry blaze, leading to a nice meal of rabbit garnished with mushrooms.

"I wonder how they are getting on," she said, earning a puzzled glance. "That is, the Perils."

"I wish we could find out," said Shāhpuhr, "but going back to Dardan—"

"—Will surely get us killed," she finished.

Abarōz sighed as she wiped her plate clean.

"I just wish that Manuchehr would send us some word."

"Perhaps he is busy," Shāhpuhr said. "Making flameproof plate cannot be a complex task."

"Don't you mean 'simple'?"

He blushed.

"Sorry. Sometimes I still make mistakes."

"But they have magick," whined Abarōz. By the new god, she hated when she did that!

"Yes, and it must take all their effort to forge it."

Abarōz huffed. She knew Shāhpuhr was being reasonable, but she felt a great impatience.

"Perhaps we will hear soon," she said with a shrug.

"Perhaps." He added more wood to the fire, illuminating Bükrek's coils as she slid toward them.

"Mother?"

"You're not going to like this," she said, "but I must ask you to leave tomorrow. Securing more ebrens is the only way we can win."

Abarōz went cold.

"You mean . . . *dragons?*"

Bükrek nodded.

"There are many in the Bērūn who distrust Sangal. They are somewhat loyal to me, but still completely wild. You must call on all your strength to become an Aswār of Ebrens—a Rider of Dragons."

"But Mother," Shāhpuhr protested, "there haven't been Aswārs for hundreds of years!"

Bükrek gave him a sad smile.

"You must revive the tradition."

Abarōz hugged her arms close.

"Dragons scare me," she said. "I heard their screams and roars the night they took my father."

"They can be fearsome," nodded Bükrek. "but not all are brutes. There is also in our nature a loving, caring side."

"To which Sangal is an exception."

"It will be fine," Shāhpuhr said, smiling down at her head. "I speak Dragon and basically know their ways. I will be there to protect you."

"Where exactly is 'there'?"

"The south," he told her. "That is where the good ebren live."

"And the bad?"

"To the north."

Abarōz gulped, not wanting to doubt him but feeling a tremor like a quake beneath Dardan.

"We should rest," said Shāhpuhr. He threw two blankets over the grass at the edge of his crackling fire.

Abarōz lay down but was consumed by worry.

"What," she asked, "will prevent these ebrens from taking us hostage in return for Dardan gold?"

Shāhpuhr's laugh echoed through the clearing.

"Who would pay our ransom?" he asked. "Besides, there is always my mother who, though kind, can be strict upon occasion." He rubbed his rear. "I still have scars where she spanked me."

"In other words, the nice dragons are scared of her?"

Her friend pursed his lips.

"If they're not, they should be."

She took this in, resting her head on her arms as she surveyed the sky.

"What are those?" she asked, pointing up to the twinkling dots.

"Axtars," said Shāhpuhr. "Mother told me they were created by Ülgen, a god beholden to Tengri. Ülgen lives above us, on the sixteenth floor of the sky, and moves the axtars about."

"But what do they do?" Abarōz asked. "Are they just meant to be pretty?"

"I can't say," said Shāhpuhr. "Mother says that some men believe they never move, but I have seen them drift across the sky."

"I suppose," Abarōz said, thinking of home, "that some think the new god created them. But that they themselves are not gods."

Shāhpuhr sighed.

"Only Tengri would know."

Abarōz stared at his crouching form. In the glow of their small blaze, he looked especially striking, his prominent nose and dark skin drawing her in.

Could we ever . . . ? she wondered, then stopped, dismissing her thoughts as nonsense. *He* was a boy of the forest, and she? A proper Dardan girl who only knew city life. How could they be more than friends with such dissimilar pasts?

Still . . .

Her mind continued to plague her as she tried to drift into sleep. Just as her dreams offered a tantalizing vision of the future, she felt a slight pressure on her upturned cheek.

If it were day, she would have flushed brighter than Mihr. As it was, she heard the roll of a tall body settling down to rest.

Had Shāhpuhr just kissed her?

The Tallying

The next morning, when Abarōz woke, she glanced at Shāhpuhr and blushed. Had last night's kiss really happened, or was it merely her wish? He looked the same as ever, sitting cross-legged on the grass and munching a crust of bread. She wondered if she should ask him, but knew she didn't have the courage. The question became moot as she saw a small speck soaring toward them: green and scaly, moving quickly across Mihr.

"Bükrek?" Abarōz asked, watching the speck descend.

"Yes," said Shāhpuhr, shielding his eyes. "Something amiss?" he called to his mother.

"I'm afraid so," Bükrek answered, sliding her coils to join them. "Sangal has made a first strike. I've come to learn he's poisoned Dardan's water, which means an attack will come soon."

"But why?" Abarōz whispered. Hadn't she told Manuchehr to keep the gold counts high? Enough to appease the Šāh and the beast who pulled his strings.

"Because he is Sangal," said Bükrek, "and lives for the pain of others."

Abarōz wanted to curse, but she wouldn't do so out loud. Instead, she thought of her zand whose members would perish from thirst.

"What can we do?" she asked, plucking at her skirt.

"Forget the south for now," said Bükrek, "and return to the zarr. Check on the Perils' progress and prepare the Dardans for war."

Abarōz felt her skin prickle, though she'd known this day would come.

"Very well," she sighed, "I guess it's back to the city. Just what I dreaded most."

"Do not despair," said Shāhpuhr, "I will go with you. And my mother can surely set us before the gate tonight."

"I will," Bükrek agreed. "though you are not yet Aswārs, you can climb on my back and hold on."

"Thanks," said Abarōz with a sickly smile.

"Well," Shāhpuhr told her, "we can see where the Perils are. So your wish came true."

"In a manner of speaking."

"We can do what we did before—creep down those stairs in the dark. Check on the Perils and persuade some Dardans to wear the flameproof plate."

"Easy," said Abarōz, her tone slightly mocking.

"It can be if we're careful. We need only avoid the guards and pretend we have business below."

"Inciting rebellion?" she asked.

"Something like that."

It was a tense wait until nighttime when Bükrek reappeared, unloosing her coils. Shāhpuhr urged Abarōz forward as his mother slunk close to the grass. Picking Abarōz up by the waist, he hoisted her so she could swing out a leg, then sit atop the dragon. He leapt behind her, wrapping her in his arms.

"No need to worry," he said as she grabbed a green spike. "This journey shouldn't take long."

Abarōz tried to nod as Bükrek took off. She felt her stomach drop to her sandals as a dragon-made wing stirred around them. Still, she wasn't afraid to look down to see green recede and sand take its place. As Bükrek gained height, her snout angling skyward, Abarōz fought to stay calm. If Shāhpuhr weren't behind her, his hands holding her fast, she would surely be on her way to the top of a dune.

Shāhpuhr was right: this journey was mercifully short. When you traveled by dragon, you nearly outshot the moon. Bükrek, knowing Dardan, flew high above the main gate to land without noise by the hatch.

"That was . . . " Abarōz couldn't speak. She just wanted her feet to hit sand. When they did, she recited a prayer to Tengri.

"Thank you, Mother," said Shāhpuhr, and Bükrek nodded before taking off again. Abarōz saw her winging her way back to the tranquil forest.

Shāhpuhr motioned her forward until they both stared down at the hatch.

"You first," Abarōz said. "If I fall on you, you won't be crushed."

"Are you sure?" teased Shāhpuhr.

Abarōz gave him a swat before throwing open the hatch. She leaned over to watch him descend the rope ladder. Though his left foot made him clumsy, he refused to slacken his pace. She came next, lowering herself before shutting the hatch.

"Very well," said Abarōz, scurrying down the last rung. "Again, to the zarr. It should be sleeptime in Dardan."

The two of them passed huddled livestock on their way to the staircase.

"Now," she urged and they both stepped down into blackness.

Shāhpuhr's fingers traced the wall in search of a nearby sconce. He found a torch sparked it, cupping the flame with his hand.

"Good thinking," Abarōz said, in a state of disbelief at having to make this journey again. Still, with the light, they made much faster progress, although each squeak on stone caused them to hold their breath. This time, they were lucky: no shadowy spies or guards emerged to surprise them. By the time they'd reached Abarōz's Hamwar, with only six more to go, she felt so light she even passed Shāhpuhr.

"We can do this," she mumbled, glancing over her shoulder to see her friend nod. Finally, after eighteen more sets of stairs, she felt a familiar heat.

She and Shāhpuhr stopped by the massive gold door where Abarōz knocked three times. This time, when it opened, they were greeted by friendly faces and not whip-wielding guards.

"Greetings," said Abarōz to a tired group of zarran. She started as Manuchehr[1] popped in beside her.

"You were expected," he said, "now that Sangal has cut off Dardan from its most precious resource . . . and by that, I do not mean gold."

"We know. Would it be possible to see what you've done so far?"

He gestured with one white wing.

"Of course."

1. https://www.behindthename.com/name/manuchehr/submitted

She and Shāhpuhr walked past newly sent guards, who, though bound, certainly looked well-fed. She stared above their heads to see an amazing sight: gold plate, piled halfway up the mine, glinting even in its dull light.

"You–you work fast," Abarōz said.

Manuchehr[2] rolled his blue eyes as he crossed his arms.

"We are Perils," he said. "We have magick. Did you expect us to work slowly?"

Abarōz gave him a smile.

"No, I guess not."

Shāhpuhr stepped forward.

"How many warriors can this plate outfit?"

"Twenty-five," answered Manuchehr[3].

"Hmm." Shāhpuhr stroked his chin. "I hope that is enough."

"It has to be," said Abarōz. "Besides, they're fashioning more."

She pointed down the tunnel to where six Perils stood in a circle, mumbling over a cauldron that bubbled over with gold. Beyond them, small bobbing lights told of the zarran at work—that, and the steady thud of their axes.

Abarōz felt an excited shiver.

"Come," she told her companions, "let's take a closer look."

She ran to the wall stacked with gold, seizing a breastplate. It was unlike any she'd seen with its small gold squares layered thickly; and, on the shoulders. sharp spikes like Šahr's idol. Lying nearby were gold pieces for forearms and calves with a separate mound devoted to weapons. Abarōz saw sleek swords and lances, plus round shields embellished with runes.

"What do they mean?" asked Abarōz, squinting down at the symbols.

Manuchehr[4] chuckled.

"They form an old Peril saying: 'When words don't work, be sure your weapons are sharp.'"

"Truer words were never spoken. Er, not that I doubt you, but . . . is everything fireproof?"

2. https://www.behindthename.com/name/manuchehr/submitted

3. https://www.behindthename.com/name/manuchehr/submitted

4. https://www.behindthename.com/name/manuchehr/submitted

The Pixel extended an arm, murmuring over the breastplates. A cascade of fire shot out, not causing a single drip.

"You were right," Shāhpuhr told Abarōz. "They are indeed possessed of strong magick."

"You didn't believe me?" huffed Manuchehr[5]. "A girl's word is better than mine?"

"No, no," said Shāhpuhr. "It's just that—"

"Please," Abarōz said "Let's save our fights for the enemy."

The Peril nodded.

"You're right," he said. "Now is the time to find warriors willing to wear this plate."

Although Abarōz nodded, she felt her stomach clench. How to approach fellow Dardans if even *one* served the S̄āh? She'd end up like her father, supper for Sangal's hordes.

Shāhpuhr seem to sense this.

"No," he said, putting a hand on her shoulder. "The danger is far too great."

"We discussed this," Abarōz fumed. "Why employ the Perils only to waste their work?" Shāhpuhr set his mouth. "Let me go," she said, but he shook her head. "This my zand," she insisted. "I lived with them my whole life and am familiar with their ways. Some will remember my father. I know this is a risk, but we must take them to win."

She saw a grudging acceptance spread across Shāhpuhr's face.

"Of course, I'm coming with you," he said as if the matter were settled.

Abarōz nodded grudgingly, not wanting to put him in danger but still glad for his presence. They both picked up golden swords.

"Ready?"

He followed her to the door which swung back without protest. Abarōz beckoned for him to follow as they marched to an area just outside the zarr. Harsh sounds of scale chains falling and the clink of metal told her where they were: among the Ōšmurdans.

She approached one with a smile. The man, gaunt and harried, continued to weigh gold nuggets.

5. https://www.behindthename.com/name/manuchehr/submitted

"Greetings," Abarōz said. "You Ōšmurdans work hard." She hesitated. "Did–did you by chance know my father? His name was Rastag."

The man ran a hand through his grey hair, looking like he'd been struck.

"I know no traitors, living or dead, to our glorious Šāh," he recited.

But his eyes, filled with worry, would not rise to meet hers. Abarōz crossed her arms.

"I take it that you did," she said.

The man took up a nugget, rolling it between his fingers.

"Be careful in your speech," he hissed. "Even in your thoughts. They say the Šāh is a Zehn̥ Xan who can penetrate our minds."

Abarōz snorted.

"That is a false rumor. If it were so, I'd be dead twenty times over."

The man seemed to untense . . . slightly.

"What is your name?" asked Abarōz.

"Pabag[6]."

"And I can see you know who I am."

"They say," Pabag whispered, "that you fled to the Bērūn. Escaped the enemy's swords to be rescued by a tree."

"It sounds strange to hear it," said Abarōz, "but that is entirely true. However, you're missing all that came after." Pabag narrowed his eyes. "The Perils have magicked gold plate which no flame can destroy. That is how we'll survive—against the dragon lord."

"Dragons?!" Pabag gasped. "Girl, you must be mad!"

"Unfortunately, no," said Abarōz. "The 'enemy' outside our gate are not men, since they have four claws and a tail."

"Saints preserve us!"

"If you Ōšmurdan fight with us, we may not need them at all."

"And just why," Pabag asked, crossing his arms, "would we do that?"

"Because the dragon Sangal is planning to attack."

"Dardan?!"

"The water was just the beginning—now, we think he'll come for all the gold."

"We are doomed!" cried the Ōšmurdan, tossing away his gold nugget.

"No." Shāhpuhr said sharply.

6. https://www.behindthename.com/name/pabag/submitted

Pabag looked at him—and his Šahrian clothes—with suspicion.

"You are not one of us," he said tersely.

"No . . . and yes."

"I've no time for riddles, boy!"

"I am an Axwaš."

"Yet you *live?*"

Pabag looked skeptical.

"As you see, all things are possible."

Pabag gave Shāhpuhr a look as if he were a holy saint.

"Indeed."

"This is what we need," Abarōz told him. "Twenty-three men and women who are willing to go to war: to protect our home from those who seek to destroy it."

Pabag picked up his nugget, turning to stare at Shāhpuhr.

"If an Axwaš can live," he said, "I will find you these warriors."

"Thank you."

"Please tell them to come to the zarr tonight. Make sure there are no spies."

"Those traitors are well known to us. They will not be asked." Pabag thought for a moment. "One question: What is 'tonight'?"

"Oh, said Abarōz. "Sleeptime."

"We will see you later then."

Sangal's Response

Abarōz and Shāhpuhr returned to the mine courtesy of the gold door. She looked over the heads of zarran to see Manuchehr and his six Perils still muttering over their cauldron as molded gold emerged.

Approaching, Abarōz made out two full suits of plate still sizzling with magick.

"Very nice," she told Manuchehr. "I especially like the way they float."

He gave her a look of satisfaction, then pointed the tip of a wing toward his latest creation.

"These are yours," he said. "Try them on to see if they fit."

Abarōz ran toward the first suit, afraid to touch the metal. But Shāhpuhr had no such doubts: He lifted the breastplate over her head, twisting back to avoid spikes. She doggedly put on the rest: the pieces for arms and legs; even a thick gold helmet whose guards flared out at her chin. Apart from its fine worked gold, the suit amazed her with its sheer lightness. She felt she could run, jump, and rush without the burden of extra weight. When she turned to tell Shāhpuhr, she found herself staring at what could be her double!

"You–you look magnificent!" Abarōz cried, then blushed at her own boldness. "A far cry from the wild boy I once found in the forest."

Shāhpuhr looked down, his jaw working under his helmet.

"You too, Abarōz," he said, "look far different from the shy girl of Dardan. But your new strength lies more than in plate: it–it permeates your soul."

Abarōz hoped that her chin guards served to hide her reddening cheeks. When she thought back to that girl: cooking, cleaning, scraping low to villains, she felt like a snake that had grown a new skin.

She and Shāhpuhr chose their weapons as the Perils continued to work: a lance, sword, and shield for each. If Sangal attacked this second, at least the two of them were prepared.

Since sleeptime must be almost over, Abarōz wasn't surprised to hear a large door opening, muted footsteps, and the distinctive swish of wool. Twenty-three Dardans made their way toward her in silence.

"Welcome," Abarōz smiled. "As one of your zand, I well know your risk in coming here: if we are discovered, we will surely all be killed." Concerned looks crossed the faces of men, women, and those about her same age. "But," she went on, "do we not take risks simply by living? Under the S̄āh, any one of us could be murdered for either his sport or spite." The heads before her nodded. "What are we?" she asked, crossing her arms. "As long as we're in the Azēr, we're like burrowing moles who will never see the Bērūn. We might as give up our lives since the ones we lead resemble more of a death."

A murmur rose from the Dardans which culminated in shouts.

"I'm tired of being afraid!" a young boy cried.

"Of scrambling for dēnārs!" yelled a woman.

"Of spies reporting our every move!"

This from an angry-eyed man.

"Then we are decided," Abarōz said. "When Sangal and his horde attack, we must be ready. Please, each of you—find a suit and weapons. I have seen with my own eyes we cannot perish in flame!"

The Dardans before her all marched to the gold-stacked wall, pulling off plate that would suit them. They helped one another with buckles before choosing a sword and shield.

None was a trained fighter, but then again neither was Abarōz. She was counting on their shared feeling: a deep love of home, one without the stain of the S̄āh.

Abarōz shot a worried glance at Shāhpuhr. She figured that with so many citizens missing from the Hamwars above, they'd soon be visited by guards. But instead of the harsh stomp of boots, she heard the scuttle of sandals.

"Beware!" shouted a man who ran in breathlessly. He nodded to two of the warriors. "We've heard noises from the top—horrible roars and screams, louder than ever! The enemy has come!"

"Yes," nodded Abarōz, "but he is not who you think." She turned to the others. "Ebrens."

A terrified Dardan woman gripped her elbow.

"What do we do?" she asked in fear.

"Get up to the first Hamwar."

Abarōz set the precedent by running to the gold door, then mounting the first small staircase to begin her ascent. On her heels came Shāhpuhr and the others.

As they sprinted past each Hamwar, she could hear the cries of terrified Dardans. Some even took to the stairs, forcing Abarōz to gesture them toward the wall. Once they saw the warriors, they stepped aside in relief.

"FASTER!" she called to Shāhpuhr, quickening her own pace. She silently counted off every stairway: twenty-five, sixteen, five, three . . . it seemed they'd never get to the top until her foot left the last step.

"The gate!" she cried, moving past milling livestock to find a bend in the tunnel. *"This way!"*

She led them to where she thought it stood, she and the others pointing their swords at five guards in a silent command. They worked a thick rope on pulleys, slowly moving the massive boulder until it provided an opening.

"Look to the skies!" Shāhpuhr yelled as they stepped into near-darkness. Māh was barely a slice, hidden behind massed clouds. At least he and a few of the warriors had the sense to seize the guards' torches.

Abarōz stood by her friend, sword and lance at the ready. Where were those screaming beasts? Had they turned tail and fled? Her answer came as a red dragon soared around the mountain, ten ebrens in tow. They formed a sky-born "V," Sangal the tip of the arrow as his flight swept lower.

Once in range, Sangal spat out a sheet of flame, engulfing three plated warriors.

Abarōz watched as the Perils' magick repelled the blast like water. This seemed to infuriate Sangal, who let loose with a roar, swooping for a second pass.

"On your guard!" Shāhpuhr hissed, holding up his round shield. Abarōz did the same when the red dragon hovered above, targeting the two of them as he vomited flame.

Abarōz felt searing heat on the other side of her shield. Orange lit up the sand and for once it wasn't Mihr. Once the heat and light faded, it was replaced by strangling white smoke.

"Y-you all right?" Shāhpuhr coughed, lowering his shield with caution.

"Yes," Abarōz said, amazed as she saw a red shape, screaming, flapping its quick way east.

"Hmmp," said Shāhpuhr with relief, "guess Sangal is like a child."

"What do you mean?"

"If he doesn't get what he wants, he huffs off and heads home."

Despite the lingering tension, Abarōz giggled.

"That may be," she said, "but he's left nine of his ebren."

"Ahhhh!" A woman cried as she was picked up in a jaw, then hurled over the sand. A second dragon twisted down, pummeling her with its tail.

Abarōz and Shāhpuhr did their best not to be taken. They hacked at outstretched claws, swiped off black talons, and stabbed at unscaled throats. But how could they and the warriors match the strength of nine dragons? So many were raked or bitten that only a few still stood.

Before she could retreat, a green ebren, as vicious as Bükrek was kind, make his gliding way toward her until, despite her plate's spikes, it lifted her by the shoulders!

Abarōz kicked out furiously, now suspended over sand. She yelled down at Shāhpuhr, but, as the dragon shot up, what could he possibly do? As the torches' flames grew small, she reacted from pure instinct: raising her sword, she struck to separate the beast from its claw!

The green dragon's screams must have been heard on the ground: they spoke of pain and betrayal; and most of all, disbelief.

Abarōz found herself falling, down toward the flat plain lighted by tiny specks.

This must be it, she thought as she tumbled; probably, to those below, no more than a speck herself.

She steeled herself for landing, hoping the pain would be quick. But instead of hitting a solid surface, she felt but the grasp of strong arms.

Abarōz craned her neck, the pulse in her ears merciless.

"Shāhpuhr," she breathed. "How did—?"

"No time for that!" he shouted. "Our side's been slaughtered—we need to go!"

Abarōz managed to nod as her boots hit hard rock.

"RETREAT!" she yelled, running back toward the gate. Hearing the jingle of plate behind her, she ran with the survivors to frantically roll back the stone.

The Magick Ball

There were only nine left—but no Shāhpuhr. Abarōz slumped against the boulder, tears running onto her breastplate. *How could she have let this happen? Shāhpuhr, so skilled and well-muscled, slain by Sangal's ebrens as if he were a babe. And it was all her fault: For her, he'd given his life for a people who'd tossed him away.*

The word *"Why?"* turned in her mind as if it were on a wheel. Tengri or Jesus or *Someone* seemed to consider death as a game like Roll-the-Rock. Abarōz looked at those who were left, most injured and bleeding. Had this small group evaded Sangal just to be killed by the Šāh?

But, from the other Hamwars, Abarōz thought she heard echoes of wailing. Perhaps the Šāh was busy trying to placate the city after the enemy struck. Abarōz could almost see him giving dēnārs to those who'd lost a loved one.

"Abarōz," said Pabag—*happily, he'd lived!*— "I am glad to see you're all right."

"Not really."

"Your friend," the Ōšmurdan went on, "was *not* taken by ebrens." Abarōz couldn't move. "He was dragged back to the city . . . by the Šāh's personal guard."

She didn't know at that moment whether to cheer or mourn. That meant Shāhpuhr wasn't dead . . . didn't it?

"Why?" she finally choked out.

"I wish I could say, but I'm no vizier. Perhaps the new god knows."

Abarōz closed her eyes. If He did, he wasn't sharing.

"Bükrek," she said dully. "I've *got* to get to Bükrek."

"Don't be foolish," Pabag told her. "The ebrens have not left."

Despite her feeling of numbness—like an empty vein of quartz—Abarōz stirred herself to think. The Ōšmurdan was right. She couldn't get to Razūr with dragons lurking outside. How then to alert Bükrek that her son had been taken captive? She'd have to be invisible or conjure some magickal spell.

People barely looked her way as she clattered down the stairs. They were so engrossed with saving themselves that another life didn't matter. Abarōz didn't know how she'd managed to get there, but when her feet hit level stone, she was faced with the gold door.

"Manuchehr!" she shouted.

With a pop, the Peril appeared beside her. His bearded face was grim.

"We know what happened," he said. "Our plate did its work, but the dragons did theirs."

"Shāhpuhr's gone," Abarōz said. That was all that mattered to her.

"Yes," Manuchehr nodded, "I fear he is lost to you."

"Never," she growled, staring up at his yellow robes. "Again, I request your help."

The Peril spread his hands.

"But what can *I* do?"

"Send a message to Bükrek that her son is held by Al-razi."

"Hmm." The Peril thought, gathering his wings close. "I suppose that's not 'actively helping'—as long as we do not fight." Abarōz closed her eyes. "We must be quite cautious . . . not to enrage the Šāh. I dare say he knows you've been to see Şahmeran, and, if you are captured, he'll torture her hiding place out of you."

Abarōz opened her lids, staring at him without blinking.

"Let him try."

The Peril gave a half smile. He clasped his hands before him, curving his fingers as if holding an unseen ball. Then, a ball took form, its blue arrows glowing to light the runes on its surface.

"Fly," Manuchehr said.

The object did just that, speeding and then disappearing through the tunnel's thick wall.

"T-thank you," Abarōz told him, crouching down by his side.

Now would come the hard part: she'd have to sit and wait.

The last of the eight warriors made her into the zarr. Abarōz couldn't meet their eyes.

"I'm so sorry," she whispered. "If it weren't for me, our force would still be whole, and Shāhpuhr would be here."

"Do not apologize," said a woman, her forearm bandaged. "We fought for ourselves—not you. We couldn't bear one more minute of groveling at the Šāh's feet."

Though Abarōz felt heavy, she still managed to nod. Pacing back and forth by Manuchehr, she mumbled a curse—both at herself, and the sluggish passage of time.

"That will not help," The Peril said, "neither the curse not the walking. I ask you to put your faith in both me and my spells."

Abarōz tried to nod. She'd seen what the Perils could do . . . that was not the issue. She just feared that Bükrek's power might not extend to Dardan.

Abarōz was glad, as always, that measuring time in the zarr was tough: it was buried so deeply that it sank below the dead. She hoped Shāhpuhr wouldn't join them as she waited for Manuchehr, but her spirits lifted when a ball of blue passed through the wall to settle in his hands.

The Peril stared down, rubbing his fingers over the runes.

"The green dragon has answered," he said, "and bids you to wait outside the hatch."

"But . . . Sangal's dragons?"

"Bükrek is a healer," said Manuchehr. "She would not lead you to danger."

Abarōz considered this. She had no reason to believe otherwise.

"Thank you. Again."

He bowed, the bottom of his wings rustling.

"Goodbye," Abarōz said to her fellow warriors. "Tengri willing, we will meet again."

She mentally prepared for another stair-filled climb. But this time, knowing that Bükrek had called her provided extra strength to her legs. When she heard the lowing of cows, she rejoiced, sweeping past them and their friends on her way to the rope ladder. Nothing could stand in her way—not even the S̃āh—as she climbed, threw open the hatch, and wriggled onto flat rock.

She cocked her head, listening. No roars or flapping of wings. No bursts of flame or smoke. Just as she untensed, letting out her breath, she found herself nose-to-nose with a . . . dragon!

Surprising even herself, she unsheathed her sword with speed.

"Abarōz, no," said Bükrek. "It is only me."

"But–but the others?" Abarōz asked as she stood.

"I drove them off," the dragon said calmly, "as I did at your first escape. They are not brave enough to face me—their master's dreaded foe."

"I wish . . . " Abarōz started, "that you'd been here during the battle."

"As do I," sighed Bükrek "but as you know, I cannot fight."

Abarōz nodded, circling back to the subject she cared about.

"And Shāhpuhr?" she asked eagerly.

"You will see," said Bükrek. "Come."

Abarōz saw the dragon flatten her coils, permitting her to mount . . . badly. She gripped a green spine with both hands, steadying herself for flight. Bükrek took off down the sand, winging her way to Razūr. Without Shāhpuhr's arms to hold her, Abarōz felt unstable. She couldn't have been more glad when Bükrek touched down by the river. Loosening her death grip, she slid to the ground.

"Shāhpuhr?" she asked again.

"You called?" a voice sounded, and, whirling, Abarōz saw him. He was wearing Dardan robes and looking more handsome than ever.

"*Shāhpuhr!*" she cried, running up to throw her arms around his neck. *Modesty, be cursed!* "How did you escape?"

"It's an odd tale," he said, returning her hug before putting distance between them. "The guards took me straight to the S̃āh, who was overjoyed to see me!"

"What?" Abarōz asked. *How could this be?*

"It seems that my name, Shāhpuhr, means 'son of the king.'" Abarōz stared at him, stunned. "And that the S̄āh has great regret for casting me out. He said he couldn't be happier to find I was still alive, and, when I told him I wished to return to my mother, he said yes! He sent her a message and she frightened away all the ebrens before flying me here."

Abarōz opened her mouth, but no words emerged. Could it be that *Shāhpuhr* was the son of the hated S̄āh? If someone had told her that she'd grow wings like a Peril, she would have believed it sooner. At last, she was able to speak.

"Er . . ."she began, blinking rapidly. "That's–that's not what I expected!"

"I know!" he crowed with a wink. "It seems the S̄āh has more wives than this river has stones!"

Abarōz laughed even as doubts crept in. There was so much to unspool: *Why* wouldn't the S̄āh cling to his long-lost son to use as a bargaining tool? Was the ruler filled with sentiment after the attack on Dardan? Had he gained respect for Bükrek's maternal bond? Whatever it was, Abarōz shrugged it away. After all, Shāhpuhr was with her, and that's all that mattered. She placed her hand on his wrist as his mother smiled down.

"You two have endured much," she said, but our struggles do not end here. I know Sangal well: he will come again to the city, probably with greater numbers."

"He wants gold," said Abarōz.

"Every last nugget," Bükrek nodded. "I think we can agree that based on last night, men are no match for dragons."

"Not even women," said Abarōz.

Bükrek's yellow eyes met her dark ones.

"We postponed your trip to the south. Now it is time to go."

Abarōz had been dreading this.

"Very well," she said. "I see clearly that to battle dragons, our side needs more dragons."

"More than one," Shāhpuhr chuckled. Abarōz sighed. "It will not be so bad," he said. "Remember, I speak their tongue."

"And *theirs* are bigger than you are!"

His shoulders shook with laughter.

"We should set out immediately," he said. "Time to pack the provisions."

Abarōz shrugged, seizing two leather packs. She grabbed every dried food in sight and filled four skis with water.

"Ready?" Shāhpuhr asked, turning toward the forest.

"No," Abarōz told him, "But that hasn't mattered before."

"Farewell," Bükrek called. "May your journey be one of peace."

Abarōz snorted. How could it be with bloodthirsty beasts waiting?

She and Shāhpuhr walked in silence past the Rōd and into the trees. Abarōz could stand it no longer—she had to ask.

"Well, how was it?"

"What?"

"The S̄āh's Hamwar!"

Shāhpuhr sighed.

"Ah, it was all very . . . rich."

"Go on!" she urged.

"Well, I've never seen so much gold except down in the zarr. There were gold threads on the draperies, life-sized idols of the S̄āh in every corner, and even a bed with solid gold sheets!"

Abarōz tried to look calm although she wanted to scream. It figured the S̄āh lived in opulence while his subjects died of thirst.

"Where," she asked, "did he obtain this thread and drapery? Certainly not from Dardan!"

"A vizier told me they're from long ago. Before the city went underground."

She paused before her next question.

"They–they didn't harm you?"

Shāhpuhr chuckled.

"Not a son of the king!"

Satisfied, Abarōz went quiet until they had walked quite a bit, clustered leaves giving way to dunes.

"Pretty," Abarōz said.

"Yes. See how their tops glow orange with the help of Mihr!"

"Still, it's unbearably hot."

"It's true that few choose to live here, but for a dragon, it's perfect."

"Why?"

"They are solitary creatures who wish to live apart."

Abarōz blinked the sweat from her eyes, feeling Mihr burn bright on her back. She paused to wipe her face and take a long swig of water.

"How much longer?" she asked, offering Shāhpuhr a skin. He gulped its contents gratefully.

"Perhaps a full day. We should find a place for the night so we can resume tomorrow."

To Abarōz, this sounded good if it meant halting their trek. She hiked up her dress as Shāhpuhr limped toward a dune, his poor foot not helping as it sunk into sand.

By the time they reached the dune, Mihr had gone down substantially.

"Thank Tengri!" Abarōz cried, slouching to rest her back on the dune. She withdrew a dried *something* from her pack, and they both ate hungrily. After that, what struck Abarōz as odd was that as the night progressed, the air grew steadily colder, until she found herself shivering!

"Here," Shāhpuhr offered, removing his cloak to throw it to her. "Try to rest. Tomorrow's bound to be busy."

Abarōz grunted, collapsing onto the fabric and wrapping it over her shoulders. As tired as she was (and as much as her calves ached), she couldn't drift off to sleep. There were so many questions: When would Sangal attack again? Would he really challenge Bükrek to another nine-year war? And what was the S̆āh's real aim in letting Shāhpuhr go free?

At some point in the night, under Māh's pale light, she thought she heard movement like someone creeping toward her. She stiffened, peering through nearly closed lids as she spotted a figure—Shāhpuhr—looming over where she lay. Despite Māh and the axtars, she couldn't see his expression. Then he crouched in the sand next to her, running his long fingers from her thigh up to her neck. He made no sound, and all Abarōz's could hear was her own blood rushing.

Then, his fingers swept upward, brushing the cheek he'd kissed, tracing her lips and jaw until they returned to her throat.

What was he doing? Was this some forest ritual? She guessed it wasn't as his hold became firmer, choking off her air.

"Sh-Shāhpuhr!" she gasped and he instantly let go. "Wh-what were you doing?"

She put a hand to her aching throat, giving a few short coughs.

"I–I'm sorry," he said, staring down at her face. "I must have walked in my sleep."

Abarōz narrowed her eyes though she wished to believe him.

"What I really meant to do," he smiled, "is this." He leaned over her, placing his lips on hers in a heartfelt kiss. "See? That's what I do when I'm awake."

Abarōz returned his smile.

"Still trust me?" he asked.

"Of course."

She rolled over his cloak as he went back to his sleeping place. She heard him sigh as his long body hit the sand.

"Goodnight," he called.

Abarōz made a sound like a word mixed with a grunt. She lay frozen in place, wondering. Could she in fact trust Shāhpuhr? Believe his tale of sleepwalking? Doubts clouded her mind as she grabbed short stretches of sleep, afraid to be out for too long.

Az

ABARŌZ WOKE WITH HER body aching—probably from thrashing around. She lay under the cloak while her thoughts ran wild. What had happened last night? Did Shāhpuhr really loathe her, as his attempt to choke her attested; or did he feel something else based on his later sweet kiss? She hadn't felt this bewildered since Archura had sped her away.

Once she rolled to her feet, she had two opposing desires: to study her friend's face carefully while averting her own. Since that wouldn't work, she chose the first, hesitating when a seated Shāhpuhr offered her some bread.

"Sorry again about last night," he said. Abarōz slipped his offering behind her back. "I'm not sure what came over me. Good thing I don't sleepwalk at home!"

Abarōz forced a grin, still not willing to eat. There was something wrong here and she was resolved to find out what.

"So," she asked, "this was the first time you've done this?"

"Yes." He shook his head. "Must be the desert winds."

Sure.

"Has it ever happened to you?" he asked.

"No," she said sharply.

"Lucky," Shāhpuhr told her, rising to strap on his pack. "We should go. Before Mihr turns us bright red."

"Very well."

Abarōz trudged beside him, not feeling quite so sorry at his limping progress. She tried to think through what had happened. First, there was the kiss. It was the second he'd given her, and both times he'd thought her asleep. Did this mean he secretly liked her but didn't want her to know? Or were his feelings more of the love/hate kind? She would never know until she asked, but based on her wavering trust, she didn't want to chance it. In the meantime, she could still feel the ghost of his lips on her own.

"How much farther?" she asked, wanting to break the silence.

"I'm not sure. I've never been here before."

"Well, what are we looking for?"

"Caves. A cluster of caves at the edge of the sand."

Abarōz sighed. Could she ever leave them behind?

They two of them made slow progress as they trudged between dunes, only pausing to drink.

Abarōz looked around.

"I don't like this," she said. "This place."

"You mean the desert?"

"If that's what it is, then yes."

"Yet Dardan is in one!"

"That's different—it's underground."

Shāhpuhr considered this as his sandal sunk into sand.

"I don't love it either," he said. "Take me back to my cool forest!"

Abarōz closed her eyes, seeing the sleepy Rōd and its tall, shady trees. When she opened them, Mihr's rays were striking mercilessly at her back.

"How much farther?" she asked again.

"I sense not too much—look!"

He pointed at pebbles leading to rocks which in turn led to a cave. Based on the size of its entrance, something big must live there.

Abarōz frowned.

"We should have brought weapons," she said.

"No no. We're supposed to be on a mission of peace."

She couldn't swear it, but she thought he'd rolled his eyes.

"I'll go in first," he said.

"I'm not going to argue."

From outside, Abarōz thought she heard sounds: a whistling and roaring, exchanged at even intervals.

"Shāhpuhr," she whispered, "I think the dragon is sleeping."

"Good," he said, grabbing hold of her hand to move forward.

"Wait!" she cried, "is this really wi—?"

Too late. They were both stepping on lumps, all of them different sizes.

"By Tengri!"

Shāhpuhr pointed down, and even without much light, Abarōz saw something glint.

"Is it real?" she whispered, stumbling to stand beside him. At their feet was a solid-gold goblet adorned by precious gems.

"Yes," said Shāhpuhr, giving a throaty laugh. "What the Šāh would not give for this!"

To Abarōz's surprise, he bent to pick up the treasure, securing it in his belt.

"Why did you do that?" she asked, her suspicions all flooding back.

A gift for the Perils," he said. "They can fashion more plate from this."

Again, his excuse made sense, but it also made her uneasy. *Was she trapped in a dragon's den with a boy she couldn't trust?*

He gave her a close-lipped smile.

"Let's move nearer," he said.

Abarōz resisted, but he tightened the hold on her hand. As they moved forward, the whistles and roars grew louder until they hurt her ears; worse, she felt a stiff breeze stirred by the snoring beast. Shāhpuhr's grip became crushing.

"Ow!" Abarōz exclaimed.

"Shhh . . ."

She wasn't afraid to admit that she was intensely afraid: as much as during the battle. If she'd been alone, she would have turned and fled, but Shāhpuhr had taken that choice from her. He dragged her up to the cave's far end where she caught a glimpse of white.

Then, she was faced with a sleeping ebren, its scales all the same color, its head on the ground like a puppy. Small shimmering wings were tucked into its side.

"We must awaken it," said Shāhpuhr, dragging her with him and tapping the dragon's snout. Two tar-black eyes opened, staring at the visitors. It must not have liked what it saw since it released a fiery stream.

Shāhpuhr jumped to the side, carrying Abarōz with him to the side of the cave. Thinking fast, he let out a series of roars.

The dragon lowered its claw, answering him at length. Despite the roughness of its language, it seemed completely calm.

Shāhpuhr turned to Abarōz.

"He says his name is Az. He is a young drake, just seventy-five, and especially fond of emeralds."

"Good to know," she said, "but what about being ridden?"

Shāhpuhr turned back to the ebren who now rested his head on his claws. There followed a short conversation in which Az let out several snorts.

Then, the dragon raised his coils, letting loose with a burst of flame that instantly heated the cave. This must have been a warning since neither of them was hit. Still, Az looked unhappy, narrowing his eyes to slits.

"Not good," Shāhpuhr said, "but you likely figured that out. Even if it saves Gehān, he will *not* submit to a rider."

Abarōz slumped. This might well be their last chance.

"Can you . . . take him by surprise?" she asked. Shāhpuhr gave her a look almost as fierce as the dragon's. "What I mean is . . . leap on his back and see what happens?"

Shāhpuhr crossed his arms, eyes blazing.

"You would have me risk my life?"

To Abarōz, his words seemed tinged with disdain.

"No, no . . . please, forget I ever—"

"I cannot disappoint Dardan, even if it means my death."

Where did *that* come from? In any case, he shook out his limbs and gave a running leap. Once on the dragon's back, he grabbed the closest spike while Az roared as if he'd been struck. The ebren reared up, extending those fragile wings, then swooped out of his lair.

"Shāhpuhr!" Abarōz shouted, running after the pair to see Az curl his coils and try to shake her friend. She could only watch, helpless, as Shāhpuhr flew over rocks to land in a heap on the sand.

She put her hands to her mouth, running over to him and kneeling. She completely ignored the flames and roars from Az.

"Shāhpuhr," she whispered, trying to search for injuries. He'd managed to incur just a few scrapes, but, from the look on his face, his dignity had been bruised.

"What am I?" he asked groggily, putting a hand to his head.

"You mean 'where'? You're with the dragon Az—you must speak to him! Tell him we mean no harm."

Shāhpuhr's gaze wandered from her to the white-scaled dragon. He rose to his feet shakily, approaching Az with caution.

There followed a long back-and-forth which to Abarōz didn't sound friendly. But she supposed that roars and screams never did. Once both parties were calm, Shāhpuhr walked back to rejoin her.

"An agreement?" she asked.

"Of sorts. Az says we can ride him back to Bükrek. He greatly respects her."

"Good work!" Abarōz crowed, almost forgetting herself by giving him a hug. Awkwardly, she pulled back.

"We should go," she said quietly.

"Ready to fly?" he asked.

"I didn't care for it with Bükrek, but yes, I suppose."

He escorted her over to Az who looked resigned to his fate. She felt his strong hands as he lifted her up. Now it was *her* turn to grab a white spike as Shāhpuhr leapt behind her. Curiously, this time, he put out no arms to hold her.

Az gave a groan, took a running leap, then soared into the clouds.

Without Shāhpuhr steadying her, Abarōz was terrified, convinced that at any moment, she would fall to her death. The white spike dug into her palms as she bowed her head so as not to see sky streaking past. Still nothing from Shāhpuhr. When this journey was over, she planned to talk to Bükrek.

The one encouraging thing about this flight lay in its sheer speed. When Abarōz next raised her head, she saw green spreading below her, the Rōd winding placidly as Az landed beside it.

The minute his claws hit the ground, Abarōz did the same. Even though she was frazzled, she remembered her manners.

"Thank you," she told Az.

He must have guessed at her meaning since he nodded stiffly. Then he, Abarōz, and Shāhpuhr all turned when they heard a rustling. Through the tall grass, Bükrek raised her green head. She seemed almost surprised to see the southern ebren, but gave him a smile and began to converse in Dragon. Abarōz could tell she was pleased: Her yellow eyes softened as she clasped her front claws.

"This," she told her son and Abarōz, "is just the beginning. With the help of Az, we must rally other ebrens." Abarōz looked down. This meant yet more forays into dark, forbidding lairs. "For now though, let us rest," Bükrek said with a wink. "Tomorrow, Az will guide you to his neighbors. He says most are a good sort."

Abarōz sighed. She hoped so. She flopped down on the grass while Shāhpuhr went off to find food. Maybe later, she could find the courage to talk to Bükrek in private. For now, the green dragon sat with Az, conversing in their native tongue.

Once Shāhpuhr returned, two waterfowl in hand, Abarōz tried to ignore him. She averted her gaze as he sought to find two rocks, merely shrugging as he started a fire. Despite the delicious smell of roasting meat, she didn't turn toward him once.

"Here," he finally said, handing her a full plate.

"Thank you," she said stiffly. "And your dragon guest?"

He waved a hand.

"Oh, I could never feed *him,*" he said. "Az is on his own."

"Not exactly," Abarōz told him, "the model of a good host."

In Dardan, his surly attitude would be taken to task. There, host and guest shared a bond that was practically sacred.

He answered her with a sneer as he devoured his meat. *Why* was he so unlike the sweet boy she'd once known? Where had he learned cruelty? Enough to try to choke her.

"I'm done," Abarōz told him, striding up to the two dragons. "Bükrek, a word?'

She nodded her green head, and Az, taking the hint, slithered off through the grass.

"Abarōz," Bükrek asked, "is something wrong? I have sensed your unease since you returned from the south."

"Yes, er . . . well . . ." It would not do to back down now. "It's about Shāhpuhr."

"I see," said his mother, still perfectly calm. "Please—tell me."

"It's just . . . since you brought him from Dardan, he hasn't been the same. He's nasty and short with me, and is unconcerned with my safety."

"Hmm," said Bükrek. "Perhaps he's merely fatigued."

"There's–there's more than that," Abarōz blurted. The dragon's yellow eyes did not even blink. "During our time in the desert, he–he tried to choke me."

Now *this* stirred Bükrek to snap her head up quickly.

"What happened?"

"I woke in the night, and his hand was around my throat. Then, when he thought I was sleeping, he kissed me—nothing alarming—in fact, he was gentle. After that . . . in Az's cave, he dragged me forcibly, and then, on the ride home, he seemed like he hoped I'd fall."

Bükrek opened her mouth, revealing those sharp rows of teeth. For a second, Abarōz thought she might be bitten, but soon changed her mind when Bükrek let out a sigh.

"I have an inkling," she said, "of what plagues my son. But, for us to be sure, we must put him through a test." She looked down at Abarōz sadly. "I fear that this involves you." Abarōz gulped. "I know I ask a great deal, but Shāhpuhr is fond of you. And the behavior you've described is not like him at all."

"I know," Abarōz whispered. "He was such a great friend before he attempted to kill me."

The green dragon nodded, serious.

"Let me tell you my plan and we will attempt it tonight. Please have faith I'll allow you to come to no harm."

Abarōz took a deep breath. She trusted Bükrek, but of course, but then she'd trusted Shāhpuhr. Still, she didn't think that a being who'd helped create the world would resort to trickery. Even dragons like Az held her in high esteem.

"Very well," Abarōz said, leaning forward as Bükrek whispered.

Night fell over the forest in stages, Abarōz barely aware as Mihr gave way to Māh. The moon was still a sliver, but one that shed pale light over a green canopy. Since their meal, she hadn't spoken to Shāhpuhr: Perhaps her critique of his hosting skills had caused a simmering anger. It was almost better this way as she took to her usual bed: one across the fire from him. She crept under her thin woven blanket, resting her head on a pile of leaves. It reminded her of Paristan—not just the sleeping arrangements, but the fear of a night visitor.

Not wanting to rouse suspicion, Abarōz mumbled "Goodnight" over her shoulder. What she got in return was a snort.

The air, cool and bracing, drifted over her cheek. Most evenings, she'd delight in the sound of the river; the creak of branches nearby. But tonight, she was on the alert as she only feigned sleep. She tried to tame her breathing though she really wanted to pant.

How long would it be? How long would he wait . . . or do nothing at all?

Abarōz suppressed an urge to shout, clamping her teeth together in a sheer act of will. Now, the sounds of the forest were haunting: wind rippling through leaves; the scurrying of an animal. She thought she might go mad until she heard him stir.

Calm, she told herself, *calm as the lifeless stone.*

Her senses seemed to heighten as Shāhpuhr crept round the fire, staying low to the grass. She tried not to stir as she saw his tall form approach. Her heart pumped so much blood she thought it would come through her ears.

A rustling.

Just like in the desert, he was upon her, one hand clasped over her mouth with her stone knife in the other.

Fear jolted through her as it had in the last battle, and, without thinking, she squirmed and bit down on his hand.

"Ow!" he shouted, "traitorous little harlot! That was your last act of defiance!"

Abarōz raised her arms to block against the knife before she felt, rather than saw, a looming shape.

"That is enough," ordered Bükrek, and when Abarōz dared to look, she saw the dragon with her son's cloak clenched in her mouth as his feet left the ground.

"Put me down!" Shāhpuhr yelled. "You both will be punished for opposing my blessèd father!"

Abarōz leapt to her feet.

"You mean . . . the S̄āh?" she asked.

"He will see you in agony! You shall feel his wrath as his guards flay you alive!"

Abarōz and Bükrek could only shake their heads. She could still hear Shāhpuhr screaming as his mother took him away.

A Gift from the Šāh

Not long after, Bükrek slithered back to Abarōz. There was no sign of Shāhpuhr.

"What–what happened?' Abarōz asked, still stunned by her friend's outburst.

His mother sighed.

"I feared all was to easy when the Šāh let him go." Abarōz stiffened—so had she. Bükrek let out a snort. "Dardan's ruler fancies himself invincible. Still, Sangal must have told him how to turn good dragons to bad."

"But Shāhpuhr isn't a dragon!"

"No," said Bükrek, "yet the Šāh has discovered a way to apply the curse to men."

"A curse!" Understanding flooded Abarōz. "There must be a way to undo it. I–I want my old friend back!"

"And I my son. I do know of a way, but it is far too risky."

"Just tell me—I'll do it!"

Bükrek looked grave.

"It is said that the blood of a dragon, drawn from its head, has the power to cure all ills."

"But we can do that!" Abarōz cried. "We have you and Az!"

"Yes," answered Bükrek, "but since this curse is dark, a dark dragon is required."

"You mean . . . Sangal?"

"Or one of his followers. The deed must be done with stealth, and ebrens aren't stealthy. That's why this task falls to you."

Abarōz opened her mouth, but before she could answer, she was distracted by a noise like wood being struck. At the edge of the clearing, she found a pitiable figure: Shāhpuhr, secured to a tree by bonds. Even in the faint moonlight, she could see the hate in his eyes—the fury in every feature.

"Whore!" he screamed.

Abarōz dragged back to Bükrek.

"I will go," she said. "To the north, where the bad dragons live."

Though it was hard to believe, Abarōz provisioned her pack again. If only Shāhpuhr could come with her! But he was the reason she went. Bound to his woody prison, he was like a mad dog . . . one who could curse in two languages.

She moved slowly toward him, taking from his belt the gold goblet he'd stolen from Az.

"Don't worry," she said, "I will make this right. It's my fault this happened anyway. If we'd never met, you could have avoided the Šāh."

He gave her a growl in response.

Abarōz turned sadly before buckling on her plate. She made sure she held both sword and shield before bidding Bükrek farewell.

"Do not let down your guard," the dragon told her. "Remember, Sangal is chaos, and his horde isn't far behind."

"Where are their lairs?"

"Not as far as the southern ebrens'. You need go about half that distance."

Abarōz nodded before marching out of the clearing. It was now early morning, Mihr's beams scattered through trees. She walked by the river, then took to a winding dirt path to emerge onto sparkling sand. It figured. Even the north was a desert. Still, she tried to keep up her spirits, remembering the old Shāhpuhr. As Mihr became more intense, she had the urge to tear off her plate, but thought this course unwise. Tengri knew what was out here . . .

Judging by Mihr's position, she must have been trudging for hours, stopping only to steal the occasional drink. Her body told her to stop; to turn back to the cool forest, but she wouldn't give up on her friend. If she didn't help him, he would surely die. It was said that the end of curses could kill, the poor victim's skin blackening and cracking. So, she walked on, her own exposed flesh burning as her boots sunk into sand. It shouldn't be too much longer . . . not long. Unless Sangal's horde decided to swoop overhead . . .

Tengri, she thought, *new god:* let me live to complete this journey. Not for me, but Shāhpuhr.

Through a shimmer of heat, she swore she saw sand turn to rock, or was it a waking dream? *No!* As she dragged through pebbles, she came to a vast row of caves, each entrance arched and open. What could these be, if not dragons' lairs? Certainly not the realm of men . . .

Abarōz approached the lip of one, dousing her head with water and blinking the sand from her eyes She walked quietly forward, now prepared for the lumpy cave floor strewn with goblets and gold. If she'd been gold-sick like the S̃āh, these gleaming riches would have called to her. But, she wasn't, so . . .

She hugged a cave wall as she made her way in deeper, light fading with every step.

Then, she heard it: the familiar whistles and roars of a sleeping dragon.

Its breath was more like a growl, wafting two puffed lines of smoke over Abarōz's head. That's when she saw the ebren. It was about the size of Az, its scales of heavy silver. It was likely dreaming of Sangal and his next attack.

Abarōz stopped some six paces from the dragon's head. Her mind whirled with plans: Should she attack without warning—take it by surprise? Or awaken the beast and attempt to bargain? Her indecision cost her as the dragon opened one eye. Of course, it was gold, and, as she quickly discovered, so was the other.

For a moment, they engaged each other in an unblinking stare. Then, instinct took over:

Abarōz raised her round shield just as the dragon spat fire. Thanks to the Perils, she wasn't charred into ash.

"WAIT!" Abarōz cried, raising a hand. "I have something for you—more treasure." The ebren raised what would have been its brow. Slowly, she swung round her pack, and with shaking fingers, removed the gem-studded goblet. "See?" she said, holding it up by its handles. "This is solid gold. With–with emeralds!"

The dragon looked interested, holding up a front claw, its pupils narrowed by greed.

"I–I need something small in exchange," Abarōz told it. She pointed to the beast's head. "Your blood. Just a thimbleful. To help my friend get well."

The ebren looked puzzled. She decided to demonstrate by lifting her sword to her forehead and cutting a shallow gash.

The dragon gave her a look he must have reserved for fools. Shrugging, Abarōz moved to its head and waved her sword at its horns.

This was not a wise move. The beast reared, its horns bumping the ceiling as it opened its mouth. Abarōz rolled just in time to avoid its orange stream. Then she did something desperate: she rolled back toward the dragon, hefting her blade and hurling it at its head! The roar that filled the cave penetrated even her helmet, but she tried to stay calm as she extended an urn, catching a few drops of blood!

"I'm sorry," she told the ebren, leaping up to remove her sword. "If you apply pressure, the bleeding will stop."

She hurled the gold goblet to the floor, dashing back toward the entrance where with her every step the dragon's cries became fainter.

"Thank Tengri!" she cried once she'd made it outside. A renewed energy filled her, giving wings to her boots. She ran back across the desert, ignoring dunes, her sinking feet, and the killing rays of Mihr. Nothing could stop her as she flew down heated sand: not thirst, not hunger, not even exhaustion as she spotted trees up ahead.

Abarōz tore off her plate once she'd reached the Rōd, wading in to wet her feet. But she didn't stay long before crashing into the clearing.

"Bükrek!" she cried, *"I've got it!"*

That was all she remembered until she woke to the sight of a large green dragon's head.

Ebrens of the South

“Abarōz!” Bükrek called down. “I was sorely tempted to use some blood on *you.*”

“Please don’t,” Abarōz begged, forcing herself to sit. “Every drop must be saved for Shāhpuhr.”

His mother smiled, then guided her back to the tree to which her poor friend was bound.

“I thought to wait for you,” said Bükrek. “It will calm him after he’s cured.”

Quite far from that now, Shāhpuhr gave Abarōz a snarl.

“Dardan harlot!” he cried, “my father will crush you!”

Abarōz turned to Bükrek.

“Has he been like this the whole time?”

“Yes,” his mother said sadly. “It’s as if he’s possessed.”

“Let’s end this now,” growled Abarōz. “How should I give him the blood?”

“He must drink it,” Bükrek answered.

“I daresay he won’t like that. How should we do it exactly?”

You must force him.”

“ME?” Abarōz cried.

“My claws are far too big for such a delicate task.”

Abarōz slumped, then crept up to her friend.

“Tengri curse you!” he shouted. “My father will see you doused in oil and burned!”

Abarōz winced.

“Shāhpuhr, you need to stop talking.”

Seeing how he was, she knew he wouldn't listen. She grabbed the urn from her pack, approached his head, and forced a trickle of blood through his open mouth.

Nothing happened. Abarōz cast a worried glance at Bükrek. Then, Shāhpuhr's body began to tremble, his eyes became clearer, and, upon seeing her, he gave a wide smile.

"Abarōz. Mother," he said. "Can you tell me why I'm tied to a tree?"

"It's a long story," said Abarōz, taking her sword and gingerly cutting him down. "Your father the S̆āh cursed you and the only thing that could cure you was drinking a bad dragon's blood."

"Blech," he spat, wiping his mouth before flexing his now-free arms.

"I think the dragon felt the same way."

"How did you do this?" he asked.

"Well, I went to the north. Exchanged the goblet you stole for a bit of blood."

"Yet you do not speak Dragon!"

"In this case, actions were better than words."

"Oh."

Shāhpuhr blinked, trying to absorb this.

"Mother," he said, "If I did anything vile while cursed, I can only apologize."

"My son, that's hardly necessary. You were not in your right mind."

He turned to Abarōz.

"The same applies to you." He looked in her eyes, face troubled. "I hope I didn't say anything unduly harsh."

"Besides calling me a harlot? No."

Shāhpuhr's olive skin seemed to lose at least three shades. He put a hand to his eyes, stemming a flow of tears.

"How can you ever forgive me?"

Abarōz crossed her arms.

"It seems I already have." She ran up to him, and, silencing her mother's voice in her head, threw her arms around him. "Oh, Shāhpuhr. I can't tell you how glad I am that you're back."

"Me too," he grinned. "Now, let's eat—I'm starving. Being cursed has increased my appetite!"

Abarōz broke from him reluctantly as they all trudged to the clearing's center.

"What is your choice?" he asked his mother. "Venison, rabbit, or partridge?"

"I'm afraid," said Bükrek, "in your 'absence,' there was only bread."

Shāhpuhr strode behind a rock, picking up his bow and quiver.

"Come," he told Abarōz, "you must join me on the hunt."

"I'll go as company," she said, "but I won't be very much help." He smiled, setting off for the trees. Avalos sprinted behind, every two of her steps equal to one of his. "How do you feel?" she panted once she'd caught up. "Are you completely well?"

"I am. I feel just like my own self."

Abarōz wanted to hold back but her curiosity wouldn't let her.

"How was it?" she asked. "When you were under the curse?"

"It was strange," Shāhpuhr said, shivering. "I wasn't aware of anything except for a swirling black mist."

"So you don't remember coming from Dardan? Or anything after?"

"No. Not a thing. I can only hope I wasn't one-tenth as bad as my father."

"Maybe that," confessed Abarōz.

"What did I do?" He stopped abruptly under the trees. "Please—tell me."

"Well . . . you tried to choke me." His face constricted with horror. "But, you also kissed me." She blushed, turning away. "And I must say it was quite sweet."

Shāhpuhr slung back his bow, his fingers resting on her chin before he lightly tugged her toward him.

"I cannot express my sorrow," he said, his eyes filling again.

"You don't have to. None of it could be helped."

"Or this."

He closed the space between them, pressing his whole body against her. A heat she'd only felt with him coursed through her like the best kind of curse.

He pulled away slightly, staring into her eyes.

"Kiss me," she whispered.

He took her face in his hands, putting his lips to hers. The kiss was so soft it was like the touch of a Peril's wings, but Shāhpuhr broke the spell.

"What am I doing?!" he cried, springing back as if she carried disease. "Abarōz, now you really *can* blame me."

"Did I resist?" she asked. "Push you away? We are both guilty, but I'm no longer sure of what."

"Very well," he mumbled, moving off awkwardly. "Let's see about that hunt."

They stayed quiet as he stalked between the trees, as silent as any deer. Finally, he found one, head bent as it grazed on grass. Notching an arrow to his string, he shot, felling the buck. Abarōz flinched, but was glad it did not suffer. Shāhpuhr picked up his kill and slung it over his shoulders. Their silence continued as they tramped back to the clearing where he skinned and butchered the animal.

He took a break to start a new fire, spitting chunks of meat. Abarōz sat by the flames, hugging her knees to her chest. She felt completely ignorant: she didn't know what her feelings were for Shāhpuhr, if he were ashamed of *his*, and if the rules of Dardan applied in an untamed forest.

She sighed.

Adrina had been right about one thing: Boys were nothing but trouble.

The source of *hers* finally stepped toward her, bearing a plate filled with meat. Abarōz happily ate, not realizing how hungry she was after her trip to the north. Shāhpuhr plopped down beside her, taking two heaping helpings. He also unveiled some bread from one of his hiding places.

After they'd finished and cleaned their plates in the Rōd, a rustling came from behind them. They both whirled to see the white dragon Az.

"Az," said Abarōz, "you scared us."

He and Shāhpuhr conversed in Dragon.

"He says," said Shāhpuhr, "you must learn the difference between good dragons and bad."

"Please tell him," Abarōz said with a wave, "I've recently gained that skill."

Az showed his teeth in a smile after Shāhpuhr's translation. Not long after, they heard the slide of more scales. Abarōz tensed, imagining silver, but relaxed when they proved green.

"Mother," Shāhpuhr told her, "you look concerned."

Abarōz noticed it too.

"I am sorry to bring bad tidings to a happy occasion. But as you know, Sangal won't rest: he never has in the past. I must ask you—all three—to return to the south. Before the next attack, we *must* recruit more ebrens."

Abarōz sighed. Here in the Bērūn, there always seemed to be trouble. It reminded her in some ways of the Tree of Life.

"When shall we go?" she asked.

"Dawn," said Bükrek. "If it weren't for Shāhpuhr, I'd change that to now."

"But Mother—" he protested.

"I insist. You just came out of a curse."

Abarōz walked with Shāhpuhr back to their makeshift beds. As they soaked in the fire's warmth, she worried about their next journey. She could only hope that most southern ebrens were as friendly as Az.

She made sure Shāhpuhr fell asleep before she shut her own her eyes. His mother had been right—he needed time to recover.

As Mihr peeked over the trees the next morning, Abarōz felt her arms being shaken.

"No," she mumbled, "early."

She heard a familiar laugh.

"In the forest," said Shāhpuhr, "this is considered quite late."

Abarōz groaned, then threw off her blanket. Her friend helped her up, and she set about—once again—filling their packs. They helped each other buckle on plate.

"This good thing about this journey," Shāhpuhr told her, "is that it will be short."

"What?"

Abarōz was not yet fully awake.

"It is the same distance, but this time we fly by dragon!"

"Right."

Abarōz looked around, hoping to locate Az. They found him down by the water, snoring away with a smile.

"Sorry . . ." Shāhpuhr told him, poking his snout. After Az lifted one lid, they had a short talk in Dragon.

"What did he say?" asked Abarōz.

"That he's not a morning dragon."

"Tell him," Abarōz groaned, "that I feel the same."

Az seemed to sense this as he patted her head with a claw. Then he flattened himself on the ground, giving Shāhpuhr a chance to boost her up before he mounted behind her.

"Hold on!" he cried, and this time, thankfully, his grip on her waist was secure.

Abarōz clutched a spike as Az spread his white wings, loping on all fours before launching himself in the air. Without Shāhpuhr, Abarōz would have been terrified, but as long as he held her, she knew she wouldn't fall.

It was so much better to soar over sand than sink into it! Abarōz didn't miss heat burning her flesh or the prospect of desert camping. Instead, Az reached the south with such speed that she gasped when he soared down.

The caves. There they were, lined up in neat rock row. Az's riders slipped from his back as they peered into an entrance.

"Could you find out," Abarōz asked Shāhpuhr, "if he will come with us? He did say he's on good terms with his neighbors."

"Sure."

Shāhpuhr conveyed the message, and Az must have agreed since he happily took the lead. He marched them inside the cave next to his, roaring out a greeting. How different this was from the north, where she'd dreaded every step! Now, she skipped over treasure, following the bounce of Az's tail. The dragon twisted and roared something at Shāhpuhr.

"He says to stay here," her friend explained.

She watched Az venture deeper, then heard *two* sets of roars. Abarōz turned to Shāhpuhr.

"What's going on? Is someone being murdered?"

"No, no," he grinned. "Az is asking his friend to join Bükrek. Before Sangal destroys his cave."

Abarōz pursed her lips, impressed.

"He should argue the law in front of your father."

Shāhpuhr rolled his eyes.

"In Dardan, the law *is* my father."

Abarōz shrugged in defeat as Az came sliding toward them, a powder-blue dragon in tow. As they entered the next cave, then the next, and finally the last, two ebrens became four until they were eight and ended in twenty-four! When Abarōz glanced down the line of dragons, each a different color, she felt a swell of pride. *They had done it!* Well, at least Az had . . .

The trip back home was joyful . . . even for a reluctant rider. Az led the flight over sand until Abarōz spotted green; then, he landed by the river, joined by a new scaly army!

Bükrek winged over trees before perching on a half-submerged rock. As she opened her mouth to speak, Shāhpuhr prepared to translate.

"I thank you," Bükrek told the ebrens, "for agreeing to join our cause. If we cannot defeat Sangal, the south will be destroyed—along with all of Gehān." From her spot beside Az, Abarōz winced. "Friends," Bükrek continued, meeting ebren eyes one-by-one. "Your presence here tells me you've agreed to accept a rider, a practice we haven't seen for thousands of years. Our first concern must be Dardan. On foot, their warriors were slaughtered. But as Aswārs of Ebrens, they will gain virtual wings." Abarōz waited, breathless, for the next sandal to drop. "Our initial step will be to recruit other Dardans to take the place of the fallen. I ask you to entrust this task to me."

Abarōz stepped forward.

"But Bükrek," she asked, "how do we get them here? The S̄āh will never permit it."

"He is not as invincible," the green dragon smiled, "as he thinks he is."

Although Abarōz nodded, a wave of unease swept through her. When she thought of the S̄āh, his guards—and the dragon who controlled him—she wondered how even Bükrek could soar over these obstacles.

As if reading her mind, Bükrek addressed her directly.

"Freeing the remaining warriors will be our first concern. To do so, we must fly to Dardan and frighten off Sangal's dragons. Then you, Abarōz, demand to be let in the gate."

"What?!"

Had she heard that quite right?

"You can't ask her—" Shāhpuhr began.

"My son," said Bükrek, "your compassion does you credit. But your friend will be flanked by twenty-five of us. Do you really think your father would harm a hair on her head?"

Shāhpuhr looked unconvinced.

"I will go with her," he said in a voice that would stand no argument.

"Of course," Bükrek smiled, "I expected no less." She turned back to the flight. "Follow me," she ordered. "Sangal and his tool the Šāh have thus far proved ruthless, so, despite our numbers, we must proceed with care."

Abarōz checked her weapon as Shāhpuhr did the same. She tried not to think of her outsized role in the upcoming skirmish. Even so, as she mounted Az, her legs trembled a little.

"You all right?" Shāhpuhr asked, swinging a leg behind her. "You've done much worse than this."

"Really?" she answered, her voice ending in a squeak.

"Of course!" He put his arms around her waist. "You fled from Dardan, then prowled her stairways to reach the zarr. You found and spoke with Şahmeran, perhaps the first to do so. *And* you braved the north to seek the means to heal me."

"Well," Abarōz mumbled, "when you put it like that . . ."

"Do not be afraid," he told her as they watched Bükrek take off. "This time, you have a force that will make my father tremble."

I hope so, thought Abarōz, gripping that white spine tight. Az spread has wings before soaring to the tip of their flight's "V." He was second in line behind Bükrek, and, at this close range, Abarōz marveled at her size.

In no time at all, they were over Dardan with ten of Sangal's ebren already in the air. But at the sight of their massive flight, they gave out roars more like squeals, then wheeled in a body, turning tail for the north.

"Cowards," Abarōz muttered, though she was hardly the model of courage as her legs continued to shake.

Once Bükrek gave the signal, her flight descended to land neatly by the main gate. She gave a nod to Abarōz who, not quite willingly, slid down Az's flank.

Shāhpuhr jumped to the ground beside her.

"Remember," he said, "I am with you, and will not let you come to harm."

This at least gave her the strength to stride up to that towering boulder and give three sharp raps. A stone peephole shot open.

"Who goes there?" a harsh voice demanded.

"Abarōz, daughter of Pabag, former Ōšmurdan of Dardan."

Abarōz heard a low chuckle.

"Spawn of a traitor! You must be mad to come back here!"

"Not entirely" Abarōz drawled, "for if you look behind me, I am joined by twenty-five dragons.

She stepped aside as one dark eye took in the unusual sight.

"Sweet Jesus!" cried the guard, "I–I must consult my master."

"See that you're quick," said Abarōz. "On the whole, dragons are not known for patience."

What went on behind that gate, she could only imagine. But she grinned as much faster than expected, the boulder began to slide. With the final groan of a pulley, it rolled from sight, allowing her and Shāhpuhr to enter.

"Father!" he exclaimed, putting a hand on his sword.

Abarōz did the same.

Had the hated Šāh deigned to greet them himself?

Yet there he stood, barricaded by guards who each bore a sharp steel pike. He surveyed his visitors with contempt.

"Filth," the ruler spat at Abarōz. "How dare you return after flouting my law?"

"I escaped," she said calmly, "after you murdered my father."

The Šāh crossed his arms over his flowing robe: one, she noted, richly brocaded in gold.

"What do you want?" he growled. "A bribe? A sacrifice?"

"Our side desires neither."

"What then?"

He bristled along with his guards' steel.

"Simple," Abarōz said. "Give us the warriors who shelter in the zarr."

The Šāh began to chuckle but no one else joined in: the sound was as hollow as he was.

"Absurd." He flicked some dust off his sleeve. "None may leave or enter the city."

"Yet, here we stand," said Shāhpuhr.

The Šāh set eyes on his son. But instead of a frown, his lips curled into a smile.

"Fourteenth son," he said. "You have lately shown me your love. Will you permit this whore to insult me?"

Abarōz looked at her friend. Would he still pretend to be cursed? Since that wouldn't get them far, she felt relief at his answer.

"Gladly," Shāhpuhr answered, "and you will not insult *her.* He sucked in his breath. "What kind of father lays a curse on his own son?" Abarōz thought she saw the guards stiffen. "You will do as she asked," Now Shāhpuhr crossed his arms. "Or the dragons outside might begin to feel . . . restless."

The Šāh tried to peek over his son's head, but he was far too squat. Abarōz knew that he knew his refusal would mean death; but, if he agreed, he would appear weak.

As always with Al-razi, self-preservation won out. His face turned sour as he balled his many-ringed fingers.

"Bring the warriors forth," he growled. "And banish those annoying Perils. Both factions have dared oppose me!"

Half his guards clattered off and they had a long way to go. As Abarōz waited, she openly eyed the Šāh: How could a man so feeble wreak cruelty on so many? Torture and kill with impunity? As she looked at his guards, she found her answer: No one held onto power without a shield of the willing.

Abarōz turned around, taking comfort in the sight of the dragons as she waited to hear boots on stairs. After a long, awkward wait; the guards returned with nine warriors, each clad in precious gold plate. The nine looked well-fed and healthy, a consequence, Abarōz thought, of being cared for by Perils.

She bowed her head to each as their guard stepped aside.

"You are free," she told them, jerking her chin at the Šāh, "from this man's greed and depravity." He gave her a look shot through with hatred. "We will meet again," she said.

"Sooner than you think! When Sangal hears of your treachery, he will rent your ebrens in two!"

"Something tells me," answered Abarōz, "that he already knows."

A Dual Training

The rescued warriors did not ride back to Razūr: They walked, half the dragons forming a cordon around them.

Abarōz watched from above as Shāhpuhr gripped her on Az. The airborne dragons flew slowly over the party on foot. As Abarōz grew impatient, both groups made it back to the Rōd where Bükrek perched on her rock.

"Welcome," she told the newcomers. "Abarōz, Shāhpuhr—well done. We may now start to join two halves of a priceless coin: dragons, and their riders." Though the dragons didn't understand, she continued in Dardan. "This bodes well, though the path before us lies hidden." Pabag nodded. "The warriors of Dardan must be trained as Aswārs." She chuckled. "This means much more than not falling. Though your armor is flameproof, remember, your dragons are not. If yours is struck by fire, not one, but two, are lost." Abarōz winced. That might be true, but it was grim. "What will take place in this forest is what you might call advanced lessons. In ancient times, it took two years to become an Aswār. We have but a few days." She turned to Shāhpuhr. "Please translate into Dragon. *Both* species must be trained: the Dardans to sit an ebren, and the ebrens to carry a rider."

The warriors, battle-hardened, struck their breasts with their fists. Abarōz saw in their eyes the glint of anticipation.

Bükrek issued one last command.

"We begin after food and rest, when Mihr is at her height."

The company disbursed, its dragons taking flight in search of food. Shāhpuhr first looked bewildered at the sight of nine more guests, but then dragged three sacks of grain from behind his "secret" tree.

"I see," Abarōz told him. "I must return to my prior life as a cook."

Shāhpuhr laughed, ripping open the sacks.

"Something tells me," he said, "you've outgrown your past."

"Regardless," Abarōz sighed, "I am here with my pestle."

Wielding her branch, she honestly didn't mind mixing, molding, and laying small mounds to dry. In fact, she enjoyed it, knowing it would help their side. When she finished, she brushed off her skirt, then ran to meet Pabag.

"Greetings," she said, lowering her head from habit. "I am so glad to see you well. Can you tell me—in the zarr—what happened after we left?"

"Thankfully, not much." He smoothed his wild grey hair. "The Perils were wonderful, conjuring us food and water. But we heard from whispers above that the aqueducts run alarmingly low. Of course, the S̆āh and his men and family get all the water they want. As for the other Hamwars: they say that drink is rationed, and some have already died."

Abarōz balled her fists.

"The Perils—are they gone?"

"Yes. When the guards came for us, they vanished. Manuchehr feared that they would follow and destroy all Paristan."

"I wouldn't put it past them."

Shāhpuhr leaned over to join them.

"My father," he said, "will seize all that he can. His selfishness is bigger than my mother."

"You learned quickly," Pabag chuckled, "despite not living among us. I'm only surprised he didn't attempt to turn *you.*"

"Oh, he did," said Shāhpuhr, "but . . . a *certain someone—*" he winked at Abarōz, "risked her life to save me."

Pabag fell silent, then turned to regard her with an Ōšmurdan's sharp eye.

"Who would have thought," he asked, "that my old friend Rastag would ever produce such a daughter?"

"I'd say no one," Abarōz told him.

"Well, I should take my leave," sighed Pabag. "You young people don't need an old man around."

Abarōz was about to protest when he stepped over grass to join the other warriors.

Shāhpuhr looked puzzled.

"What did he mean?" he asked.

"Simply," said Abarōz, "that in this situation, three people is one too many."

"Oh."

Abarōz blushed. She felt shy as he took her hand, crouching with her under pretense of checking the bread where he kissed her cheek lightly.

"Shāhpuhr!" she cried. "Not in front of the Dardans!"

"I'm sure many have children. Why would a kiss cause them such grief?"

Abarōz put her face in her hands.

"Because such behavior is not allowed until marriage. Even then, signs of affection must be exchanged in private. Surely your mother told you?"

He vigorously shook his head.

"She taught me our zand's language—but not all its customs. What was the chance of my ever having to know them?"

Abarōz's face cooled.

"I suppose you're right," she said primly, rising without his help. "Just remember that we are Dardans and, er . . . when it comes to . . . things like kisses, easily shocked."

He rose without effort.

"I'll keep that in mind. Thank Tengri, those Dardans weren't raised here! In the forest, they would see things they could never forget."

Abarōz turned aside, clearing her throat.

"Shouldn't we," she asked, "be joining the others for training? I'm hoping that someday I can ride by myself."

"Not me," Shāhpuhr whispered, putting his hand on the small of her back to guide her back to the Rōd.

Abarōz shrugged. She knew she should say something, but . . .

By the time they got there, all the dragons were back. Bükrek flew over, settling at her son's side. As she spoke in Dragon, he translated.

"She says," he told Abarōz, "that since ebrens haven't been ridden for centuries, the instinct has been lost. But it may be regained, starting with trust in their Aswār." He cocked his head, listening. "She says they must always be aware of the precious life in their claws. Not to make too-sharp turns, or to plunge groundward too fast. If their Aswār falls, they must try to retrieve him. Or her." Abarōz smiled. "She wants the ebrens to practice taking off, flying, and landing as if a rider were on their back. She says that when their Aswār first mounts, it will feel quite strange."

Abarōz took all this in, watching as scales of every hue flashed and swirled above her. The dragons were being cautious: not flapping too fast or speeding like an arrow. Their turns were slow and deliberate; their landings soft and prolonged.

"Excellent!" Bükrek called, raising a claw in approval. "Now, in the midst of battle, you might have to move evasively, which brings us to our Aswārs."

Abarōz saw them off to the side, where they'd been herded into a circle to be dwarfed by their future mounts. Without wanting to attract notice, she motioned to Shāhpuhr and joined the warriors. Surely, Bükrek would let them?

"I believe," the dragon said, "that learning to be an Aswār is more difficult than learning to carry a rider."

"Oh no," Abarōz breathed.

"But," Bükrek went on, "after training, I'm fairly confident that no one here will fall."

Fairly?

Abarōz found her eagerness, as always, tempered with layers of fear.

This is not the time, she scolded herself. *After all, you've ridden Az . . .*

But never by yourself.

"Unlike the horse," said their teacher, "an ebren will not stand for a bridle, bit, or saddle. That is why you must rely on your body alone."

"What's a horse?" Abarōz whispered to Shāhpuhr.

"It doesn't matter," he said.

She resisted the urge to grab his hand. So, they would have to fly with nothing: Apparently, Aswārs didn't need help.

She tried to pay attention.

"Now," said Bükrek, "the true art of the Aswār rests in their arms and legs. Arms to steer by spike, and legs to control speed. It's quite simple: just a touch with the shins to slow, and a gentle kick to go faster." Even though the banks of the river were cool, Abarōz started to sweat. After all, she'd lived her whole life where the biggest beast was a camel. And Bükrek expected her to control a whole *dragon?* One twenty times her size? "Shāhpuhr, Abarōz."

Abarōz snapped to attention when she heard her name. "Since you've already ridden, please demonstrate for the others. On two separate ebrens."

By Tengri! Abarōz's moment had come and she could barely move. How could she be an example when she was so clearly inept?

Abarōz stared after Shāhpuhr as he leapt atop a black dragon. She decided to stay with Az and made an attempt to mount. He had to lay flush against the dirt until she swung a leg over.

Long before she was ready, Az spread his wings and took off.

"Whoa!" Abarōz protested. "Aren't *I* the one who steers?" She gripped his closest spike tight as Az roared off over the trees, and, without Shāhpuhr, Abarōz almost tumbled. *"Slower!"* she cried, kicking him with her heels. The dragon puffed white smoke. "I know," Abarōz said, "that you know I don't know what I'm doing. Sorry."

Az shook his head, going wherever he pleased, but not, she had to admit, as fast as he usually did.

She saw a blurred black object from the corner of her eye: Shāhpuhr, applying just the right pressure as his dragon darted and soared.

If only . . . Abarōz sighed, testing her hold on the spike and the force of her kicks. As Az circled back to the river, she even relaxed a bit, until he thrust down his snout and sank like a Dardan stone! Trying to salvage her pride, Abarōz didn't scream, but was not exactly aware when her dragon landed. She toppled to the ground, mixing her pride with dirt.

The gathered warriors clapped: surely, not for *her?* She pointed at Shāhpuhr, who'd jumped from his dragon's back as if he were born to it. She had to face the truth: *He* was already an Aswār while she should crawl back to Dardan.

"Very nice," Bükrek called. "From both of you." *Right.* "Time for the rest to try."

Abarōz looked up, her body drained of strength. She was grateful when Shāhpuhr helped her to her feet.

"You were amazing!" she told him, nearly brushing his hand. "And I . . . well, I could be the S̄āh's entertainment."

"Nonsense! The longer you rode, the more confidence you developed. Just get a feel for landing and you'll be an Aswār yet."

This made her feel slightly better as she turned to watch the warriors. They had all mounted an ebren and some even looked ill. Once the dragons and riders took off, she caught expressions of horror from the latter and even a tumbling body before Bükrek saved the day.

Abarōz had never felt joy at the misery of others, but she confessed to a sort of relief at not being the only bad Aswār. One or two of them in the air were hanging off their mount's flank.

"Time to land!" Bükrek called, and the ebrens staggered in, hindered by novice riders. "We will continue our lessons today and through the night if we have to." Abarōz sighed. "Sangal has not been idle. Archura informs me he plans another assault. That's why we'll train every minute until we're called to the battlefield."

Bükrek, Abarōz saw, was not one to exaggerate. For the next three days, she, Shāhpuhr, and the warriors barely touched Gehān as they spent their time in the sky. Though her backside was sore, she could feel herself untensing, even acquiring skill as she steered and prodded Az. The others too seemed more comfortable, with fewer falls and mistakes. Shāhpuhr was even bonding with his black dragon, whose name, he said, was Catanes.

Even though they were small in numbers, this time, Abarōz hoped, they'd be on more equal ground . . .

She was taking a rare break in the clearing, Shāhpuhr at her side, when Bükrek swooped over, calling them all to the river.

"It is time," she told the assembled dragons and Aswārs. "Sangal grows tired of waiting for Dardans to perish from thirst. Şahmeran has sent word that he will besiege the city."

Abarōz regarded her solemnly. If this had come from Şahmeran, it was assuredly true.

Shāhpuhr gave her a wink.

"We will be fine," he told her, "now that we have dragons."

But not enough riders, Abarōz's mind whispered.

She tried to give him a smile, but her lips wouldn't obey as she thought back to the last battle. Where over half their force had been slaughtered. Where she'd been carried off. But, Shāhpuhr was right. With ebrens of their own, they would present a much better front. But that might not be enough.

Battle of the Ebrens

Abarōz surprised herself by being among the first to mount. Like the others, she wore gold plate; secured her blade in her hand. As Mihr's crown became a half-circle, Bükrek issued the order, and their flight of twenty-five rose above Razūr. But how many would return?

As the dragons formed their "V," Abarōz felt a swell of pride: it was she, after all, who had set this force in motion: Bükrek; the Perils; the zarran.

"Father," she whispered as Az gained height, "if I do nothing else, I promise to avenge you."

The prospect seemed near as she trailed Bükrek and Catanes. She'd even developed an understanding with Az—as long as she didn't kick him, he'd obey her commands.

As their flight headed east, Abarōz saw that Mihr, who had played hide-and-seek with Dardan's mountain, now revealed her whole self to hang over the city.

This was it. Time to get revenge and free her zand from the enemy: one with claws and a tail; the other swathed in gold.

Below them was the main gate, desolate in the desert. Until it was joined by dragons: Sangal's horde, swarming like angry wasps, their numbers so great the north must be empty.

"Steady!" Shāhpuhr called back. "Remember—right will always prevail!"

Will it? Abarōz wondered, pressing her shins against Az. As the dragon flapped harder, they came closer to the horde which looked even more imposing. More ebrens had swooped from behind the mountain, darkening the sky and obscuring the clouds. One came straight at her, grey tail held upright as it opened its mouth to spew flame. Abarōz felt something tickle her breastplate but she remained unscathed.

"Ha!" she cried. "Time to fight fire with fire!"

She nodded down to Az, who required no signal as he too spat fire. The grey dragon roared, then wheeled, its backside now facing them. And, to Abarōz's amazement, flames burst from its *tail!*

How could this be? Dragons who blazed from both ends? But, as she surveyed the enemy, she saw that they all had this skill. To avoid the grey, she turned Az's spike to the right, steering him to wheel . . . right in front of another beast! This one was silver and growled its displeasure—was it the one she'd taken blood from?

In any case, this time, Abarōz did more than sit. She urged Az to fly at top speed, then confront the silver head-on so it would expose its throat. One slash of her sword and a spurt of blood later, the dragon came tumbling down.

"That's the way!" Shāhpuhr cried, thumping a fist to his chest. He and Catanes took on two ebrens who seemed like they'd rather be elsewhere.

Az roared in annoyance, pointing a claw at a trio of dragons who looked like orange triplets. Now Abarōz trembled. She was only one, and they were in swooping fast.

"Shāhpuhr!" she yelled, but he couldn't get away. Abarōz took a deep breath, then turned Az fully around. "You know what to do!" she told him, and he certainly did. Raising his spade tail, he let out a stream of red which dispersed over three orange forms. This was followed by screaming and a hasty retreat.

"Nice work," Shāhpuhr called, sending his own two foes down to Gehān. "Should we join up?"

"Yes," said Abarōz, jerking her chin toward a menacing purple and yellow. They flapped together toward Az and Catanes.

"I've got your back!" Shāhpuhr shouted, hefting both sword and lance.

He was true to his word as he dodged double flame. Thinking fast, he split up their two assailants so Abarōz could take on one. Still clutching Az's spike, she gripped her lance in her other hand and threw it, hitting her purple mark. At the same time, Shāhpuhr steered Catanes under the yellow one's belly, allowing him to avoid its flames from both ends. Once Catanes fired his own, yellow went down to meet purple before the Dardan gate.

"Very nice," Abarōz called to Shāhpuhr, who lowered his head in a bow. "Do you know how our side is doing? Overall?"

"I don't think we've lost many—I've only seen four defeated."

"Good," she said, watching a handful of dragons flee screaming from Bükrek.

"You mother," she yelled to Shāhpuhr, "has quite the effect!"

He smiled but still looked wary, and his caution was justified: four ebrens were flying their way, two-by-two. The first pair gained height to hang over Az, while the second assaulted Catanes.

Abarōz's limbs shook. She knew that this fight was the worst one so far. Her two new foes, silver and gold, shot flames from mouth and tail: she could feel them on her helmet, and suspected her breastplate was next. Az thankfully wheeled so her exposed flesh was spared, but she realized that any minute, it would be scorched by fire.

"Az!" Abarōz called to the dragon's head. "What should we do?"

The white dragon shook his head, as trapped as a zarran in the mine. After hurling both her weapons, Abarōz was left with only her shield. She closed her eyes as she felt heat swell from above: then, to her horror, Az gave a cry of pain before smacking into the sand.

When Abarōz awoke, the first thing she saw were two heads, both worriedly looking at her.

"Shāhpuhr?" she asked groggily, trying to restore her vision. At the moment, she saw four of him.

"How are you?" he asked, running his hands down her sides. Her plate had been removed. "Does this pain you?"

"No," Abarōz croaked, accepting a skin from him and gulping down cool water. There was just one thing on her mind. "Did we win?"

At her grassy bedside, Bükrek shook her head.

"I fear not," she said. "Sangal called in reinforcements, and we were overwhelmed."

Abarōz shut her eyes. She wanted to sit up, but wondered if the effort was even worth it.

"How many?" she asked. "How many did we lose?"

"Seven," Shāhpuhr answered. "Aswārs and dragons."

Something ripped at Abarōz like an ebren's claw. She opened her eyes to face her two friends.

"It can't be!" she cried. "Were they not afraid of Bükrek?!"

"Some," said Shāhpuhr, "but, alas, not enough. Sangal's hold on his horde seems only to increase."

Abarōz couldn't help the tears sprinkling her face. This war, she feared, was lost. They would never recover.

"Do not cry, my child," said Bükrek. "There are more dragons yet stirring in the south. Like the ones who gave their lives, they are willing to fight for freedom. They know that Sangal will come for them—it is just a matter of time."

The subject of dragons stirred something in Abarōz.

"Az?" she whispered.

"He died bravely," Bükrek told her, "in a cause he truly believed in."

"And Dardan?"

"Safe for now," said Shāhpuhr. "Once we retreated, Sangal's horde did too. I suppose they weren't too eager to break through solid stone."

"Good."

For the first time, she was glad of Dardan's caves.

Bükrek smiled down at her.

"You should get some more rest."

The green dragon slid off.

"Always the mother, that one," Shāhpuhr grinned. "Careful, or she might start teaching you Dragon!"

"I wouldn't mind. But, Shāhpuhr—" Abarōz ran her fingers over the length of her body, amazed to find it whole. "How–how did I survive?"

He plopped down beside her.

"I returned my debt to you by stealing that purple dragon's blood. You know the rest."

"I–I don't remember."

"That's because your spirit was sleeping."

"Oh." Abarōz wiped away more tears. So . . . Shāhpuhr had saved her life. She felt incredibly grateful, and at the same time humbled. "Thank you," she whispered.

He bent to kiss her cheek.

"We are now even."

They shared a quiet moment after the frenzy of battle. Abarōz put up a hand to stroke his stubbled jaw. Shāhpuhr was her very best friend, and, just maybe, something more . . .

The mood was shattered as she thought of Dardan again.

"The city," she choked, "will soon run out of water. Once all are dead, Sangal will clear out the mine."

"I imagine," said Shāhpuhr, "that my father will let the zarran live."

Abarōz felt a rage that bubbled into her throat.

"Of course," she snapped, "for the Šāh lives to serve Sangal."

"Both he and the dragon share an unnatural love of gold."

Abarōz nodded, rising shakily to her feet.

"Were you," she asked, "able to save any others with the dragon's blood?"

"Yes. I took enough to heal four. I was too late for the others."

Abarōz felt course through her a strange mix of cheer and dread. But the former won out as Shāhpuhr came to stand by her side.

"We must go south," she told him, "to gather more ebrens. But . . ." He stared. "Of what use will they be with only nine Aswārs?"

"Do not worry," he said, placing an arm around her shoulder. "My mother will solve this. Remember, she is a healer."

But enough of one, wondered Abarōz, *to free more Dardans from the yoke of the Šāh?*

The Gurg Kamāl

Seated atop my stone dais, I overlook my horde. I have already doled out punishments, cutting the wings from an ebren who dared to flee prematurely; taking some tails as prizes to subtly warn the rest.

Really, do I have to do *everything?*

I stare down at my pitiful ebrens, none gathered too close, and prepare to issue a screed like none they've heard before.

"I am enraged and disgusted," I bellow, "at your retreat from Dardan when victory was in our claws! Once Bükrek's ragtag forces admitted defeat and flew home, what was there to stop you from storming the city gate?!"

As always, I'm greeted by silence: They all know my temper, and in case they do not, I spit a billow of fire above their cowardly heads.

"Now," I cry, my voice echoing on stone. "We must wait for the death of the aqueducts before I can seize my gold."

I see a few ebrens—leaders—nod briskly with vigor.

Sycophants.

"Luckily for you," I say, "I intend to recruit a new ally. One who will feast on Bükrek's filthy force!"

I hear a low murmur—just the effect I sought. With the drama of a Greek behind his mask, I turn to my lair's entrance and beckon with one large claw.

"Ebrens!" I shout. "Meet the Gurg Kamāl!"

I have to chuckle as most of my horde steps back. Their first glimpse at my new friends is just what I had hoped: a mixture of awe and fear. For the Gurg Kamāl are truly terrible creatures with the form of a dragon but the head of a wolf.

"Greetings," I say in their uncouth Dragon. I feel a heady rush to see the leader bow deeply. "Friend," I address him, not bothering with the rest. "You might have heard of my quarrel with the city of Dardan."

This leader raises his head and stares with yellow eyes.

"Great Sangal," he answers, "word had traveled far. Even to those in Abaxtar."

I nod, satisfied. Good to know that my actions do not go unremarked.

"I have called you south," I say, "in order to swell our ranks. My hated rival Bükrek makes war against me in favor of men. But with your pack behind us, they will all visit the grave."

The wolf-head's eyes glow brighter.

"Forgive me, King," he says, "but for risking our lives, my pack requires a favor."

"Of course," I purr, fully prepared. "Once Dardan is ours, you may have the enemy's plate." The wolf-head looks at me skeptically. Foolish, foolish creature. "Do you think this below you? It is Peril-made and flameproof!"

I see the fire of greed in his pant. Now that he's caught in my trap, he cannot gnaw his way out.

"I agree," he says, thumping a claw to his chest. "For this magick plunder, we fight."

"A wise choice," I answer, showing off all my teeth. If he had dared to deny me, I would have killed him and made another—one more willing—the alpha in his place. "Please," I tell my new friends, "feel free to remain among us until the next battle dawns. Tell me—what is it that you eat?"

"Meat," says the alpha. "Not cooked—we like it raw."

"As do we. I shall see that your needs are met."

I motion to my second-in-charge, whispering into his ear.

"Fly to Dardan," I tell him, "and retrieve all human corpses. Our wolves will feast well tonight."

A Spinner of Time

"Bükrek."

In the clearing, Abarōz approached her hesitantly, since with a fight looming, the dragon must be preoccupied.

"Yes, Abarōz?"

She and Shāhpuhr walked before his mother, *all flanked by warriors and ebrens.*

"Your son and I were just talking, and . . . we desperately need more Aswārs. Before Sangal's next strike."

Bükrek looked down, extruding smoke through her nostrils. This meant she might be angry or merely lost in thought.

"I am hoping," the dragon sighed, "there is something I can do. It would right two evils."

Abarōz's curiosity was like a living thing.

"What?" she asked eagerly.

"You know that Sangal and I visit here every millennia. My primary task is to try to heal the world. But I do have another gift . . ." Even Shāhpuhr looked surprised. "I am a Spinner of Time. When I'm not in Gehān, I spend winters asleep in my ocean. But when I awaken in spring, it causes new life to blossom."

"You mean . . . " Abarōz asked, "that you *create* the seasons? Is that how you spin time?"

"Partly," said Bükrek, raising her head with a smile. "But I can do something else. Every thousand years, for one time only, I am allowed to spin time."

Abarōz stared at her yellow eyes.

"You mean," she asked, "you can undo what's been done?"

"Under the strictures I've stated, yes. But I cannot remove Sangal, or go back more than a century."

Shāhpuhr looked a bit hurt.

"Why didn't you tell me?" he asked.

His mother let out a sigh.

"I did not think it would be needed," she said, "to spin time during this visit."

"But now?" asked Abarōz. "Is now the time?"

Bükrek looked over her head.

"I sense that it is."

"What part of time will you spin?" Abarōz was so eager she couldn't keep still. "Prevent Sangal's horde from joining him? Not let the S̆āh rule Dardan?"

Bükrek considered these choices.

"I could stop Sangal's ebrens from joining him, but he would simply find others. As to the S̆āh: his is an ancient dynasty, passed from father to son. If he does not rule, then one of his sons surely will."

"Why not Shāhpuhr?" asked Abarōz.

"No," he said firmly, "I've no wish to be S̆āh. I fear that over time, I'd become as depraved as my father. Besides, his viziers would be happy to kill me."

"What then?" cried Abarōz, stomping one sandaled foot.

"We know we need more Aswārs," Bükrek explained, "but since the horde has lost its fear of me, they cannot be retrieved from Dardan." Abarōz closed her eyes, wanting to scream. "However, your father—"

"What?"

"—and the other Axwaš who've been lost these hundred years. If I could bring them back, we'd have quite a force, for their numbers are sadly large."

"But . . ." As thrilled as she was at a chance to see her father, Abarōz was troubled. "Most of them," she said, "were cast out at birth like Shāhpuhr. Will we be an army of babes?"

Bükrek chuckled.

"Do not forget," she said, "those who suffered maladies later—they too were discarded. So we will have more than babes."

Abarōz turned to Shāhpuhr, lacing her fingers with his. If Bükrek's magick could work . . . if they could be gifted with warriors . . .

She tried not to tremble.

"My father . . ." she whispered. She could hardly imagine seeing him . . . taking him into her arms . . .

She turned to Bükrek.

"You–you really think you can do this?"

The green dragon nodded.

"With the help of Tengri, I can."

"THEN WHAT ARE WE WAITING FOR?!"

Abarōz's feet left the ground.

"Very well," said Bükrek. "I must fly alone to undo the wrongs of the past. You two wait for me here."

Abarōz nodded—she was willing to wait forever.

"All right?" Shāhpuhr asked her.

"More than," she said softly, wiping tears from her lower lashes. "May Tengri smile upon your mother and aid her in her task."

The Funnel of Time

As she soared, Bükrek glanced down at the ebrens gathered by the Rōd. Most looked exhausted, lying full-length on the grass. Though she desperately wanted to gift them with riders, she could only hope she was doing the right thing. Even for an immortal, it was sometimes hard to tell.

During her last three visits to Gehān spaced every millennium, she had not called on her special gift. Sangal had been quiet in his lake of fire, while the cave cities endured: surely not a heaven, but not in jeopardy either. Across the rest of the world, zands made their way from place to place and empires rose and fell. Gehān continued to turn; people intermingled and killed one another in war. Iifn other words: more of the same.

The one cruelty that always disturbed her—made her flinch and look away—was the fate of the Axwaš. Bükrek had tried her best—she had after all saved Shāhpuhr—but was afraid to save all lest Sangal emerge from his lake. But that hardly mattered at present: he was here, he was chaos, so what could be the harm?

Bükrek lifted her face to the clouds as she flew to her heavenly home. If only Tengri, great sky god, could give her a sign that what she sought was holy! Still, she rose higher, past light-bringer Mihr, to a cloudless patch where the air grew chill. She hadn't been up this far for five hundred years, and, in five hundred more, to this place she would return.

After giving a final push, Bükrek tucked in her wings, buoyed by a strange current even she couldn't feel.

I must still my mind, she thought, concentrating her power. She began to loop in a circle which became steadily smaller. *Intent,* she reminded herself.

"Time," she spoke aloud, "unravel your weave on my air-wheel. Allow me to work my gift."

She saw she was now at the center of a raging tornado, but rather than dirty-white, its funnel was multicolored, with swatches of blues and reds straining to escape.

"Spin," she commanded, and the funnel reversed its motion, swirling so fast that all its colors merged. Bükrek kept a calm mind as she thought of the Axwaš, conjuring newborns and those of all ages who tossed inside bending air walls.

"Undo," Bükrek said, "the evil that has been done."

The helpless human forms hovered upon their backs, driven down by that wind which Tengri alone could control.

She and her Axwaš now floated, free of the funnel's constriction.

Again, she passed Mihr, who warmed the air around them; then flapped over the trees of Razūr with its ribbon river and clearing.

Bükrek landed on its green space, followed by drifting Axwaš gently down. She wondered how they'd react to the soft feel of grass.

The Axwaš

Abarōz paced nervously, the prints of her sandals flattening the grass.

"Try to relax," said Shāhpuhr with a smile. "There's nothing we can do until my mother returns."

"I know," she breathed, holding her arms to her sides. "It's just that—"

"—Your father. How strange it will be to see him after his death."

"I knew I would," said Abarōz, "but only in the next world." She continued to her pacing. "How long," she asked, "do you think it takes to spin time?"

Shāhpuhr shook his head.

"I've no idea. Hopefully, less than a thousand years."

Abarōz narrowed her eyes. She was in no mood for joking, and consulted the sky so often, her neck began to throb.

"Where *is* she?" she hissed, shielding her eyes from Mihr. "I can't see through those clouds!"

"Hear something?" asked Shāhpuhr, cocking his head.

Abarōz did the same, straining to hear the flap of wings.

"Look—it's her!"

She was so excited she grabbed Shāhpuhr in a hug. Then, remembering that Axwaš were Dardans, she pulled away. As Bükrek's green form came closer, Abarōz saw she was surrounded by a swarm of falling figures.

"Are they . . .?" Abarōz asked, letting her tears flow freely. *"Father!"* she called to the bodies that set down, each face pale as an angel's, all eyes firmly closed.

"FATHER!" she yelled again, bending down to examine the Dardans. Stumbling past a circle of newborns, she made her way to the others, all unmoving and asleep. She didn't recognize most—they must have been discarded far before she was born—but when she came to one pale face, she felt her own take on the same hue.

"Father," she whispered, dropping to her knees beside him. She looked up at Bükrek. "Is he . . . are they . . .?"

"Alive," the dragon smiled. "Restored as they once were. Just give them a moment."

Abarōz could not: she threw herself across Rastag, kissing his cold brow and cheeks.

Shāhpuhr came up to kneel beside her, taking her hand.

Then, Abarōz felt a heat—Rastag's flesh coming to life!—and she saw his eyes open as blood ran into his face.

"A-Abarōz?" he forced out, even attempting to sit. "Is it—is it really you?"

"Yes, Father!" she cried, hugging him where he lay. "How . . . how do you feel?"

"Odd," said Rastag, leaning back on his elbows. "The last thing I remember, I was being eaten by ebrens—"

"Do not think of it," she whispered, stroking his grey-flecked hair. "You have landed in a new world. One where evil has been unspun to give you another chance."

"And these?" he asked, pointing to the Dardans around him. Most were now awake, serenaded by the cries of babes.

"Axwaš," Abarōz told him. "Like you, all who were sacrificed over the past hundred years."

"Can it be?" her father mumbled, accepting her help to stand, his face now half-a-foot from Shāhpuhr's.

"Erm . . . Father, Rastag of Dardan; this is Shāhpuhr of Razūr. He is son to the dragon who brought you here and—" she blushed, "—a very good friend of mine."

The two men's dark eyes met, her father's gaze intense.

"Not *too good,* I trust?" he asked.

Abarōz giggled.

"No, Father. Shāhpuhr has been helping to free our zand from the Šāh."

"May he be spat on by snakes!" Rastag roared. "Then, fed to the wolves!"

"I quite agree with you, Pid," sad Shāhpuhr. "I am ashamed to be his blood son."

Rastag clapped him on the arm.

"You will be judged by your own deeds."

"Let Tengri make it so."

Abarōz smiled, glad that her father was fair.

"Well," Rastag asked, looking around, "where in Gehān are we?"

"This is Razūr, Father," said Abarōz. "A forest not far from Dardan."

Her father shivered.

"May I never live to set eyes on that place again!" Abarōz exchanged a glance with Shāhpuhr. Her eyes told him to save this matter for later. "Tell me," Rastag asked wearily, "what have I missed since my death?"

Abarōz started—it was just such a strange thing to hear.

"Well, we fought the Šāh's master Sangal in two battles." Rastag gave her a stare. "Both times, it didn't go well."

"Sangal, "said her father. "Is he not some dragon of myth?"

"Unhappily, no," she replied. "He lives and commands a horde of ebrens."

Rastag looked troubled.

"You can never win," he told her.

"We can now," insisted Abarōz, "for we have ebrens of our own—and riders!"

She spread her arms to encompass the hundred or so Dardans there. Her father gave her the same sort of chuckle as he had when she was five.

"If you say so, daughter."

"I do," she said, putting an arm around his waist. "It won't be long before you're a fearsome Aswār!"

Her father looked terrified.

"I hate ebrens!" he spat. "Let them return to myth!"

"I understand, Pid," said Shāhpuhr, "considering your last meeting with them."

"Hmmp," Rastag snorted. "At least one person has sense!"

Abarōz tried to smile. She could only imagine how strange talk of Aswārs and ebrens would be to him.

"Do not fear, Father," she said. "So much in Gehān has changed. The dragons of the south help us—even the magickal Perils!"

"Son!" Rastag cried, "is my daughter in her right mind?"

Shāhpuhr smiled.

"She is. And speaks truth."

"This I will have to see," mumbled Rastag.

Abarōz squeezed his shoulder.

"You will."

She walked with him and Shāhpuhr to their usual cooking place. As Shāhpuhr headed off to the river, she regarded her father. He looked the same as he had the night he'd been taken: the same lines etching his face; the same tautness to his jaw. He'd been weighted with care before the Šāh's cruelty and being brought back hadn't helped. She sought to lift his spirits.

"The Perils," she said, "have made us flameproof armor!"

He scowled.

"Then why don't they wear it?"

"They aren't allowed to aid us . . . actively."

"Dark witches!" he spat.

"You'd be surprised. They really are quite elegant."

Her father regarded the stacked sticks before him.

"These ebrens," he said. He must have been thinking of fire. "How many on your side?"

Abarōz looked down.

"I don't know. We lost many in the last battle."

Rastag shook his head.

"And you expect to get more?"

Abarōz brightened.

"Yes! There are more who would join us."

"And how are they summoned?"

"We . . . must journey south."

"You and not me!" cried Rastag. "I am *not* leaving this spot. The worktime I mount a dragon is when Perils dance in my head!"

"Yes, sir," Abarōz answered from habit. She saw Shāhpuhr returning with a long string of fish. "Time to eat. I'm sure you're famished."

They all shared an ample meal before their sparking fire. Rastag ate with gusto, his expression one of bliss. The other Axwaš were fed by Bükrek, who distributed meat and mushrooms. Abarōz shook her head. Whatever her source, the green dragon provided a feast.

Once they were finished, Abarōz noticed her father's head sinking.

"Please, Pid," she told him, "you must rest. You have gone through something not many live to speak of."

"True," he muttered, lying down by the sputtering fire, and falling quickly to sleep.

"So," Shāhpuhr asked as he led Abarōz off. "Did seeing your father match all your wishes?"

"No," she said frankly. "I assumed, in light of his treatment, that he would rally against the Šāh. Instead, he is more cautious than fourteen Hamwars of Dardans."

Shāhpuhr smiled.

"I'm sure he'll change his mind—once he sees our ebrens."

"That's what I'm afraid of."

Bükrek's Plan

When Rastag awoke, he joined a circle of Dardans: some getting re-acquainted; some meeting for the first time. Abarōz was relieved to see a host of five Axwaš taking care of the babes.

"Well," she said to Shāhpuhr, as they wandered down to the river, "now we have both dragons and Aswārs. What next?"

"If I know my mother," he answered, "lots and lots of training."

"My father will be so happy."

They both exchanged a grin as Bükrek came slithering up.

"All is well?" she asked.

"Yes. Thank you," Abarōz said with emotion. "For saving my father and all the others."

"I only did what was right."

"If you don't mind my asking," said Abarōz, trying not to sound too curious, "where do we go from here?"

"I believe," Bükrek told her, "we need more than dragons and Aswārs. Surely Sangal will not sit still until he's gathered more allies."

"What did you have in mind?" asked Abarōz. "Are there more clever creatures here? Like the talking tree man?"

Bükrek shook her head sadly.

"I fear not."

"Well . . . what about other places? Gehān is said to be large."

"It is indeed," the green dragon said. "And crossed with zands and creatures who are either fearsome or friendly."

"I say," said Shāhpuhr, "we try to find the *last* kind."

His mother smiled.

"I will think on it. In the meantime, try to rest. We must all be at our best."

Abarōz and Shāhpuhr treaded back to the clearing where she saw her father. As this eventful day would soon give way to night, she nodded to his friends, then took his elbow to lead him.

"Father. May I sleep by your side tonight?"

"Of course. I would welcome it."

She gave him her blanket as Shāhpuhr stirred a fire. Before long, they were all sprawled out on the grass. Rastag must still be weary for he was the first to close his eyes, and the rhythm of his breathing, even his dreaded snores, made Abarōz feel she was home. Now that he was free of the Šāh, he did seem less jittery: no more peering around every corner fearing a spy would jump out.

If he could only, Abarōz thought, *commit himself to their cause, her world would be near-perfect.* Of course, with Shāhpuhr on the other side of the fire, she didn't have far to go!

She fell into a tranquil sleep roughly interrupted by something poking her shoulder.

"Go away," she mumbled, turning. The annoying prods continued.

"What?" she snapped, her lids fluttering open.

"Come," said Shāhpuhr, reaching out a hand. "My mother wishes to speak to us."

"She keeps strange hours," Abarōz yawned, rising with his help to stretch the sleep from her limbs. It must be well into the night, the silver light of Māh embracing their silent camp. Shāhpuhr led her over the clearing to where his mother stood.

"I am sorry to disturb you," said Bükrek, "but I told you I would think on it."

"And you have?"

Abarōz suppressed another yawn.

"Yes. I can hardly keep secrets from my son or the hero of Dardan."

Abarōz blushed down to her chest.

"Surely you don't mean me!"

"You are the one who inspired this rebellion. Never forget who you are."

Abarōz fought a silent battle: Was she really that girl in gold plate, the one who rallied the zarran; Or a maid of Dardan, lately afraid to talk to a boy?

She blinked, trying to pay attention.

"—Old legends," Bükrek was saying, "of a dark land to the north. It lies far beyond Sangal and is said to harbor strange creatures, unknown to all but the gods. There is the myth of the Erbörü, savage men with the power to turn into wolves. Even as an immortal, I have never set eyes upon them."

What was she going on about? A distant lands and wolves? Abarōz hoped that the dragon hadn't let time-spinning break her. Even Shāhpuhr seemed skeptical.

"But mother," he asked, "how can these Erbörü help us?"

Exactly. They might not even exist.

Bükrek folded her claws.

"They would be a powerful ally. And, I have a sense that wolves lie in our future."

"Are we not descended from them?" asked Shāhpuhr.

"Yes, but keep that to yourself. Men do not like to hear about an animal ancestor."

Abarōz rolled her eyes. This meant nothing to her, but the wolves of the north surely did.

"Bükrek," she questioned, "what if these wolf people tear us apart? There is nothing to stop them."

"The Erbörü," said the dragon, "were exiled eons past. No others on Gehān will suffer their presence."

Abarōz found herself feeling bad for them.

"That's unkind."

"I heard some time ago that they wished to rejoin the world. Whether or not they still feel the same is something unknown to me."

"So . . ." Abarōz stood and thought. "You're saying that if we offer them a way out, they might fight on our side?"

Bükrek smiled, sharp teeth on display.

"You are clever," she told Abarōz, "but do not let it lead you to trouble."

"Too late."

"Mother," asked Shāhpuhr, "do you mean to send a party north?"

"I do," she sighed. "In order to conquer Sangal, we must expand our reach."

Abarōz saw Bükrek's face shining with bands of moonlight. The dragon had been a great friend, her city's foremost champion. Who was she, a girl of Dardan, to oppose one of her world's creators?

"I'll go," she said slowly.

"Oh no," protested Shāhpuhr, "this journey is not for you."

"Do you intend," Abarōz asked, "to venture so far by yourself? To a land so little known?"

"Abaxtar," he whispered. "I have heard the name."

"And that equips you to go?" Abarōz was furious, placing her hands on her hips. "Since you know the name, you will surely proceed in safety?"

"No," Shāhpuhr huffed, "but I will feel much better knowing *you* are kept safe."

Abarōz snorted.

"That is far more absurd than an edict of your father's! You will 'feel better' if you put yourself in more danger?"

Bükrek, who'd been watching this discourse as if they traded blows, decided to intervene.

"That is enough," she said. "My son, your feelings are honorable, but you cannot do this alone. If Abarōz wishes, she must be allowed to go."

In a sudden fit of pique, Abarōz stuck out her tongue.

"Best put that back," groused Shāhpuhr, "or you might lose it."

Abarōz crossed her arms, narrowing her eyes.

"That's settled then." Abarōz turned to Bükrek. "When should we leave?"

"At sunrise."

Based on the lightening sky, that shouldn't be too much longer.

"Come on," she bid Shāhpuhr, taking his hand in hers. "Let us sleep while we can."

He grumbled something as they both returned to the fire. But he must have felt forgiving since he tossed her a blanket.

"Thanks." Once they lay down, side by side, she extended an edge so it covered him too. "Truce?" she asked.

He rolled over to face her.

"I was not angry," he said, so close she could feel his breath. "But from what I've heard of Abaxtar, it is not a place for a girl."

Abarōz wrenched herself up.

"So that's your real objection? I should go back to cooking and cleaning—make sure I have a large dowry so I can attract a husband?!"

He put an arm on her shoulder.

"Of course not! I only meant—"

"That girls have no place in war. Now that I know how you feel, I'll be sure not to get in your way."

She seized back the blanket, wrapping herself in its layers.

"Abarōz," Shāhpuhr whispered. "We both know you're a fierce fighter. You learned to be an Aswār in just one day!"

"Hmmp." Abarōz still felt upset, but wanted to hear him say "Sorry." "Go on."

"Must I? You've fought in two battles, infiltrated two cities, and gone up against ebrens. What I said about Abaxtar—I just don't want to see you hurt. I . . . I've come to care for you."

Abarōz felt a shiver.

"Really?"

She rolled toward him in her cocoon.

"Yes."

Shāhpuhr unraveled the blanket enough to reveal her neck. He covered it with light kisses, working up to her jaw, then her lips.

He bit down gently on her bottom one, causing her to whimper. Encouraged, he brushed his tongue against her teeth, and she let him in, reveling in the sensation. This could have gone on until dawn if she hadn't remembered Rastag across the fire from them.

"Shāhpuhr!" she hissed, pushing against his chest. "We mustn't. My . . . my father."

He groaned, then changed his position so they were back to front.

It was going to be a long night.

In Search of Friends

Just before dawn, Abarōz woke and walked to her father. Curled on his side, he looked like a sleeping child. But she couldn't forgive herself if she left without saying goodbye.

"Father," she whispered, crouching by his side. He mumbled, turning over. *"Father,"* she said louder.

He shot up, putting one hand on her throat.

"Who are you?!" he hissed.

Abarōz answered through coughs.

"F-father, It's all right—it's–it's me."

His arm fell to his side.

"Forgive me," he said. "You startled me." He glanced at the red-streaked sky. "It is early."

"Yes." Abarōz did something she had never done in Dardan: gave his arm a squeeze. "Father," she told him, "I must tell you I need to leave. I'm here to bid you farewell."

"Ah." He looked somber. "I return from my own journey only to have you make one."

Abarōz sighed.

"It can't be helped. Or you may have come back for nothing."

"I wouldn't say that," he smiled, "for I've been able to see you again."

Abarōz blinked away tears. She had to stay strong—for him.

"Do not worry, Father," she said, stroking his grizzled face. "I'll be back before you know it."

"May Tengri make it so."

She put down her hand reluctantly, rising to stand above him.

"I will return," she said. "And we'll be together again."

He gave her a smile so full of love that she had to turn away. When she found Shāhpuhr, he sensed her sadness and bent to kiss her cheek. She was thankful for this and the sight of two loaded packs, gold plate roped to the deerskin.

"Ready?" he asked softly, motioning toward the Rōd. Bükrek was not to be seen, which Abarōz thought was deliberate: they had already said their goodbyes.

The forms of sleeping ebrens dotted both banks of the river. As Shāhpuhr approached Catanes, Abarōz's hands flew to her mouth.

"Shāhpuhr! I don't have a dragon!"

This awoke Catanes, who smiled up at his rider. The two of them exchanged roars.

"He says," Shāhpuhr told her, "that the blue at his side, Iotapa[1], proved her courage at Dardan."

Abarōz looked into eyes the same color as the dragon's scales. She walked slowly to the ebren's side, and once Shāhpuhr relayed that his friend needed a mount, Iotapa[2] hugged the ground.

"Thank you," Abarōz told her, feeling a twinge for Az. But she tried to push away thoughts of her last disastrous ride as she leapt atop Iotapa.

The dragon unfurled her wings, taking off to soar past water and trees. Lulled by her ride's smoothness, Abarōz relaxed her death grip on Iotapa's spike. Hearing a nearby flap, she turned to see Catanes where Shāhpuhr rode with both hands free.

"A master Aswār?" she teased.

"Not quite," he smiled. "Give me another two years."

They continued in silence, Mihr flaring brighter the farther they flew. The sky turned a burnt-orange as they soared above Sangal's lair.

"Ugh," shuddered Abarōz, thinking of her adventure there. "You don't think the north ebrens will attack?"

Shāhpuhr shook his head.

"They are far too arrogant to expect anyone in their space. In this case, their hubris is *not* a flaw!"

1. https://www.behindthename.com/name/iotapa/submitted

2. https://www.behindthename.com/name/iotapa/submitted

Abarōz laughed, impressed that his mother had taught him something of the Hrōmāyīg. He had really missed nothing by not growing up in Dardan.

At last, they were free of the desert and approaching a tree-lined land. Abarōz looked down. She had never been this far north and she was frankly afraid.

"Shāhpuhr," she called, "are we sure this journey is wise? To venture to a place only spoken about in whispers; to attempt a bargain with wolf men. If this isn't madness, what is?"

He shot her a wry grin.

"I can't dispute you," he said, "but when have the two of us been anything but mad?"

She couldn't maintain her frown.

"True," she told him, "but this Abaxtar is not Šahr. The customs will be unknown to us—even the language!"

"We have no idea," Shāhpuhr said, "of what lies ahead in that strange land. But if there's one thing I trust, it's my mother. My faith in her equals my faith in you."

Abarōz felt a glow as if she could fly without a dragon.

"Thank you," she smiled. "I return the feeling fully. Unless, of course, you're under your father's curse."

He laughed.

"I can't blame you."

"So what are we looking for when it comes to this Abaxtar?"

"When I was young, Bükrek told me tales. She said it lies in the northwest and is heavy with trees. The forests there make Razūr look like a pinprick."

Abarōz shuddered to think of this wood and its creatures. The wolf men might well be the least of their worries. She tried to distract herself by looking down at the landscape. After just a short time aloft, she spotted a vast spread of water.

"Is that an ocean?" she asked.

"No," answered Shāhpuhr. "It is a sea of black."

Abarōz leaned over cautiously.

"But all I see is blue."

"Still, My mother says it is called the Black Sea."

"Oh," she gasped, amazed that she couldn't see the opposite shore. "I've never seen anything like it."

"Nor I. The Bērūn contains many wonders."

And dangers.

"Will we reach the forest by nightfall?"

"Oh yes. Not to Abaxtar, but the north ones that lie before it."

Abarōz felt her skin prickle: yet another unknown.

As the dragons flapped on, she saw the Black Sea give way to green thickets. The further they flew, the more dense they became, and the less Mihr warmed them.

"Where are we?" she asked.

"In the north I spoke of. It is a good time to land."

Abarōz didn't need to guide Iotapa as Catanes aimed for the ground. They set down their claws in a green clearing where both riders jumped off. Abarōz looked around warily.

"There," Shāhpuhr said cheerfully. "That wasn't so bad!"

"I'm not worried about the journey—it's the destination that scares me."

"There are no Erbörü here, so you don't have to worry."

"But," asked Abarōz, "*what else* might be hiding?"

He raised his shoulders, spreading both hands. The two ebrens, in need of rest, closed their eyes and sprawled out full-length.

"One thing is sure," he said. "These woods have never been cut."

Abarōz nodded—even she could tell. These trees towered so high they seemed to reach past Mihr.

"What should we do now?" she asked.

"Besides not harm the trees? We rest."

"But *we* only rode!"

Shāhpuhr let out a low chuckle before pulling dried meat from his pack.

"Eat," he said, tearing off a small chunk for her. He cocked his head and listened. "I don't hear any large creatures, so I think we're probably safe."

Abarōz let out a breath. How she wished that he *knew.* She startled at birdcalls unlike any she'd ever heard. They were wild and screaming, though Shāhpuhr took no notice—of them. He seemed more concerned about her.

"I take it," he said, "you don't much like the outdoors?"

Abarōz gulped.

"I like Razūr since it's calm and safe. But here?" She swept her eyes to a low-hanging branch. "Anything could happen."

"That is so," said Shāhpuhr, "but I find the more wild the place, the better I like it."

"Why?"

"I don't like to be bored. Not knowing what or who I'll meet keeps me on my toes."

"I don't know," Abarōz sighed. "Give me a Dardan without the S̄āh, and I could be perfectly happy."

"Buried in stone?"

She sighed.

"Well, I didn't mean it that way. But I'd like the safety of a city mixed with a touch of Mihr."

Shāhpuhr grinned.

"Perhaps you'll achieve that someday."

Abarōz sighed.

"I doubt it. But in the meantime, at least we don't have Al-razi."

Shāhpuhr motioned over the clearing.

"Here we are free," he said.

"You're right. That at least is something."

"There is no one to watch us," he whispered, sidling over to where she sat. His face now inches from hers, he bent to touch her forehead. "Whatever we do will never be told. By the sky god, I swear it."

Abarōz closed her eyes, all her emotions colliding. Should she continue to follow the old ways—those of Dardan—or give herself up to Shāhpuhr's? At last, the warmth she felt for him made her decision easy.

"Kiss me," she ordered, surprised at her own boldness.

His eyes shone as he put his arms around her. At first, his kisses were gentle, soft lips upon hers; then, he deepened them, allowing their tongues to explore. Someone let out a groan and to Abarōz's shock it was her!

Shāhpuhr's hands caressed her throat before moving down to her sides. Abarōz felt a heat that had long surpassed warmth: it scorched like an ebren's flame. Even though she flushed, shy at her lack of experience, she placed her hand in his hair, raking through the long strands.

"Abarōz," he panted, and his fingers swept upward to right below her chest. "May I?" he whispered, and all she could do was nod. As his hands caressed her breasts she lost all sense of place: she could have been here, in these woods; sequestered in Dardan; or in Şahmeran's den, with its falls and flowers.

"More," she begged, and he lay her down, his own body flush with hers, every inch of their flesh touching. Abarōz felt his groan vibrate as the friction between them grew. Was this really it then? So many visions passed through her mind: Adrina, scolding; her father, disappointed; the entire city of Dardan wagging its finger under her nose.

"WAIT!" she yelled, startling Shāhpuhr with a hard push. "I know," she said, her breath coming in gasps, "that with you, I am free, but . . . my old life is watching."

He caught his own breath before he rolled to his feet.

"It's all right," he said. "You must tell me if I go too far. I may not have grown up 'civilized,' but I fancy myself a good man."

"You are," Abarōz told him. "I've never known a better one."

He bowed, and she felt she could trust him (and herself) to slowly rise and move toward him, placing her lips on his.

When they pushed apart, he gave her a lopsided grin.

"I hope you don't hate me."

She playfully smacked his arm before they stood in silence below the cathedral of trees.

"Abarōz?" he asked. She prepared herself for anything. "I think we should stay here tonight. That way, we can get a fresh start in the morning."

"Whatever you say. After all, you *are* a boy of the forest."

He laughed, her humor dispelling any unease. Shāhpuhr walked the dragons, picking up fallen branches, and, before long, a merry fire sparked. He sat on a fallen log, then beckoned for her to come over. Even though their thighs touched, she felt completely safe. Gazing over at the sleeping dragons, Abarōz let out a sigh.

"If only," she said, "life could always be like this: no wars, no Sangal, no S̄āh."

"That would be perfect," he answered, "but you know that Gehān is not. We must learn to work with her flaws."

Abarōz smiled as she stared at orange flame dancing. She and Shāhpuhr sat together until Mihr's rays disappeared. He set out two blankets on moss.

"Rest," he said, lying down. "Tengri knows we'll need all our strength tomorrow."

"Yes," said Abarōz, thankful for two things that warmed her: him . . . and the fire. After feeling Shāhpuhr's embrace, she had no trouble closing her eyes.

The next morning, Abarōz woke to the harsh call of birds. Why were they still there? They sounded annoyed, affecting her the same way. What was it about these woods that brought forth such terrible sounds?

Shāhpuhr rose to his feet, then stamped out the fire's ashes. Abarōz got up and gulped down a flat piece of bread. As Shāhpuhr dined on dried meat, she walked out to Iotapa whose blue eyes were now open.

"No," Shāhpuhr said.

"I'm sorry?"

"We can't fly over the forest. Might as well wave a red cloak to tell every creature we're here."

"Oh. We walk then?"

He nodded, strapping on his gold sword and handing Abarōz hers. He turned to roar at the two dragons.

"Ready?" he asked Abarōz.

She only stared as Mihr poked through the trees.

"Not really," she said, "but as always it doesn't matter."

Shāhpuhr didn't smile.

"Stay by me," he ordered, making for a nearby thicket. "We don't know what to expect."

Abarōz sighed, wishing he'd kept that to himself.

She trailed him by two hands' breadths as he dove into the woods, taking a dirt path north. The farther they walked, the denser—and darker—it seemed this forest became. There came a time deep inside when Shāhpuhr unloosed his sword to cut away thick hanging branches.

Abarōz' gloom increased in proportion to that around her. She grew more apprehensive as she heard the scuttle of creatures, some on dirt and some on wood. She even gave a small cry as a leaf hit her upturned face.

Why was she here again?

She bumped right into Shāhpuhr as he abruptly stopped,

"Wha—?"

"Shhh."

He had his blade in both hands as he sniffed the air.

Abarōz tried to look over him, but of course he was too tall. Then, she heard a deep growl, and it wasn't coming from him: She saw a small dark brown form launch itself at his throat.

"Ah!" he cried, swinging his sword in a death blow.

The creature, small as a dog, lay bleeding on the dirt.

"Wh-what was that?" asked Abarōz.

"A xūg."

"Di-did you h-have to kill it?"

"Don't be deceived," he said, "by that sweet furry face. The xūg has cutting claws and is a fearsome predator."

"But it's so small!" she cried.

"Size is not the issue—it can bring down a full-grown deer."

"Oh."

Abarōz felt relief she was with a boy of the forest.

"The only good thing," he told her, sidestepping the body, "is that xūgs are hated by wolves."

"I see. So when we find them, let's tell them you killed one—before they tear us through."

Shāhpuhr's shoulders shook as he laughed.

"Remember," he said, "the Erbörü are more than wolves."

"I wish I could take some comfort in that."

Shāhpuhr turned to face her.

"We cannot become complacent: my mother says these woods are filled with bears and big cats."

"Now you tell me."

"Though these may seem tame compared to the beasts of Abaxtar."

"Is that supposed to be encouraging?"

He didn't have an answer as he cut his way down the path. If one more branch snagged Abarōz, she was going to confront Şahmeran. As they made their slow progress, Abarōz felt a chill. Although the air was mild, she felt that the trees were smothering her. *And she had lived in a cave!*

Such thoughts just frightened her more, each rustle of branch or leaf causing her to jump. She nearly cried out to Shāhpuhr when he stopped before her: there, to the side of the path, was a modest thatched hut. It was hardly remarkable, except for its leafy location, and the stilts that held it up. To Abarōz, they looked like the giant legs of a chicken!

"Baba Yaga," Shāhpuhr breathed. "We must have made it to Belarod."

"Is that the name of the hut?"

"Oh no, she's a—"

"Hello," came a voice as the crooked form of a woman emerged from the hut. She was a bit hard to look at, what with her long face, crooked nose, and black hat that rose in a peak. In one hand, she clutched a broom, and Abarōz had a feeling she did more with it than sweep.

"Greetings," said Shāhpuhr as she approached, though he kept his sword close.

"You are not . . . children?" this Baba Yaga asked. Though her accent was strange and some of her words unknown, Abarōz understood her.

"Er, no," she said. "We consider ourselves full-grown."

"Pity, for I had hoped to (strange word) you."

Abarōz turned to Shāhpuhr.

"What did she mean to say?"

"I'm not sure, but I think she hoped to eat us."

"WHAT?"

"It is said she devours children."

"Blech."

The old woman squinted over her nose before shuffling closer.

"Let *us* hope," whispered Abarōz, "we are not the exception."

Baba Yaga, now across from them, gripped her broom and gave them a stare. Abarōz almost felt that the witch could see her insides.

"Are you aware," asked the woman, "that I am more than a (?) of children?" Both travelers shook their heads. "Well, I am. You hardly hear it in stories, but I have been known to give advice to passers-by."

"Really?' Abarōz gulped.

"Come, child—"

"I'm *not* one!" Abarōz cried.

The old woman frowned.

"Let's not stand here and quibble. My advice is said to be wise."

"V-very well," said Abarōz, "what do you have to say to us?"

Baba Yaga smiled, transforming from fearsome to mild.

"Don't think I don't know what you seek—why you tread these woods. The Erbörü are fierce with no tolerance of strangers. You must approach them slowly, hands over your head. And . . ." she chuckled, "I'd put away those swords."

Abarōz grew impatient. What kind of advice was this?

"One more thing," said the witch. "Never disturb them when the moon is full. They'll make *me* look like a rabbit." This, at least, was helpful. "Now Dardans, take your leave, and follow the crooked path. When you hear a howl in the distance, you must set down your weapons."

"Thank you," said Shāhpuhr. "When I return home, I'll inform Bükrek of your gifts."

The witch gave a throaty chuckle.

"Oh, she knows."

With a vigorous last wave, Abarōz followed Shāhpuhr back into the forest. Abarōz had to admit Baba Yaga no longer scared her, but she was left with just one question: *Why* the legs of a chicken?

The Erbörü

"Follow the crooked path," said Abarōz, thinking how her parents would disapprove. But the path that emerged past the hut was as straight as a Dardan stone. It wasn't until they'd traipsed through a copse that it suddenly turned on itself. Shāhpuhr no longer needed to hack as they strode the narrow walkway which twisted so harshly it almost made Abarōz sick.

"Where is this leading?" she mumbled to Shāhpuhr's back.

"Hopefully, to the Erbörü."

"Is that really something to hope for?"

Just as she thought she couldn't take anymore, the dirt path straightened. Abarōz was glad, but not at the sight of dead trees strewn across the trail. They were forced to scamper over them, and Abarōz wasn't pleased at her growing number of scratches. If this didn't stop soon, she'd have to wrap her palms.

Thankfully, the wood maze was finally replaced by moss. This was more than welcome since it was easy to walk on.

"Where do you think we are?" she called to Shāhpuhr.

"Abaxtar. It is said that no one who enters these woods ever emerges."

"Now you tell me!" cried Abarōz.

Shāhpuhr shot her a wink.

"If I truly believed the myth, I never would have brought you."

Abarōz opened her mouth, then closed it. She really had no response.

"We must be close," said Shāhpuhr, sniffing the wood-scented air. *"Wait!* Did you hear that?"

"What?"

"A howl," he said, "and it's being answered."

Abarōz strained to listen, her senses much less acute. But now she could hear two wolves, their high-pitched cries prickling the skin on her arms.

"Put down your sword," said Shāhpuhr.

"I don't really kn—"

"We must trust Baba Yaga. Why would she lead us astray?"

"Er . . . she eats children?"

"Shhh!"

Shāhpuhr set down his blade before raising his hands. Abarōz sighed, but did the same, thinking that, compared to this, war was practically easy. As they waited on spongy moss,

Other wolves joined the chorus, their keen so eerie that Abarōz wanted to scream. Why did they even do that? To frighten prey before they slaughtered it? All she knew was that she stood here, unarmed, waiting to be devoured. How her father would mourn . . .

There came the crackle of branches as a solitary figure emerged.

Thank Tengri, he was a MAN, though his clothes were odd, made entirely of deerskin. His face was severe as he gave them an unblinking stare, eyes filled with dislike.

"Greetings," said Shāhpuhr. "As you can see—" he nodded up toward his arms, "—we mean the Erbörü no harm."

The man crossed his own arms.

"I understand you," he said, "for your tongue is similar to ours." Shāhpuhr started to smile. "Whether I believe you or not is an entirely different matter."

Shāhpuhr's face fell as the man brought up a spear. Abarōz saw its shaft was of wood with a sharp stone tip. She felt that if she were going to speak, the time was now.

"You should!" she burst out. The man narrowed his eyes. "Believe us, that is."

"And why, strange girl, is that?"

Abarōz didn't like being called that, but she had thought the same about him.

"Because we know a way to end your isolation."

The man practically snarled.

"Indeed."

"If you'll just let us—"

"The choice is not mine," he said. "It must be approved by the council."

"Oh."

"I am Berislav[1], by the way, pack leader to the Erbörü."

Abarōz couldn't help it—the words slid out her mouth.

"But . . . you're not a wolf!"

Berislav[2] half-growled.

"Are you foolish enough to judge me by my appearance?"

"I—"

Before she could finish, Berislav[3] dimmed, in the hold of a silvery glow. Thin tendrils whirled around him, blurring faster and faster. Once the glow faded, Abarōz let out a scream: The being who stood there was Berislav, but his head had been swapped for a wolf's!

"Did you think," asked the pack leader, "I must wait for the full moon?"

Abarōz tried to dislodge her tongue from the roof of her mouth.

"Er . . . Baba Yaga—"

"Does not know all!" yelled the wolf. "How can she when she never ventures this far?" Abarōz tried to nod, but her neck seemed frozen. "We have not seen other creatures since fur men rode the plains. We have been exiled for something we cannot help."

"That is unjust," said Abarōz, and she truly believed it. But rather than placating Berislav, her words made his yellow eyes blaze.

"We're the same as other predators," he cried, "those who rent with fang and claw! Why is it only us who endure the pain of solitude?"

"My mother," Shāhpuhr told him, "is Bükrek, a dragon of creation. She wishes to let you know that if you fight for our side, you will be welcomed back."

"Fight!" the[4] wolf man spat. *"Who are you to us?!"*

---

1. https://www.behindthename.com/name/berislav

2. https://www.behindthename.com/name/berislav

3. https://www.behindthename.com/name/berislav

4. https://www.behindthename.com/name/berislav

"The people," said Abarōz, "who might be able to free you." Panting, Berislav opened his mouth to reveal sharp incisors. Abarōz tried to ignore them. "This council—how often do they meet?"

"Once every quarter moon. We could call it tonight."

"Do you think," Abarōz asked, "we could go with you? Present our proposal to end your pack's isolation?"

Berislav thought, his yellow eyes flickering.

"I will consider it," he growled. "In the meantime, I suppose you are my guests."

His voice held contempt at the thought of himself as a host. Still, he led them to a small cave where they all stooped to go in. Abarōz looked around: the small space didn't disturb her—she was used to caves— but she couldn't say the same for the bones strewn over the floor.

"Stay here," Berislav snarled, then turned and slunk out.

"Well," said Abarōz, sinking against a wall. "I almost thought he was going to eat us."

Shāhpuhr took a place at her side.

"The Erbörü," he said, "are not known for their manners."

"I suppose we can't blame them, since they've been alone for so long."

"True. Now we must trust Berislav to call his council together."

"I hope we can."

Abarōz took some dried meat out of her pack, but the sight of all those bones instantly killed her appetite.

"What do you think is going to happen?" she asked.

"It will not be easy even if we're allowed to attend. We must inform the council that their foe will be dragons."

"Don't forget the Šāh and his men."

"Being wolves," Shāhpuhr said, "I think they'd rather enjoy them."

"Ugh." Abarōz shuddered. "What kind of ally is this?"

Shāhpuhr closed his eyes.

"One that we need to win."

As the shadows outside the cave lengthened, the two of them followed instructions, not daring to venture out. Finally, Berislav's form framed the entrance. At least, Abarōz *thought* it was him: though he was now all wolf, she recognized his face.

"Very well," spat their reluctant host. "We agreed to let you speak." He shot them a hungry look. "Just try to be brief."

Abarōz nodded as she and Shāhpuhr stooped out of the cave. Berislav loped ahead, leading them deeper into the forest over which one quarter of Māh presided. Abarōz picked up the scent of moss comingled with wood. Though a bit dusky, the smell was not unpleasant.

At last, Berislav halted before a good-sized dirt clearing. He raised his snout and issued an echoing howl. Abarōz saw wolves slink in, forming a loose circle, but their shapes varied: some were men with wolf heads; others all wolf; with a last group that sprouted wolf parts like furry legs and a tail. It was all so bizarre that she stayed close to Shāhpuhr.

Berislav put on out a paw, showing them where they should sit. Happily, they were not far from the boulder that raised him above the pack.

"Erbörüs!" he cried. "I must request your indulgence. The high council has agreed that these two strangers—"

"Rip them apart!" a half-wolf shouted.

"Kill them now and allow us to feast!"

Abarōz felt a bit hurt since this had come from a man.

"SILENCE!" Berislav ordered, his alpha shout effective. "They wish to be allowed—"

"All men are false!" yelled a man with dripping fangs.

"They will betray us!" came another cry.

"I cannot disagree," said Berislav, yellow eyes glinting with moonlight. "But before we set upon them, let them have their say."

Abarōz gripped Shāhpuhr's hand. These creatures made the S̄āh look merciful. Still, she managed to smile as Shāhpuhr set forth their proposal. The wolves were mostly silent, a few emitting low growls.

Once he'd finished, Berislav looked over the circle.

"I am no tyrant," he said, "and as is our custom, we vote." Several furry heads nodded. "All in favor?" he asked.

Both hands and paws shot up—from about half of those gathered.

"All opposed?"

Again came the odd display, and Abarōz knew the result would literally mean life or death.

"Interesting," growled Berislav. "It seems we have a tie, and it falls upon me to break it."

Abarōz stared at his eyes, wondering which side he'd choose. Wolves were said to be cunning, so . . .

Berislav lifted a paw, black nails shining. In his animal form, he gave nothing away.

"Very well," he said. "I have no desire to fight in a war for men." Abarōz crumpled. "However . . . what I like less is living as a pariah, reviled by all of Gehān." She picked up her head. "My great-grandfather, and his before him, knew of the dragon Bükrek. She returns to us often to heal and remake the world. To rejoin the pageant of creatures, we must trust both her and her son."

While half the wolves snarled, they made no move to attack. Berislav turned to other matters, nodding in dismissal to his guests. Abarōz and Shāhpuhr walked to a copse beyond the clearing, both of them soaked with sweat.

"That–that was close," she said.

"Berislav is a good man."

"Let's hope his wolf self is too."

She tried to catch her breath; stop the shaking in all her limbs.

When she could speak, she said, "We must find a way to let the pack know when it's time to bring down Sangal."

Shāhpuhr shook his head.

"Don't be deceived," he said. "Wolves are remarkable hunters, but Sangal is chaos itself."

All Opposed

The two of them trekked back to Berislav's cave to await his return. The more Abarōz thought, the more elated she felt.

"We did it!" she told Shāhpuhr as they crouched in the low cave.

"Yes. I can hardly believe it."

"You are not," came a voice, "out of these woods just yet."

Abarōz turned to see Berislav slinking in.

"What do you mean?" she asked.

"Our pack will not aid you until your final fight. Bükrek will understand."

"I thought as much," said Abarōz. "But how do we contact you?"

"Send a dragon," he growled. "I assume you know more than one."

"Yes."

"Be sure to leave enough time, for we wolves must travel by land."

"Of course," said Shāhpuhr. "We really can't thank you enough. Your help may well mean the difference between Gehān's rebirth or destruction."

Berislav chuckled.

"As it did for you this evening. Now, have a care as you make your south You never know what you'll meet."

Abarōz clenched her jaw. Couldn't they even travel without the risk of attack?

"Thank you," she told Berislav, retrieving her pack from his cave. "And for what's it worth, I like you best as a wolf." He opened his fierce jaw in what might have been a smile. "Oh! My friend here slew a xūg. Just thought you'd like to know."

The wolf nodded, pleased.

"Goodbye!" Abarōz called as she and Shāhpuhr crawled through the entrance. "We hope to see you soon." She turned to her friend. "Or not?"

Shāhpuhr only shrugged as he took the lead on the straight path. Abarōz hated to travel at night, but the sooner they returned to their ebrens, the better. They trundled along in the near-dark, Abarōz's mind refusing to calm.

"Do–do you think . . ." she asked at last, "that our mission was too easy?"

"How?"

She sighed.

"I expected more of a fight."

"Don't worry girl—you've got one."

That voice was *definitely* not Shāhpuhr's.

"Who are you?" he asked, raising his blade with both hands.

A low growl emerged from the forest, followed by two loping forms. Wolves. Abarōz too hefted her sword.

"The question is," asked the first wolf, his fur a mottled brown, "exactly who are *you?*"

"If you'd been at the council—" Abarōz said.

"Oh, we were," said his friend, a handsome grey.

"Then you know who we are," said Shāhpuhr, "and what was agreed to."

"Yes," said the brown. "A decision made by only half our pack."

"Berislav—" Shāhpuhr began.

"—Is a fool!" spat the brown. "To entangle us in a man's war. To trust the word of a dragon, who'd as soon blast us to ash!"

"No," protested Shāhpuhr. "My mother—"

"Hold your tongue, boy," the brown ordered. "The great Berislav may believe he has the final say, but my friend and I do not. Better to rot in the north than be betrayed by men!"

"Your pack took a vote," said Abarōz, trying to keep her voice steady. "What do you intend to do?"

"This."

The brown leapt for Shāhpuhr's throat, lifting a paw to smack his sword to the dirt.

"Shāhpuhr!" Abarōz cried, slashing at fur with her blade. All she could do was hold the grey at bay as the brown growled over Shāhpuhr, pinning him to the ground. The larger wolf was drooling, his exposed fangs reaching for

flesh. Abarōz closed her eyes and brought her sword down flat to smack the wolf's rump forcefully. When she could look, she heard a whimper.

"I'll do worse," Abarōz warned, "if you don't leave us alone."

She stood guard over Shāhpuhr, gold blade glinting.

The grey turned to his friend.

"Come on, Jaroslav, no use getting stabbed if they'll let us go."

Jaroslav's green eyes flamed as he slunk away from Shāhpuhr.

"Very well," he snarled. "But don't think this is over."

The two wolves slipped back between trees as if they'd never been. Abarōz knelt beside Shāhpuhr, relieved to find him whole. She offered her hand, helping him rise to his feet.

"That–that was close," he said shakily. "If it weren't for you, Abarōz, I'd be Jaroslav's late supper."

She grinned.

"That would never happen. Besides, you don't have enough fat."

Shāhpuhr laughed, but she could tell by his stiff shoulders he hadn't completely recovered.

"I–I suppose we should get on," he said.

"Right. In case Jaroslav has more friends."

Eager to leave, they stepped up their pace, first finding the crooked path and then the one heavy with trees. Tengri and the new god must both be with them since no more creatures appeared.

"I am glad," said Abarōz as she scrambled over a tree trunk.

"For what?"

"That this part of our journey at least has not unleashed a surprise."

"Say nothing," Shāhpuhr told her, "until we find our ebrens."

The night sky—what they could see of it—grew fainter when they reached Baba Yaga's. Though a fire burned in the hut, the witch herself did not emerge. Perhaps she was lying in wait for foolish children to pass. In any case, Abarōz shuddered when she saw those distended chicken legs.

"Almost there," Shāhpuhr called back, and Abarōz couldn't wait. As light fell upon trees, revealing each leaf, he led her into a clearing.

"Thank Tengri!" she cried, running up to their dragons and hugging them. "I almost thought we'd never see you again!"

She was answered by roars and smoke.

"How have they been?" she asked Shāhpuhr, who conferred with them briefly.

"They said it's been quite boring not being able to fly."

Abarōz grinned. That made sense.

"Well, tell them their wait is over."

Shāhpuhr did, swinging a leg over Catanes as Abarōz mounted Iotapa.

"I never thought I'd say this," she told him, "but I'm looking forward to riding."

"An Aswār!" yelled Shāhpuhr as the two dragons took off.

Abarōz smiled, gripping her spike.

"Getting there, I suppose."

As they soared south, they flew over forests which went from thick to dwindling. Once Abarōz spotted the desert, she leaned forward in excitement, knowing they'd soon be home. Mihr gave them her brightest rays when they set down on the Rōd's bank.

"Abarōz!" A man with grey hair ran toward her, arms outflung. Before she could answer, he picked her up, swinging her round in a hug. "The green ebren would not tell me where you were. Of course, I feared the worst."

Didn't *everyone* in her family?

"I apologize, Father. I couldn't reveal our mission. But you are the first one to know it was a complete success!"

He let her feet hit the ground.

"A father," he said hoarsely, "should *always* be the first."

Abarōz nodded, blinking rapidly.

"Thank you, Father."

"For what?"

"For caring. About me."

He set his jaw, since as a Dardan male, he was not permitted to cry. Instead, he walked away swiftly, shooting her a last glance over his shoulder.

"Abarōz," said Shāhpuhr, causing her to start. "We should find my mother—tell her about the Erbörü."

"Right."

They both ran to the clearing. There, they found Bükrek sitting atop her coils. When she saw them, she slid over quickly.

"What news?" Bükrek asked.

"It is good," grinned Shāhpuhr. "The wolf pack took a vote and agreed to help us. Before our last battle, we are to send them a dragon."

"Did they behave?" his mother asked.

Abarōz thought this rather strange.

"For the most part," he said. "There were two objectors but Abarōz drove them off."

"Good." Bükrek nodded, but her coils seemed tense. "You cannot imagine how much I feared for your safety."

"Our trip wasn't that bad," said Abarōz. "Aside from a child-eating witch, a xūg, and a two-wolf attack, things went rather well."

Bükrek did not look amused.

"I'm just glad you are here and that the Erbörü were cooperative. This last, above all, may save Gehān from Sangal."

Abarōz had her doubts. The wolves, though fierce, could still be assailed from the air. Yet, she trusted Bükrek and wasn't in the mood to argue.

"Go now," the dragon urged. "Rest from your journey. I have a feeling that before long, we all will need our full strength."

From the towering rock in my lair, I try not to murder Kavad. I'd sent a dragon to "persuade" the annoying traitor to come. Now, as this filth kneels before me, I notice the shake of his shoulders. Coward.

"Great Sangal," the pitiful Dardan whimpers.

"Spare me," I snarl. "I will speak and you will listen."

The man's brow hits the ground.

"What," I ask, "is the state of affairs in your city?"

At that, the insect looks up—actually gives me a *smile.*

"The best it can be," he says. "For us." I ignore the implication that we are in any way equal. "The aqueducts run low; the people so disheartened they cry out from thirst. I tell you, mighty Sangal, the time for victory is near. Once the Šāh runs out of water, he'll come begging for your terms."

"Hmmp." How dare this cockroach take a familiar tone *with me?* I express my displeasure by blowing black smoke through my nostrils. Still, I need him . . . for now. “I am glad to hear it,” I say. “But what I fear most is Bükrek—and her flight of ebrens.”

The Dardan dog, clearly afraid to speak, makes a feeble attempt.

“Wha-what can be done?” he asks.

I have to stop myself from blasting him into cinders.

“We must strike Bükrek where she stands,” I say, “in her bucolic little forest. If we can destroy her ebrens, she ceases to be a threat.”

Kavad nodded, not daring to look in my eyes. He knows that every second spent here could mean his potential demise.

“Go now,” I order, waving a claw in dismissal. “If there is anything new to report, you will hasten here with all speed.”

The mongrel nods, his forehead brushing my floor. I feel rather perturbed that he is still alive. Happily, that condition will not be permanent.

Interim

Abarōz and Shāhpuhr took his mother's advice: they sought the clearing, where they feasted on birds brought in by other warriors. After they'd finished, Abarōz lay on the grass, content to stare sideways at Mihr.

"What are you thinking?" asked Shāhpuhr, sinking down beside her.

"That we are lucky," she said, "to be here at all."

He chuckled.

"That's only because you fought off two vicious wolves."

Abarōz considered this.

"Yes," she answered, "Yes, I suppose you're right." She felt a blaze of pride as she thought of their time in Abaxtar. "What do you think we missed here?"

"A great deal of training, most likely."

"Hmm." Abarōz couldn't imagine how hard Bükrek must have pushed everyone. "Do you think . . .?"

"Yes?"

"That if Sangal attacked right now, our side would be ready?"

"To be frank—no. We weren't gone long enough for the Dardans to become Aswārs." He shot her a grin. "Not *everyone* learns as quickly as you."

Abarōz closed her eyes, hearing the soft hum of bees.

"I guess if it really comes to it, they can fight on foot."

She opened her lids to see her friend frown.

"Like the first battle? You honestly want a repeat?"

"No, but now we have ebrens who at least can fight Sangal's."

"True. But Aswārs on dragons is really our best defense."

Abarōz sighed, plucking a blade of grass. She wanted to see for herself how much progress Bükrek had made.

"Come on," she said, grabbing Shāhpuhr's hand to pull them both up. "Let's go back to the river and check on the Axwaš."

He shrugged, and they made their way to the bank, where dragons seemed to be everywhere: on the ground, taking off, landing, and soaring above their heads. Each bore a gold-plated rider who, though not at ease, were neither screaming nor falling.

"How goes it?" Shāhpuhr called his mother who sat on her usual rock.

"Not ba—NO! *Do not cover your ebren's eyes! How can you expect her to see?!"* She turned back to her son. "Like this."

"Are they ready," asked Abarōz, "to fight on dragonback?"

Bükrek's yellow eyes dimmed as she beckoned them closer.

"I will tell only you two, but no. They can barely keep their seats, much less swing a sword. But will they be forced to, and soon? I fear the answer is yes."

"Sangal?" Abarōz breathed.

"I'm amazed he's waited this long. He must have something in mind: training new allies or waiting for Dardan to die. Probably both."

Abarōz stepped aside to allow a white dragon to land. The female Dardan on its back seemed relieved to be on the ground.

"How was it?" Abarōz asked her.

The would-be warrior climbed off her mount.

"Frightening," she panted. "And . . . exhilarating! To be out in the fresh air, not buried in a cave—this was always my wish!"

"And the flying?"

The woman practically beamed.

"*Magickal.* Such a feeling of freedom! So different from Dardan's constraints!"

Abarōz returned her smile.

"I know just what you mean. Well . . . best of luck. I sense we're all going to need it."

The woman heaved off her helmet, freeing her long, dark hair.

"Thank you," she said.

Abarōz froze.

"For what?"

"For giving us . . . all this." The woman swept an arm over Bükrek, her gold plate, and all the dragons around them. "A chance to get back at the Šāh. I was made Axwaš because I had a sore throat. No children of mine should suffer a similar fate."

Abarōz nodded, overcome. Lately, her reason for escape had been pushed aside: by the return of her father; the trip to Abaxtar. But, as the woman waved goodbye, that reason struck her as if she'd been doused with water: *The Šāh. Revenge.* For Rastag and all the others.

"Shāhpuhr," she said, "let's find our dragons and practice."

After an intense session where they learned to dodge fellow Aswārs, Abarōz patted Iotapa. Shāhpuhr did the same with Catanes, then gave her a wink.

"Come with me," he said.

"Where?"

"To the forest. I have a taste for rabbit."

He ran back to the clearing to retrieve his quiver and bow, then led her down a shady path. From high branches, the birds chirped sweetly, no doubt exchanging the gossip.

"Better?" he asked with a grin.

"Than Abaxtar? Just a bit."

The trees relaxed under Mihr's rays, hosting their feathered guests while sheltering small animals. There was nothing dark or menacing—no worries of some unknown beast skulking out to assault them. Razūr was so perfect, so pleasant, it reminded Abarōz of the snake queen's garden.

Shāhpuhr found his rabbit—not to mention two fat partridges—and trudged back to his unlit cookfire. He set it ablaze and prepared their meal as Abarōz searched for her father.

"Father!" she called, shielding her eyes from Mihr. *"Rastag!"* She spotted his shaggy grey head bouncing in her direction. "Come, eat!"

"Thank you, Daughter," he said, looking more than usually weary.

"Has Mother been working you hard?" asked Shāhpuhr.

"Oh yes," Rastag panted, "but I can't say I really mind. It is far better than weighing gold all day."

Abarōz smiled, pointing to a flat rock where they both sat down.

"Bread?" she offered from a newly-baked store.

He bowed.

"Thank you," he said, tearing off a corner. "This warrior life makes you hungry!"

Abarōz laughed, so glad she could be with the two people who meant the most to her.

They shared a hearty supper topped off by delicious berries. All around, Abarōz heard the murmur of Aswārs as they discussed their day.

Now Mihr seemed to move quickly, speeding away from Dardan. Abarōz tried to imagine how miserable life there must be: most everyone parched, even children; fearing the return of Sangal and the wrath of Al-razi. This couldn't go on for much longer—not while the aqueducts emptied and cracked. Abarōz knew the Šāh must be stopped before just he and his family were left.

Sangal's Revenge

The next morning was not unusual. Mihr rose as always as the Dardans ate a light breakfast. Abarōz awoke next to her father, smiling at his ruffled grey hair. Across the sputtering fire from them, Shāhpuhr tossed in his sleep.

The ebrens were down at the river, though Bükrek remained to oversee her warriors. Her coils were messy, sprawled casually across the grass. The only smell in the air wafted from burning cookfires.

That's when it began.

At first, they were just pinpricks, small splotches of color drifting over the clouds. As they approached, a few details emerged: a curving neck; an outflung tail. Then, as they continued their westward flight, Abarōz saw what they were: Sangal's horde, some two-hundred strong, wheeling over the forest. At this rate, they would be over the clearing in minutes!

"Aswārs!" Bükrek called out, her coils now tightly strung. "Put on your plate, take your weapons, and mount your ebren immediately! Do not pause for *anything!*"

Shāhpuhr, now wide awake, sprang to his feet to help Abarōz. Once he and Rastag were ready, the three of them merged with a crowd as fluid as a gold tide.

"Catanes!" Shāhpuhr shouted.

"Iotapa!" Abarōz cried.

Her father ran for his own ebren as their two dragons found *them* amidst the frantic flapping. They slithered over and flattened, permitting their riders to mount.

"Let's go!" yelled Shāhpuhr as the two settled in. The dragons' claws left the ground, leaving the river behind. Once they reached treetop level, Abarōz saw they were surrounded by their own flight and its riders. There was just one thing missing.

"Where are they?" she called, searching the sky for Sangal's horde. They had seemingly vanished, leaving only Bükrek's ebrens.

Abarōz was no general, but she figured it wasn't good to lose sight of the enemy. Her stomach clenched as she glanced at her fellow Aswārs: They were doing their best, but most sat at an angle.

Ugh, she thought, *after Shāhpuhr, I might be the best rider up here.* It was a sobering truth, made worse as the horde reappeared, twisting over treetops. They screamed out Sangal's anger while maintaining a disciplined "V."

Outnumbered. Recalling their last fraught battle, Abarōz felt ill. Again, their side would lose. Go down to flaming defeat. And, with dragons and riders unready, the toll would be catastrophic!

Almost by instinct, Abarōz steered by spike to help out Shāhpuhr with two ebrens.

"Ha!" she yelled as a purple beast flapped toward her, spewing a spigot of fire. Happily, due to her plate, she emerged without a smudge.

Now his grey friend joined him, grey scales striped with red, the two of them hemming her in by flanking Iotapa.

"No!" she yelled and felt her dragon shake. Then, she screamed, white wings charred and smoking.

Abarōz hung onto that spike as time seemed to slow, then stop, letting her observe her own legs kick up, followed by the rest of her, but the new direction was *down.*

I'm going to die, she thought, *and so will everyone else.* She tumbled, near-weightless, her eyes heavy with sights: first was a camel-shaped cloud, then the Rōd, and, rising to meet her, the triangular tops of trees. How sad. She, "the Hero of Dardan" to be crushed by wood.

As her muscles tensed, Abarōz was vaguely aware of the absence of a spike. This had barely registered when the trees below her bent, forming a leafy hammock to set her down gently. From her spot on the ground, Abarōz shook her head. What had just happened? Did the trees work together? Whisper to each other before enacting a plan?

She groaned to her feet, amazed to be unhurt. Iotapa was not to be seen, and Abarōz feared the worst. Was she just bad luck to dragons? Should she end her stint as a rider? In any case, she approached her two woody saviors and embraced their trunks.

"Thank you," she whispered, to hear a rustling, "You're welcome."

Abarōz knew who that voice belonged to and it wasn't Archura: It was Şahmeran, queen of snakes and nature, who had saved her life today!

"Queen," Abarōz muttered, "I believe it now—you really are *everywhere.*"

Turning in every direction to see nothing but trees, Abarōz wondered where she was. Somewhere near the river, she thought, but without Shāhpuhr, she was completely lost. Should she try to find her way out of these woods even if that made her more lost? Or sit at the foot of the trees who'd saved her, imploring Şahmeran for help? Just as she'd decided on the latter, Abarōz heard a faint call—sounding strangely like her name.

"Hello!" she shouted, cupping her hands to her mouth. "I'm over here!"

She realized this was foolish since she might be alerting the enemy, so she hid behind a trunk.

"Abarōz!" she heard again and the voice seemed even closer.

Abarōz wondered what to do: Should she answer? She could have sworn she now heard flapping and it was coming from above. Looking up through a net of leaves, she might have seen a hint of black . . . which resolved into a dragon that landed in the dense thicket. Abarōz blinked, but the dragon was still there.

"Shāhpuhr?" she whispered.

From Catanes' back, he vaulted to the ground.

"Abarōz," he said softly, throwing his arms around her although they both wore plate. "I was so frightened. I saw Iotapa fall."

She pursed her lips, tears forming. If only she hadn't picked the blue dragon, she'd still be alive right now . . .

"It is all right," said Shāhpuhr, stepping back to regard her face. "Like Az, Iotapa chose this fight. They are both great ebren heroes."

Removing her helmet, Abarōz wiped her cheeks. War, she'd discovered, was not all glory and honor.

"We should go," Shāhpuhr told her, motioning to Catanes. Abarōz got on first, Shāhpuhr swinging behind her. With little room to take off, the black dragon pumped his wings.

Soon, they soared over the trees while Abarōz replaced her helmet.

"What's happening?" she called back. "How is our side faring?"

"Not well," he said. "There are simply too many."

She nodded. This was no surprise, but a small part of her had hoped . . .

She forced herself to refocus on the two ebrens flying for them, screaming their intent to kill.

But with two swords and two lances, not to mention their plate, the two Aswārs were rewarded by their foes' dual tumble.

"Oh well," Abarōz mumbled, "what a shame for Sangal."

"Thank Tengri!"

Abarōz had no need to steer as Catanes streaked past Mihr. Then, she saw something beside her which made her cry out.

"Look!" she said, pointing.

There was her father, joined by two Axwaš, bullying three of Sangal's horde until they turned and fled.

"Such courage!" Abarōz yelled, flashing Rastag a sign. She couldn't believe how he'd grown: from a meek Ōšmurdan to a man who dared ride a dragon!

Though her pride held her up, the sheer number of enemy ebrens began to gnaw at Abarōz. What's more, many Aswārs had been unseated, presenting a tasty target as they formed a troop on the ground.

Scatter and run! Abarōz wanted to scream. At least some could survive. But before she could get out the words, she was met by an eerie sight: a host of dragons, wingless, with the heads of wolves. They were more frightening than the Erbörü as they slithered out of vines, directly toward the warriors. These bunched up, shields over heads and flanks, to form a giant turtle. But the wolf heads merely snarled, tongues lolling over their fangs.

Abarōz turned away, hearing the first sounds of the onslaught. Howling, growls, and the cries of men broke the calm of the forest. What Abarōz heard was a massacre and she didn't know what do.

"Shāhpuhr!" she cried. "Can we help them from the air?"

"I don't see how," he sighed. "It is too dense for us to swoop. And if we land, we'll become more prey."

Abarōz snuck a look groundward. She was revulsed by horror, seeing the wolf heads claw aside metal as if it were made of sand. Creeping red pools, the blood of Axwaš, spilled over the ground in a second unthinkable sacrifice.

Had Bükrek rescued these souls only to have them die again?

Thoughts of the green dragon led Abarōz's mind to wander down the path of who else could help them. Their own dragons were scattered, so there could be no unified flames; and Catanes couldn't prevail alone against so many wolf heads. They had no other allies, unlike the clever Sangal—no one to swarm the ground and attack this vicious foe.

"Wait," Abarōz said, her voice surprisingly steadily. *Şahmeran. The snake queen had just helped her—would she be willing to do so again?* Abarōz closed her eyes and pictured the garden cave: white Marans crawling everywhere; the two-headed queen on her throne.

Şahmeran, she thought, *I know it's asking a lot but we desperately need you. Please! Don't let the Axwaš die.*

"Did you say something?" asked Shāhpuhr.

"No, I–I don't think so."

But someone must have heard her. As both riders looked on, the ferns and plants below them became a writhing mass, snaring most of the wolf heads in a symmetrical green net. Abarōz shook, resting her head on Catanes' neck.

Şahmeran was everywhere.

Now, the sounds from the ground became high-pitched whimpers. The warriors, reprieved, hefted their swords and lances to slash at their ensnared foe. In minutes, it was over, the still-free wolf heads slinking away in defeat.

"Thank Tengri!" Shāhpuhr cried.

"No, thank Şahmeran!" corrected Abarōz.

The triumph below brought forth a swarm of Aswārs. They steered their dragons toward Sangal's with renewed vigor. Both riders and dragons were fierce, taking on two to their every one.

Abarōz wheeled Catanes toward an opposing flight, the sky now so full of ebrens that Mihr's light was diluted. These four soldiers of Sangal didn't seem very bright: rather than flaming Catanes, they aimed for his two riders.

Abarōz thrust out her sword, stabbing upward until she reached a belly. There was a roar and a rush of wind as one ebren went down. The other three looked startled but continued their assault. Catanes didn't take kindly to this as he opened his mouth, biting down on an orange neck. His friends took the hint, wheeling swiftly to find a less deadly opponent.

"That was good!" Abarōz yelled, trying to lift their spirits.

"Yes," said Shāhpuhr wearily, "but look at how many are left."

Abarōz looked. He was right. Despite their valiant efforts, Bükrek's side was simply too small. Though Abarōz saw swords fly, lances strike, flames bouncing from plate, she knew from experience that sheer will wasn't enough. She and Shāhpuhr remained in the air, repelling the foes that came at them, but she could tell from Catanes' pants that the dragon was weary. How long would it be before he lost his strength and fell twisting to the ground?

She inadvertently looked down to see the unwelcome sight of more wolf heads slinking in! How many did Sangal have? In any case, no green barrier formed to protect the dragonless warriors. Abarōz placed both hands over her ears to drown out the screams.

In her state and theirs, she felt it was too late to call on Şahmeran. Since nature remained unmoving, the snake queen must have moved on. How many disasters a day did she have to deal with on Gehān? Abarōz's head swam.

Just as it seemed that the Axwaš would die again, Abarōz saw a flight of five dragons flapping toward them—led by a much larger green one.

Bükrek! She had finally come. Though she herself couldn't fight, those behind her dropped down like arrows, pelting the wolf heads with flame. When a stray wolf dragon was dragged off by sturdy black claws, the rest, who numbered some twenty, went crying back to the vines.

Now Abarōz felt some hope. That was one enemy vanquished. But another, unexpected, was soon to torment them.

At first, she heard only a whistle, high and shrill against the clouds. Then the red form of Sangal emerged to soar over his horde. He seemed to be taking a count, looking unhappy as he flamed from head and tail. He pointed his snout at Mihr and let out a piercing scream, inspiring his followers to decamp with him toward the north.

That rare emotion—joy—coursed through Abarōz like the heat she felt for Shāhpuhr. *Had they really . . . won? Defeated Sangal's forces and sent them winging home?* The notion seemed so farfetched she didn't think it was real.

Once Catanes circled to land on the bank of Rōd, she and Shāhpuhr jumped off.

"Did that just . . . happen?" she asked, shaking her head to clear it.

"Yes," he said, eyes gleaming. "We did it. We beat Sangal back to his lair!"

An Enemy behind the Lines

Abarōz gave him a hug, then scanned both banks for her father. When she spotted him, sweaty and tinged with blood, she ran to throw herself into his arms.

"Father!" she choked.

"My Daughter!"

He threw off his helmet and buried his chin in her hair. Could this be the same stern patriarch who used to lecture her daily?

"Are you all right?" she asked, pointing to the blood.

"Of course!" he roared, "these stains came from an enemy ebren."

Abarōz collapsed against him, making sure he wasn't in danger from her shoulder spikes.

"What about you?" he asked, kissing the top of her head.

"I'm fine. Had a rough landing, but a friend gave me her help."

"I am glad of it." Rastag turned toward Shāhpuhr, who was waiting impatiently. "Go now," he told her, "and stand by your future husband!"

Abarōz blushed. Had being brought back by Bükrek turned him into a matchmaker?

She ran back to Shāhpuhr, hoping he hadn't heard her father's speech. Since his face wasn't red, she assumed he hadn't.

Bükrek flew in with her flight, setting down on her rock and beckoning both of them to her. As Abarōz entered the river, the cool swirl of water felt wonderful on her ankles.

"I am overjoyed," said Bükrek, "that you two emerged unscathed. It is the same for most of our flight."

"And the Aswārs?" Abarōz asked.

Bükrek stared into the water.

"Fifteen lost, I fear. It is not a significant number, but to those who loved them, each death is a tragedy."

Abarōz bowed her head, recalling how she'd felt when her father had first been seized. It was like a gaping wound and she sought to distract herself.

"Why," she asked, "did Sangal turn tail and flee?"

"I can only conjecture," said Bükrek, "he was in a rage over the Gurg Kamāl."

"The wolf heads?"

She nodded.

"Also, his losses were greater than ours, I should say by two-to-one. If he hadn't retreated, our sides would have been equal, and he knows he would have lost."

That gave Abarōz an idea.

"While he's off sulking," she asked eagerly, "why not go to Dardan and free it?"

Bükrek shook her head.

"What occurred today," she said, "is by all accounts a victory. But you are mistaken to think Sangal will abandon the city.

As Abarōz sighed, Shāhpuhr touched her hand.

"What is next then?" she asked.

Bükrek looked over their heads as if trying to see the future.

"I wish I knew. We have found new friends, but so has he. The Gurg Kamāl will prove far more deadly if Dardan is breached."

Abarōz groaned. Why was it that in her life, a step forward was followed by two steps back?

"Cheer up," enthused Shāhpuhr. "We won, remember?"

"Of course."

"For now, let us celebrate," said Bükrek. "But when Mihr rises anew, we must continue training the Axwaš."

"We can no longer call them discarded," Shāhpuhr said. "They are the reborn, and have proved their great worth today.

His mother gave him a loving smile.

"My son, you speak the truth. No person can be discarded so long as there's good in the world."

Abarōz felt her eyes glisten. Bükrek had molded a man that any mother would cherish.

"Shall we?" Shāhpuhr asked, bowing toward the clearing. "Hungry?"

"After today? Oh yes."

They threaded their way through dragons to arrive at their usual cook spot. Shāhpuhr lit a fire, then ducked behind a tree, emerging with two cakes of bread.

"Mmm," said Abarōz, "and to think I made these myself!" He chuckled, then shared a jam made from red berries. "Delicious," she said between bites. "Almost worth fighting a battle."

"Almost."

"Do you think," she asked, "Sangal will strike again soon?"

Shāhpuhr wiped jam from his lips.

"I don't know his mind like my mother."

Abarōz sighed.

"For once, it would be nice to know *something.*"

He smiled as they devoured boiled mushrooms. Abarōz reckoned it must be twilight based on the sky's purple streaks. So they had fought an entire day. Even the thought made her weary—all she wanted was a blanket and a pillow of leaves. She hadn't been this tired since . . . well, the battle at Dardan.

Warriors drifted around them, some still clad in plate like her and Shāhpuhr. If Sangal had something planned, they'd at least be partially ready.

The soothing crack of sparks soon gave way to another sound: the stomp of an Aswār's boots as he dragged another man with a rope.

Bükrek, always aware, slithered up to the newcomers.

"Who is this?" she asked, regarding the dusty prisoner.

"A traitor!" cried the warrior, lifting the man by the top of his cloak to turn and face the dragon. He placed a burly forearm around his captive's neck. "I found him walking back from the north."

"What is your name?" Bükrek asked kindly.

The man's face didn't move.

"Wait!"

Abarōz heard a cry, then saw her father striding toward them. "I saw him arrive as he deserves!" he spat. "Greetings, Kavad."

"You know this man?" Bükrek asked.

"All too well. He is the one who betrayed me." Rastag moved closer so his face was inches from Kavad's. "How many others?" he asked. "How many others were sacrificed so you could gain the Šāh's favor?"

Kavad didn't react.

"What of it?" he said, bored. "The Šāh will soon prevail, aided by mighty Sangal."

Abarōz stepped closer, one hand on her sword.

"What are their plans?" she asked. "To destroy Dardan through thirst, then seize all her gold?"

Kavad laughed.

"What makes you think I would tell you? You, daughter of Rastag, are the true traitor here. You've done nothing but inspire rebellion. It is not I, but you, who should be taken captive."

Shāhpuhr leaned forward, a low growl in his throat.

"You will show my friend some respect!"

He pulled back a fist.

"Ha!" Kavad laughed. "Do you really think that you—and the rest of these misfits—can defeat the deathless red dragon?"

"It might interest you," said Abarōz, "that he just turned tail and fled."

Kavad's face briefly flashed with surprise.

"No matter," he said. "There are still the Gurg Kamāl."

"Not many," said Abarōz, "for most were conquered by vines."

This caused Kavad to drop all pretense of calm.

"No matter!" he spat. "Sangal will call upon others. His reach across Gehān is endless."

"It does not extend here," said Bükrek.

"It will!" Once he commands Dardan's gold; every zand, pack, and flight will fight on his behalf!"

Abarōz snorted.

"You have to buy your allies then?"

"Whorish daughter of a traitor—"

"That is enough," Bükrek said sternly. "Take him away," she ordered his captor, "and keep him under strict guard. He may be of use to us later."

The Aswār nodded, leading his prisoner off. Abarōz turned toward Bükrek.

"Are you . . . going to have him tortured?"

"YES!" cried Rastag. "Stone him with hot coals!"

Bükrek folded her claws.

"That is not our way," she said, "or we become the enemy." Abarōz nodded, noting the dragon's troubled eyes. "For now, I must think. Before Sangal strikes again."

She gathered her coils to slide across the grass.

"Come on," Shāhpuhr told Abarōz, "let's get back to our supper."

Abarōz gestured for Rastag to join them, but she no longer felt hungry. What other appalling creatures could Sangal entice to his side?

An Uneven Exchange

Abarōz and her friends enjoyed one day of peace. The next afternoon, two visitors entered their camp, their relation the same as Kavad's and his guard.

What was this? Abarōz groaned. *More strangers come to harass them?*

But as the two dragged toward her, she observed that one was more than known to her.

"MOTHER!" she cried, as Adrina's captor thrust her forward. "What–what are you doing here?"

She and Shāhpuhr rose from their seats on the grass. As a precaution, they both still wore their plate.

The S̃āh's guard forced a smile.

"Just paying a friendly visit."

"What is it you want?" asked Abarōz.

"Nothing that you can't give us."

She stiffened. This guard's behavior was unusually cheerful.

"Are you going to tell us?" Shāhpuhr asked. "I take it you didn't come here simply to unfold riddles."

Abarōz heard the flap of sandals as a man ran through the clearing. Turning, she saw her father, gripping his sword of gold.

"Rastag," the guard nodded. "How pleasant to find you well."

Her father's face went pale with anger.

"Husrav," he spat, "I wish I could say the same."

"Relinquish your sword, Ōšmurdan, or I'll cut your pretty wife's throat."

Rastag looked conflicted, but complied by dropping his blade.

"Why is she bound?" he asked. "My wife is loyal to the S̃āh."

"A sentiment which, I fear, is not shared by you or your daughter."

From under his helmet, Husrav's eyes shone coldly.

"I assume," said Rastag, "you wish to haul me back to Dardan. In exchange for my wife."

"Clever," Husrav grinned, "but not clever enough."

"What then?" growled Rastag.

"A request so easy it stuns in its sheer simplicity." Husrav pointed a steel-encased arm at Abarōz. "Your wife for the girl. This is the wish of Al-razi."

As he spoke his master's name, he looked up, as if he expected the S̆āh to alight from heaven.

"NEVER!" both Rastag and Shāhpuhr yelled.

"Pity," said Husrav, "your wife's throat is white and supple."

He pulled down Adrina's blouse, resting his sword on her neck.

"NO!" Rastag shouted. "Adrina may have her faults, but she doesn't deserve this."

Panting, he faced off against Husrav, a warning in his eyes. If Abarōz stayed silent, someone was going to die.

"Wait." she said, her head lighter than when she'd tumbled into the forest. She waited for her eyes to clear. "I will go."

"YOU CAN'T!" Shāhpuhr shouted.

"But I must."

Abarōz thought of her mother, non-nurturing at the best of times. Still, Adrina had borne her, and attempted, in her way, to model a woman's role. A mother was still a mother even if she wasn't maternal. Rastag shuffled toward her, talking softly.

"Abarōz . . ." he said. "New god forgive me, but she is not worth your life. We know she never cared for either you or me—only dēnārs from the S̆āh."

Abarōz nodded, acknowledging this to be true. Still . . .

"Daughter," Adrina choked, recoiling from the blade at her throat. "Your father lies! Always have I loved you. Protected you from immodesty." Abarōz rolled her eyes. She'd never heard such falsehoods. But Adrina went on. "I groomed you," she pleaded, "to be an ideal wife. To master the household arts so your husband would never be wanting."

Abarōz sighed. From her mother's perspective, Adrina had only done right. How could her mother know, strangled by Dardan, that there was another way?

"I said I'd go," Abarōz repeated, lifting her chin to meet Husrav's eyes.

"Excellent!" said the guard. "Let us make a proper exchange."

He beckoned Abarōz to him, deftly shifting his sword to her throat. Then he released her mother, pushing her roughly toward Rastag.

What Abarōz saw at that moment was Shāhpuhr's face. He looked drawn and pale, like an Axwaš about to be sacrificed.

"No, take me too!" he cried. "How the S̄āh will reward you for an additional captive! Besides, I am his fourteenth son!"

Husrav stared at him in distaste.

"He didn't ask for you," the guard mumbled.

"But I escaped from his Hamwar! Surely, he wishes to punish me!"

"Shāhpuhr, stop," hissed Abarōz. "Think of your mother."

"Still tied to her cloak?" Husrav sneered.

"No," said Shāhpuhr. "That is why I insist I must go."

Husrav shrugged.

"All right. The boy may be worth more dēnārs."

He sheared off Adrina's bonds, transferring them to Abarōz. For assurance, he bound Shāhpuhr's wrists before him, and collected all weapons.

"Heed me, Rastag, and let your dragon mistress know. Any attempt on your part to retrieve these two from Dardan will result in painful death." He gave a sardonic grin. "And not just for them."

Rastag looked disgusted as Adrina ran to him. She made a motion to embrace him, which he hastily shrugged off.

"I agree to nothing," he spat, "but will not endanger my daughter's life."

"Very wise," said Husrav. "I take these two prisoners in the S̄āh's name, blessèd be his reign."

"May he die by his own hand!" Rastag yelled.

"S̄āh forbid!" cried Husrav. "Have you not heard he is now the equal of Jesus?"

"A god," Abarōz gasped. She'd always suspected that was his aim.

There was no more time to think as Husrav pushed her and Shāhpuhr from the clearing into the woods.

A Little Torture

Abarōz stumbled on the way to Dardan, she and Shāhpuhr moving awkwardly without the use of their hands.

Husrav, she raged internally. *Couldn't he at least have brought a camel?*

Still, the journey was short and Mihr concealed by clouds. Husrav stopped at the city gate, round boulder in place, then began pounding and yelling.

"Open for a vizier of the Šāh!"

A small stone grate flung open to reveal a dark eye. Seeing Husrav, those inside permitted him entrance, rolling aside the boulder. When they caught sight of his captives, their smiles were filed with delight.

"Not so fiery now?" a guard asked Abarōz, giving her a push. "Where's you ebren, *traitor?*"

"Is that not the king's son?" asked another. "The one made Axwaš but who lived."

"How pleased our god the Šāh will be."

Bowing her head, Abarōz let Husrav shove her forward. If not for her position, she would have protested, and loudly, but what good could that do her now?

"Up with you," Husrav ordered, his voice bright with the prospect of dēnārs. Shāhpuhr trailed behind as they descended to Hamwar Three, its staircase guarded by what seemed a small army. Not a facial muscle moved as the prisoners were marched past.

Abarōz snuck a look. She'd never been here before, and the opulence overwhelmed her. There was so much gold! In life-sized idols of the Šāh, rich threads woven in carpet, even the servants' robes. She felt at once awed and appalled, considering that most Dardans would never touch this metal.

Abarōz thought that on this Hamwar, no one would believe that they were in a cave. Every inch was covered with curtains and carpets, the spill of a large marble fountain mocking those dying of thirst. So much anger spiked within her that she barely noticed when she faced the god-king himself.

"Ah!" breathed the Šāh, sitting on a couch of silk cushions. "Husrav, one hundred extra dēnārs for you."

"My Šāh, you are too generous!" Husrav fell to his knees. He glared at his prisoners. "Girl," he told Abarōz, "you will kneel before Him who commands you body and soul!" He forced her down by the shoulder, and Shāhpuhr reluctantly followed. "Prostrate yourselves, you dogs!"

If it weren't for her friend, Abarōz would have spit in Al-razi's face. As it was, she touched her forehead to the carpet.

"And what have we here?" asked the Šāh, before Shāhpuhr did the same. "Our . . . son, is it not?" He squinted down. "How you must have missed being in Our presence!"

In what world? Abarōz wondered. *Certainly not this one.*

"What to do?" asked the Šāh, drumming his ringed fingers on a goblet. Husrav recognized the question as one he was not to answer. "We think . . ." purred the Šāh, "We shall torture them lightly after consigning them to Our dungeon."

"My savior?" Husrav said.

"Yes," the Šāh nodded, causing his gems to clink. "Though We would prefer death, this ensures the green beast's compliance."

He quickly lost interest in his prisoners as he palmed a fat ruby. Four guards stepped up to haul the two of them out.

Before she was dragged away, Abarōz turned her head.

"You are no god!" she spat. "In truth, you are barely a man!"

"Extra torture for that one," the Šāh called from behind her.

They were led down a few Hamwars: Abarōz counted four. So it must be Hamwar Seven where the rumored dungeons lay hidden. Once off the last staircase, the prisoners' eyes were covered and they stumbled down a long tunnel. Abarōz felt the sticky heat that could only be Dardan's as she was pushed harshly forward and heard a steel door snapping shut. She wanted to unbind her hands so she could throw off her blindfold. But Shāhpuhr, with his woodland skill, somehow managed to free them both.

They surveyed their surroundings. They were in a moldering cell about the size of four closets. The rock walls were peeling, the iron bars were rusted, and the smell was sickening, like rotten eggs mixed with vomit.

"Nice," Abarōz said as they slumped against a wall. The cell, of course, was completely bare.

"What I expected," answered Shāhpuhr, "from our great and glorious S̄āh."

"That's blasphemy!" a guard yelled from the other side of the bars. He looked slightly dejected. "Too bad we can't impale 'em or put 'em on the cross."

"Our Lord said to torture them *lightly,"* answered a second guard. "I'm supposin' that must mean fire."

Abarōz stiffened, her skin growing hot as if already put to the flame. Of course, this method was safe here: in Dardan, what was in danger of burning?

"Retrieve the fuel," the first guard ordered, and Abarōz heard a grunt as someone clanked off. In minutes, he had returned with an armful of torches, their tips wrapped in some sort of white material. He went back to pick up an urn overflowing with tallow.

"Let's get this done," said the first guard, inserting an iron key into the cell's rusty lock. "Tie 'em back up," he drawled, and two of his men marched forward to bind her and Shāhpuhr with chains to rows of big iron rings embedded into the wall.

Abarōz struggled against her bonds.

"You don't want to do this," she said, and she heard her voice shake.

"In fact, we do," said the head guard from his post outside the bars.

"I am only a girl, "she pleaded, "and he is just a boy. Do you not have children of your own? Would you want them to suffer this way?"

"My children," said the head guard, "are all polite and modest. They do not make war on the city or disrespect our god."

"You mean Jesus?' Abarōz asked, desperately stalling for time.

"Our beloved Sāh," he replied, "He who can do no wrong."

"And burning people alive? That's considered right?"

The guard chuckled.

"In this case, yes."

"Please." Shāhpuhr spoke from his chained position beside her. "Torture me. You can do whatever you want. Just leave her alone."

"Sweet," grinned the head guard, stomping into the cell. "I must say I'm almost touched."

"Shāhpuhr," Abarōz whispered, barely able to turn her head. "Our plate. They don't seem to know."

He nodded, taking a breath as the head guard hovered.

"There," said the guard, "and there. Only a few more."

He set the torches in sconces which ran down both sides of their bodies after dipping their tips in the urn. A hard substance coated the linen as he used flint and rock to kindle one torch. Wielding this like a candle, he lit them all in succession. Now the cell, formerly gloomy, seemed as bright as Mihr.

"Haven't had to do this recently," the guard grumbled, "but I guess it stays with you."

Abarōz wished it hadn't as her skin and plate glowed with heat.

"Don't worry," said the guard, "in an hour, these torches will burn out. I trust you'll enjoy them till then." Abarōz had her doubts as he motioned his men from the cell and locked the door behind them. "Farewell!" he told them. "Hope you're fond of fire."

Abarōz heard boots against rock until the sound faded. She tried to shrink from the flames, each mere inches from her, but she'd been chained so tightly she couldn't move. Not to mention, this close, the torches were blinding and emitted thick white smoke.

"Sh-Shāhpuhr!" she coughed.

"I–I'm . . . all right," he managed to choke. "It's–it's mostly hitting the plate, but—*Ow!*—that one got my thigh."

Abarōz closed her eyes, no longer able to look. Her plate did repel flames, but where she bore none, like her upper arms, her skin erupted in pain.

She didn't want . . . to show weakness . . . yet, despite her resolve, she let out a series of screams.

"A-Abarōz!" Shāhpuhr called, his own yells now joining hers.

This merciless searing surely could not be survived. No being in Gehān would be able to last a full hour.

"Had enough?" called a voice as the head guard unlocked their cell. "Regrettably, our god said to torture you *lightly* . . ."

He threw a bucket of water over the flaming torches which promptly hissed and smoked. His men came in and did the same until Abarōz was soaked and the fires were extinguished. But the skin of her upper arms was now a disturbing white.

"Take 'em down!" yelled the head guard, inspiring two others to unravel their prisoners' chains. "Looks like you'll be a bit . . . crisp . . . during the rest of your stay here."

Abarōz thought he shot her a grin before marching his men from the cell. Her ears barely registered the harsh click of a lock.

She and Shāhpuhr slumped down, every move an agony.

"Are–are you . . . badly burnt?" Shāhpuhr asked in a whispered moan. He too dripped with water.

"I–I don't know," Abarōz groaned, looking over the now seeping wounds on her arms. She could still feel the phantom heat of the torches.

Using the last of her strength, she forced herself to examine the space of their small cell. Was there *anything* they could use as a balm for tortured flesh? Iron and chains were out, which left the torches themselves. Could the animal fat which ignited them possibly ease their anguish?

Through her shivers of pain, Abarōz not-so-patiently waited: for what was now white liquid to cool. When she thought enough time had passed, she scuttled on her knees to reach the lowest, nearest torch, removing its cloth which dripped with a sticky substance.

"Here." She crawled to Shāhpuhr who slumped against a rock wall. She fell to his side, and mainly using her forearms, applying fat to his blistered thighs. "B-better?"

"Y-yes," he said, his lower body spasming. "L-let me do it for you."

He took up the cloth and, as gently as possible, applied the tallow to her burns.

Abarōz cried out since the slightest touch was like being poked with hot irons. But, as she clenched her teeth, she did feel her pain ease slightly once the fat oozed over her wounds.

"W-we shouldn't s-stop," she said, biting down a groan. "K-keep using it."

Shāhpuhr nodded, moving her carefully so a wall braced her back.

"H-how?" she asked, "d-do we ever g-get out?"

Shāhpuhr winced, a mix of pain and despair.

"I–I really don't k-know."

Hard as Gold

The only sign in Dardan that sleeptime had become worktime was the lighting of torches. But here, on the unlit Seventh Hamwar, Abarōz couldn't tell one from the other. Or when the head guard would decide to resume their "light" torture.

In the meantime, they weren't permitted to die: twice a day, some unseen body slid two trays under the door, and though the meals were foul—moldy bread and runny soup—they were certainly better than nothing, along with the two cups of water they were allotted each day.

Probably the same as the other parched "inmates" of Dardan.

Over the next four days, measured in trays, she and Shāhpuhr spent their time coating their burns with fat. It did have healing properties, for new skin gradually formed to replace the old. Abarōz found she could now move her arms without groaning, and Shāhpuhr had stopped clutching his blistered thighs. Between meals, they exchanged plans, minds focused on one thing only: *Escape.*

"The iron bars," Shāhpuhr whispered. "I know how to make fire—what if we light a torch and try to burn our way through?"

Abarōz sighed.

"That might work if they were gold: my father says it melts quickly. But the iron here must be from ancient days—before Dardan left the Bērūn. In any case, it will likely hold up to flame."

"And the lock?" asked Shāhpuhr, unwilling to give up. "If we could just make a key that fit—"

"With what?" Abarōz said. "Neither of us are smiths. For that, we'd at least need a shaman—or Peril." She forced herself upright. "Wait. The Perils—they can't help us—*but* they already have."

"Our plate?" questioned Shāhpuhr, running a hand over his hair. "How would it help against iron?"

"It's not just *any* gold," said Abarōz. "If it can repel flame . . . can it perform other magick?"

Shāhpuhr stared into the darkness.

"I suppose it won't hurt to see."

Holding her breath against the stench, Abarōz removed a shin guard. She crawled up to the cell door, smashing it against a bar. Other than a dull clang, her action had no effect.

"Perhaps." she said, "we need a sharp, straight edge."

"We have no weapons. Husrav took him."

"Tengri curse him," she mumbled. "Do you think . . . that we could *make* an edge?" She held up her lightweight shin guard. "Take one of these rounded pieces and try to hammer it straight?"

"How?" asked Shāhpuhr. "Something tells me the guards did not leave a knife."

Abarōz looked intent.

"Then we make the plate of hammer."

She handed it to him.

"Er—"

"You said you could make fire."

"Yes."

"I suggest you do so. Before they bring our next meal."

Shāhpuhr looked unconvinced, but still searched the entire cell. Over time, its stone had cracked, leaving a scattering of small rocks. He chose two—one harder than the other—and proceeded to rub them together.

"Hurry," Abarōz cautioned, every sense alert for the guards. She knew if their "god" commanded it, they would make an unscheduled visit. "Anything?"

Shāhpuhr sighed.

"These aren't ideal," he said. "Not the kind I use at home."

"Please," Abarōz pleaded, holding back her tears. "Try."

Her secret fear was that the head guard, seeing them "recovered," would put them to the torch again. She watched, balling her fists, as Shāhpuhr kept smashing the rocks.

"Ah!" he cried, and Abarōz saw he was close. A tiny spark had kindled where the two rocks met—only to flicker out.

"You can do it," said Abarōz, and she knew that he could. "I–I believe in you."

He smiled.

"No one has told me that except my mother. May Tengri help me to earn your faith."

He took up his task again, the muscles in his lean arms straining.

"Look!" Abarōz saw a small spark. Grinding the rocks anew, Shāhpuhr heightened it, and Abarōz approached with care, lighting a fat-soaked torch. *Light! And heat!* More importantly, not directed toward *them.* She cradled the torch like a babe as it cast shadows onto the walls. "Your turn," she whispered, handing the flame to Shāhpuhr.

"Yes." He seemed puzzled. "Exactly what do I do?"

"Try," she said, "to melt the gold into an edge."

He nodded, sheltering the torch with his body as he brought it up to her shin guard. The flame barely smoked as gold drops fell to the floor. Abruptly, Shāhpuhr halted.

"This will not work," he said. "The plate will end up molten."

"Very well." Abarōz seized back the torch. "We must wait for the flame to cool."

"What?"

"Trust me," she told him, setting the torch back in its sconce. After an hour, it flickered off, and she went to grab it again.

"We need to mold the gold."

Wielding the still-hot torch, she touched it to her shin guard, sculpting an edge that was straight. Well, almost . . .

Shāhpuhr looked on, impressed.

"Now," said Abarōz, we must wait for the gold to cool."

They watched it as if it were a precious nugget, Shāhpuhr finally taking the plunge by reaching out a finger.

"Ready," he said, seizing it and kneeling by the cell door.

Abarōz kept watch as he worked at an iron bar near the bottom. Though it probably shouldn't have, the plate scraped off a few chips, exposing the white beneath.

"Shāhpuhr!" Abarōz cried, throwing her hands in the air. "I love you!" She said a silent prayer that he couldn't see her red face. "I mean, er . . ."

"I understand," he said quietly, returning to his filing. "We must hope that the guards don't notice when they deliver our trays."

"They won't," Abarōz answered, trying to distract him from her hasty words.

What had made her say that? Declare her feelings *here?* Couldn't she have done so in the far more pleasant Razūr?

I've ruined everything, she thought. *He'll never say it back now. He'll just think I was caught in the moment and confused love for excitement . . .*

She wanted to break the silence, but didn't know how. Especially here, in *Dardan,* when such declarations—outside marriage—were not only shocking but banned!

"I–I'm sorry," she mumbled at last, her face heating up like a torch. "I should not have spoken so. Like a–a . . . brazen harlot."

Shāhpuhr tossed back his head and laughed.

"From you," he said, "I have learned that our zand is strange. Torture is gladly permitted but speaking one's feelings is not." Abarōz bit her lip. She had to admit he was right. "I'm going to keep cutting. Please listen for footsteps."

"That won't be hard," she said, "since they sound like charging camels."

Shāhpuhr looked up and grinned. He worked until steel boots sounded, ate his meal along with Abarōz, then continued chipping away.

"I wish I could help you," said Abarōz, staring down at her arms. Although they were healing, they bore thick blisters, and were still halfway useless.

"Do not worry," Shāhpuhr said, finishing up for the night. He huddled in a cold corner where Abarōz joined him for warmth, curling into his back. Even though they'd made progress today, her thoughts still kept her from sleep.

Had she meant it? she wondered. *Her hastily cried "confession"? Did she really love Shāhpuhr, or had torture shaken her mind?*

In-between meal deliveries, Shāhpuhr kept to his task: After just six mealtimes, he'd made impressive progress, breaking one bar in half and working away at a second. Eight more trays, and Shāhpuhr, now practiced, was proceeding at a blazing pace, cutting through three bars total with a fourth on the way. If they could just bend out the rods, this might be a way to escape.

Another mealtime, and Abarōz leaned over, watching Shāhpuhr grind away. With a last scrape of metal-on-metal, the fourth bar sprang apart.

"*We need an opening!*" she cried, wishing she weren't so helpless. But Shāhpuhr was determined, lifting Abarōz's shin guard and pounding the edge against bars. Two began to droop slightly, a space of just inches between them; one completely came off; and the last stubbornly held.

Fueled by anger, Shāhpuhr banged the gold repeatedly, efforts so loud that Abarōz feared discovery.

"Are we close?" she asked, seeing his long hair streaked with sweat.

"Just . . . a . . . few—" He pounded three more times, then rose with a look of triumph. "I'm through."

Abarōz knelt, arms held stiffly, peering at her prayer made real: a hole, not large, but perhaps just enough for each of them to squirm through!

"Remove your plate," said Shāhpuhr, and he gingerly helped her, taking care not to graze her burns. Now significantly less bulky, Abarōz first thrust her feet, then legs, between the twisted iron. She felt Shāhpuhr pushing her from inside the cell. "Just—a—little—bit—more . . ."

Abarōz was out, shooting across the floor as if she were greased in tallow. When she made her way back, Shāhpuhr handed over her plate—piece by piece.

"You next," she whispered, motioning him to join her.

He nodded and shoved out his plate, following it with his feet and long legs. Abarōz bit back her pain, extending her arms enough to help drag him through. They now lay side-by-side, panting, looking up at their former cell. But Abarōz knew time was short: They needed to find the stairway, clamber up seven Hamwars, and force themselves through the hatch.

One look at Shāhpuhr told her he knew this too, since he buckled his plate back on, urged her to do the same, then took off running down the tunnel. Abarōz heard him groan each time his foot hit the ground.

"The stairs," he gasped, "where are they?"

She abruptly took the lead, knowing Dardan as well as he did the forest.

"This way!" she hissed, seizing his hand and dashing full-tilt in the dark. She practically flew to the staircase, glad to see its torches unlit. The Šāh must not have wanted his secret dungeons discovered.

"Damn!" Abarōz breathed, barely mad at herself for cursing. On Hamwar Six, they ran into a vintner trundling his wares. "Sorry!" she yelled, pushing him to the wall.

"Warriors!" the man spat. "Always happy to drink my wine, but not a care when you spill it!"

She and Shāhpuhr continued their climb, but it must have been worktime since they kept encountering others: a mother with two small children; a wild-eyed man; and a trembling Ōšmurdan on his way to report a tally.

"Hurry!" Abarōz called to Shāhpuhr. The more people who saw them, the lower their chance of escape. Still, she hadn't heard guards running after them. But that didn't mean minions and spies wouldn't put them in jeopardy . . .

Abarōz felt her lungs strain as they dashed up to higher Hamwars. Thank Tengri *this* journey hadn't begun in the zarr! At last, despite their injuries, the two of them reached the top level and were lowed at by a cow.

She reached the rope ladder first, ignoring the pain in her arms as she mounted. Then, she heard a clatter and whipped around. An angry guard was heading straight for Shāhpuhr!

"Stop!" the man shouted, "for the love of our god king!"

"I am his son," Shāhpuhr said calmly, "and even *I* do not love him."

"Blasphemy!" yelled the guard, already hefting his spear. That's when a body—Abarōz's—swung over and dropped on his head.

"Ahhh!" the man called, hitting the floor with a clang. "Guards! Help me!"

"Shhh," Shāhpuhr admonished, pushing the edge of the fellow's cloak directly into his mouth.

"Your so-called god," he said, "enjoys binding and gagging." To press home his point, he retrieved some rope by the pens, securing the man's arms and legs. "I'm sure they'll find you," Shāhpuhr smiled, "after one or two sleeptimes."

The guard gurgled something but Abarōz didn't care: She flew back to the ladder, scrambling up its rungs before flinging open the hatch. She crawled out as best she could, making room for Shāhpuhr. As he emerged behind her, she breathed in fresh air and pointed her chin at Mihr. After so many days underground, she felt as reborn as an Axwaš. But there was no time to pause as she and Shāhpuhr helped each other up. Though they did their best to run, their pace was achingly slow as they groaned with every step.

"Shāhpuhr," Abarōz panted, "we've got to go faster!"

They both gritted their teeth, struggling through the pain. If they couldn't manage more speed, they would probably be caught.

"Look!" Shāhpuhr cried, pointing up to the clouds. A black form swooped down—one with two wings and a tail. *"Catanes!"* The dragon glided over their heads before landing beside his Aswār. Shāhpuhr limped toward him, embracing his scaly neck. "Thank Tengri!" he breathed.

He turned to Abarōz, seating her gently on the ebren: Taking his place behind her, he roared to Catanes, who promptly took off.

Despite the ache of her arms, Abarōz began to enjoy the feel of wind on her face. She hadn't quite realized how precious freedom could be. And she was determined to share that feeling with other Dardans.

There was no sign of Sangal's horde as Catanes arced northwest. Had the red dragon given up after his last defeat? Or was he skulking in his lair, laying plans for more chaos? Abarōz tried not to think of their foes as they landed among their friends.

In the clearing, Bükrek was waiting, one claw raised in welcome. At her side was Rastag, his face flooding with joy.

"Father!" Abarōz cried, sliding to the grass to embrace him.

"Daughter," he whispered, their tears mingling. "It has been so long . . . I feared you were lost to me."

"It was no simple task," she said, "but we escaped the Šāh. He is far more depraved than even I could imagine."

Rastag stepped back, eyeing her blistered arms.

"He will pay for this," he hissed, "in treasure and in blood."

"That is our hope," said Abarōz, turning to Shāhpuhr. "He and Sangal must be driven out of Gehān."

"I think they will be." Bükrek smiled down at the two of them. "If you can flee the S̃āh's cruelty, anything is possible

"What did we miss," asked Abarōz, "while we were away?"

"I'm glad to say very little. Sangal seems intent on waiting for the last Dardan to die before he assaults the city." Bükrek cocked her head. "What did you observe there?"

"Hard to say," sighed Abarōz, "since we were mainly locked in a cell. But I noticed that most of the people looked careworn and parched."

The dragon nodded.

"I'm not surprised. What we must look out for now is a second attack on us. Sangal will be eager now that you have returned."

"And—the wolf heads?" asked Abarōz, feeling a chill.

Bükrek chuckled.

"The Gurg Kamāl have proved useless in open spaces. But I fear that Sangal will turn to even worse creatures."

That's when Abarōz broached a subject that had weighed on her mind.

"What about us?" she asked. Her audience of three looked puzzled. "Why can't *we* find other allies besides the Erbörü? Surely, there must be some out there."

"While you two were gone," Bükrek said, "I allowed my mind to wander. Who else might we call upon? Who best to aid us? I settled on Şahmeran, whose help saved us before." Her yellow eyes glinted. "You, Abarōz, are the only living being who has entered her cave. I ask you to return and beg for her intervention."

"Why now?" Abarōz asked, uneasy.

"It is hardly an easy task." Bükrek folded her claws. "A last resort, as they say. But, this late in the war, we have very few choices."

Abarōz sighed, then shot a look at Shāhpuhr.

"Very well," she conceded. "But your son and I need to heal."

"Of course! You will need all your strength to enter the gate of Šahr."

"And luck," mumbled Abarōz.

"That I cannot deny." Bükrek turned to Shāhpuhr. "Son, use your store of cooking fat to apply to all wounds. That will speed your recovery."

"Yes, mother," he said, linking his fingers with Abarōz's. Rastag let them move off to settle upon the grass. "I can't believe," said Shāhpuhr, "we were able to flee that cell. I honestly thought they'd put us to the torch again."

"Yes." Abarōz shuddered, remembering that searing heat. "The S̄āh would torture us 'lightly' until we both died."

"A moment."

Shāhpuhr rose with a groan before darting behind a tree. When he returned, he clutched a simple clay jar.

"Animal fat," he said, dipping in his long fingers. "Just like the tallow in Dardan."

"Don't remind me," said Abarōz, starting as he covered her arms with white stuff. As always, it stung, but afterwards would soothe. Then they reversed, Abarōz applying the balm to Shāhpuhr's blisters. He lay back with a happy sigh.

"Now," he said, "we have time to relax."

Abarōz settled beside him.

"Yes and no."

"What do you mean?"

"I'm thinking of Şahmeran."

"And?"

"Finding her cave will not be like before. We only know where she lies in relation to the zarr."

"You're . . . you're not considering going through Dardan?!"

"By the new god's beard, no! I will never go back while the S̄āh still reigns."

"What then?"

"I know as much about entering Šahr as I do of pleasing Al-razi."

"I too am ignorant—on both points, I fear."

"Well, I suppose we should walk there—riding a dragon might draw attention." He laughed. "Then we need to get close to survey their defenses."

"Simple!" cried Shāhpuhr, though his smile belied his words.

"In the meantime," Abarōz said, "let's try not to dwell on the future. Concentrate on healing and enjoying our families."

"You'll get no objection from me! I just a need a meal that is neither stale nor runny."

Adrina

The next week passed too quickly, Abarōz feeling dazed as if she'd drunk too much wine. She'd never known such happiness—resting, feasting, and spending time with her father. She and Shāhpuhr healed steadily thanks to his soothing balm. She never wanted these days to end, but time, so often ruthless, had other plans in store.

As did Abarōz.

She knew she couldn't postpone any longer, so she walked to the edge of the clearing where her mother was bound to a tree.

"Adrina."

Abarōz tried to keep the tremble out of her voice. Her mother sat, cross-legged, at the base of a wide trunk, a hood flung over her face. Abarōz stooped to remove it.

"Ah, Daughter."

Her mother blinked up as if Abarōz were a stranger.

"I have returned from Dardan."

"So I see."

"Are they treating you well?"

Now color splotched Adrina's face.

"Yes. If you call being tied up 'well.'"

Abarōz let out a breath.

"You knew the bargain: myself in exchange for you."

"Yet here you stand."

"Yes. I guess there's no harm in freeing you, since the S̃āh would be more than happy to blame you for my escape." She circled the tree, undoing thick knots. "Better?" she asked, walking round to face Adrina.

"I suppose," her mother spat as she rubbed both wrists. Her dark eyes were filled with venom. "Some daughter you turned out to be! A thorough disgrace to our family! I'd rather kill you myself than accept such a stain."

Abarōz felt a numbness starting at her feet. Could she *ever* satisfy her mother? Make her see that her selfishness had torn apart their family?

"Adrina," Abarōz said quietly. "You never cared for me: not when I was dutiful; and now, when I am not. Whatever guise I take is of no importance to you."

"Clever," hissed her mother. "You were always too quick for your own good. You've turned your father against me—ensured I cannot go home!"

"And what a home," Abarōz told her. "Where the man you worship burns your daughter alive. Not to mention killing your husband."

"I will not hear it!" her mother shrieked, rising to stumble on unused legs. "Blasphemy! Sedition! Get away from me, whore!"

The numbness had spread upward; gripped Abarōz's head in its hands. She could only stand and watch as her mother walked away.

No matter, she told herself, shaking her limbs to restore feeling. She'd never been close to Adrina, never less so than now. Of course, she was her mother, the only one she had. She must, as the new god preached, learn to turn the other cheek.

By the time she went back to Shāhpuhr, she thought she had recovered. But he saw it all on her face, offering a gentle hug and a soft kiss on the cheek.

"Each of us has one outstanding parent," he murmured into her hair. "I suppose, in this world, that's all that we can ask for."

Abarōz nodded, letting her tears flow free. He was right, as always: She must learn to be grateful for the blessings she'd been granted.

Two Plans

I grow so tired of my wretched horde and the useless Gurg Kamāl! I've had to resist a constant urge to throw them in my lake of fire!

Imbeciles! Dogs! To give way to Bükrek and her ebrens ridden by cripples who had once been rightfully killed! It was almost too much to bear, but I have borne a great deal since Gehān came to be. Now, I must find other creatures to bolster my sorry ranks: ones who can guarantee victory when I next assault Dardan. How tired I am of waiting for mortal men to die! But I, an immortal, need not wait any longer: as commander of chaos, patience is not my strength.

There is no use consulting my minions: they share one mind among four. And as for that blackguard Kavad—I will slay him on his visit. No, it is *my* task to put an end to Bükrek; to smash my way to the gold that still lies in the zarr. As for that fool Al-razi . . . I have to laugh. The corpulent 'god' annoys me—even his bribes lose their sheen. I intend to feast on his flesh after I seize his riches. And when *I* am ruler of Dardan, his petty revenge and dungeons will look like a child's plaything. From my tall rock, I breathe out white smoke. It is well past time to set my plan in motion.

"Go," I order my second-in-command, "and take ten dragons with you. Fly north to Abaxtar and persuade the Yaryond there to join me. If they refuse, flame one to death." I smile. "It's quite amazing what a little killing can do."

I have dwelt in this cave forever, overseeing the natural world.

And I do not like, at present, what occurs beyond these walls.

I sigh from both my heads as I coil upon my throne. At heart, I am a healer, and cannot abide the destruction wrought by Sangal and his lot.

Always, he has lived; always, so have I. But he's never caused so much harm as in this present war. Thoughts merge from both my minds—from my years of living on Gehān. And they tell me that if I remain uncaring, all in nature will die.

I have already intervened once: against the Gurg Kamāl. I could not stand aside and watch them murder the Axwaš. My vines and plants are forceful, but I command so much more: the storm-tossed ocean, the lava-spewing volcano, the temblors that shake the ground. These, of course, are extreme, not to be deployed unless I must. But I believe that my subjects can help Bükrek and her friends.

I gaze down at my children as I prepare to address them. They know I only do so when the world explodes outside.

"Marans!" I cry, causing a giant writhing across the floor of my cave. From my snake's mouth, I tell them, "The dragon of creation Bükrek is sorely in need of our aid." I watch my white snakes approach, some forming a mound at a feet. "Sangal roams with impunity, waging war on man and beast. It is up to you, my Marans, to form a force against him."

I hear a great hissing from tens of thousands of throats. To others, the sound might be nothing, but to me, it is sweet: the sound of perfect assent.

"Thank you," I tell them, bowing my woman's head. "When the time comes, we will enter the battle. In the meantime, I ask this Maran—" I point to one, "—to make his way to Razūr. Once there, seek Bükrek and deliver my promise."

"Yes, Şahmeran," the Maran says over the rising hisses. "Will you open the second door?"

"Of course." I smile from both my mouths. "I must ask you to leave at present. My trees have whispered that a flight of Sangal's ebrens are winging their way north."

The New Gate

The morning after she'd seen Adrina, Abarōz rose with reluctance, cursing her own mind. In the night, no dreams or half-dreams had come with plans to enter Šahr, then discover Şahmeran's lair. Both tasks seemed impossible: She'd need more than dreams to guide her.

Abarōz found Shāhpuhr by the embers of a breakfast fire where he handed her two scrambled eggs. Where had he managed to find them? Still, she wasn't surprised: when it came to the forest, he was a true master.

"Feeling better?" he asked, offering a seat on the grass.

"I–I don't know. I'm glad to have decent food, but saddened since my mother will never change."

"I'm sorry."

"You didn't create her."

"Well, next time I see Tengri, I'll tell him he made a mistake."

Abarōz smiled, her bad mood dispelled. Shāhpuhr could always make her laugh.

"Er . . ." he started.

"Yes?"

"Not sure if it's good or not, but your arms have completely healed."

"So have your legs."

"That means . . ."

Abarōz sighed.

"Time to journey to Šahr."

After they'd finished their meal, they loaded their packs and buckled on their plate. Seeing them from across the clearing, Bükrek motioned them over.

"Children," said the dragon.

Abarōz stiffened.

"Please don't say that to Baba Yaga!"

Bükrek smiled, though her face was tinged with worry.

"What you're about to attempt requires incredible courage." The dragon looked down. "I wish I could give you specific advice: Just stay alert at all times. I have heard rumors that Šahr has aligned itself with Dardan."

"Oh no!"

Abarōz covered her mouth.

"This makes your mission doubly fraught. I would trust no one except Şahmeran herself."

"If we ever get there," Abarōz mumbled.

"If anyone can," said Bükrek, "it will be the two of you."

Shāhpuhr approached his mother and gave her a heartfelt hug. Abarōz touched her hand to one of the dragon's front claws. Then, they picked up their packs and headed for the river.

"Farewell," Bükrek called, "I expect to see you shortly."

"Dragons," Abarōz told Shāhpuhr, "seem to be relentlessly hopeful."

"Not Sangal," he said, leading her over the bank which was packed with snoring dragons.

"Speaking of which," said Abarōz, "he may very well have his ebrens outside of both cities. Let's agree—if we see them, we run. Away."

He nodded, glancing down at his angled foot.

"Be sure," he told her, "not to wait for me."

"I'll be sure," she said, "to wait."

He rolled his eyes but she pretended not to notice. Now they were in the forest treading its eastern path. All here seemed peaceful, birdsong echoing down from the trees. Too soon, they were clear of Razūr and sinking into sand. This journey was so familiar they might as well name the dunes.

"Have I mentioned recently," Abarōz asked, "how much I hate the desert?"

"No, not for some time. But, please, feel free."

Despite what lay ahead, she managed a smile. At least they had a short walk before being set on by dragons. This morning, a swirl of clouds blocked Mihr's killing heat. The landscape they trod didn't vary: sand in one form or another. But when Abarōz spotted the mountain overhanging Dardan, she reached for Shāhpuhr's hand.

"See anything?" she asked, directing her eyes to the sky. No ebrens emerged; no flapping of wings could be heard. "Phew," she breathed. "Guess Sangal's occupied elsewhere."

Once they came to Dardan's gate, she knew just what to do.

"Get down," she whispered. "We have to crawl past." He hit the sand when she did, those pesky grains tickling her knees and elbows. "Ouch," she said, making sure to keep her head low.

"Shhh," Shāhpuhr warned, and they must have looked like two beetles. As they crossed the boulder, no small stone hatch slammed open; no steel-plated guards rushed out.

Finally, they arrived at the cave's side not too far from the hatch. Abarōz stood up, lending a hand to Shāhpuhr. No one would see them here.

"That was our first goal," Abarōz said. "The second will be much tougher." She looked to her left where the city of Šahr must stand. But she'd never seen it—from the front—and wished she could keep it that way.

As they crept steadily west, Abarōz guessed that Šahr's gate shouldn't be far.

"Get down," she whispered, nearly doubling over as she hugged the ground. Shāhpuhr followed her lead, both of them rounding Dardan's far corner. Every muscle tensed as Abarōz peered ahead. When they arrived at the northwest wall of Dardan, she didn't know what to do. "Where is it?" she hissed, seeing no sign of another city.

Shāhpuhr squinted, leaning forward. From his sigh, she knew he saw nothing.

"Great," she said, crossing her arms. "Does Šahr even exist? It must because we've been there!"

"We did not dream it," agreed Shāhpuhr.

"But what if the entrance is guarded by some kind of magick?"

"If it is, I haven't heard it. Not from my mother, anyway."

Abarōz felt better as she studied a small cliff ahead. She discovered that its face was not wholly natural: there were signs and symbols that could only be carved by men.

"It's here somewhere," she said. "The only question is where?"

Still crouching, they went toward the cliff where they saw more intricate runes. Then something caught Abarōz's eye: finely etched edges crowned by a peaked roof. Šahr's zand had hidden their entrance carefully.

"Look," Abarōz pointed to the subtle city gate. "It is really beautiful, but how do we get in?" Shāhpuhr shook his head as he withdrew his sword. Abarōz doubted it would be useful against multiple guards. She sighed. "This is the hard part."

"Perhaps," said Shāhpuhr, "there's a second entrance like Dardan."

Abarōz smiled widely. What an excellent thought! But then the doubts started nagging.

"I don't know," she said. "These people seem to excel at keeping outsiders *out.*"

Still, they crept further west, past that daunting gate. They moved to a side wall, brushing their fingers on stone in hope of finding a door.

"Careful!" Shāhpuhr shouted, raising his blade abruptly.

"Ah!" Abarōz stepped back so fast it felt like she had flown. Crawling toward them across the sand was a *very large*, off-white snake. *"Kill it!"* she yelled from instinct. Shāhpuhr strode toward the serpent. "NO—WAIT!"

There was something she recognized . . . the snake's unusual size . . . its color and unmarked scales. *Şahmeran!* This was one of her Marans . . .

As the snake lifted its head, staring up with vibrant blue eyes, Shāhpuhr returned its gaze.

"What's wrong?" he asked Abarōz. "Have you developed a fondness for snakes?"

"No," she said, "but this one is special and I think it might be a sign."

"From the snake god?" asked Shāhpuhr, keeping his eye on the real one.

"In a way." He didn't put down his swords "These white snakes belong to Şahmeran. And this one . . ." she bent down, "may have been sent to guide us."

"Hmmp," Shāhpuhr was unconvinced. "Don't you think that's a bit farfetched?"

"In a land filled with dragons, and a boy whose mother is one?"

"Don't forget the Perils and snake heads. I guess I can't argue with that." Sheathing his blade, he bowed down to the snake. "Šāh Serpent, if you would—please lead us to your queen."

The snake stuck out his forked tongue, then turned to retrace his slithering. He looked like an unwinged ebren . . .

"Shāhpuhr," she asked, "do you think it speaks Dragon?"

Shāhpuhr beamed, hissing more than usual as he addressed the snake. It responded in kind, using both short hisses and long.

"It worked!" Shāhpuhr cried. "He says he comes from Şahmeran and wants to lead us to her."

"Do I hear an apology?" Abarōz jabbed his ribs. "Even though you finally believed me."

"You were right, and I am indeed sorry."

"Hmmp."

The snake continued its slide, twisting around a stone corner to what must be the rear of Šahr. This wall, like the gate, was carved with elaborate symbols.

"Could you ask him," she told Shāhpuhr, "where these signs all came from?"

There followed a hissing exchange before Shāhpuhr turned back to her.

"He says the walls were carved by craftsmen many ages past. Before Šahr was forced underground."

Abarōz nodded, hurling a "thanks" to the snake. He hissed in return, his color so stark against sand that he made the perfect guide. At last, he halted where the runes were especially dense, then raised his coils, swaying.

"Is he all right?" Abarōz asked. This must be some kind of ritual practiced by his kind. The Maran before her began a rhythmic hissing and quickened his sideways dance. This had a peculiar effect: Silver dots rained down the wall like a speckled curtain. "What—?" she began, but then the dots came together, bouncing away from the wall to create more runic symbols. They formed a dizzying circle which spun sideways, then disappeared, leaving instead a small door with a gold handle. Abarōz wanted to turn it, but the snake leapt on, using wrapped coils to push.

Once the door opened and she peeked in, what she saw were smallish hills, all manner of flowers, and a luscious green carpet. Eagerly, she went through, Shāhpuhr at her heels, until the snake turned and hissed out a scroll's-worth of Dragon.

"Oh." Shāhpuhr looked disappointed. "He says I may not enter."

"That's hardly fair," snapped Abarōz. "Why not?"

Shāhpuhr hissed to the snake.

"He says he can't tell us, but that we should trust Şahmeran."

Abarōz huffed. She deeply felt the injustice of leaving Shāhpuhr behind after he'd repeatedly saved her life. But, she knew from Dardan that most rules couldn't be broken . . .

"Very well," she told the Maran, trying to hide her annoyance. "Shāhpuhr, I'll find you here?"

He nodded, slumping against the stone.

The Maran's blue eyes met hers before he slithered ahead. With each step she took, Abarōz became more amazed: This garden was just like the one in the new god's book: perfect, nothing amiss, its broad-leafed trees framed by thundering falls. Abarōz hadn't witnessed these wonders when she'd been here last, but was glad to have the chance now.

She followed her serpent guide as he pushed past the others, so plentiful they not only covered the grass, but formed high coiled mounds. They were all the same whitish color and Abarōz grew so intrigued she had to be hissed at to notice the Tree of Life.

Thank Tengri, it was still here, guarded by its small dragon, branches stretching to the sky. Just a few steps away, Şahmeran curled on her throne, her two mouths wide with smiles.

"This is unexpected," her woman's head said. "But certainly not unwelcome."

"Oh." Abarōz stood before her, staring down at her snake head. "So . . . you did not send your Maran to me?"

"Oh no," her woman's head laughed, the sound as soothing as a spurting fountain. "I sent him to Bükrek in order to offer my help. But since you are here, he needn't travel so far."

Abarōz stood for a moment, trying to take this all in.

"You . . . plan to help us again?" she asked.

"Of course. We cannot have Sangal ripping apart our world."

"I will certainly tell Bükrek."

Şahmeran stretched out her heads so two pairs of eyes scrutinized Abarōz.

"How have you been, my dear?"

"Well . . ." Why was it so hard to answer? "Up and down, you could say. With your help, we won the last battle, but then my friend and I were thrown in a cell by the S̄āh. I'd rather not think about it."

"I see." The snake queen stretched out her coils. "There might be more bad days ahead for, as we speak, Sangal's ebrens land in Abaxtar."

"Oh no."

Abarōz balled her fists. Thoughts of the wolf men betraying them made her shudder slightly.

"We cannot anticipate," Şahmeran said, 'all that is to come. Not even me." Abarōz looked down. "Just know when the time is right, my Marans will fight on your side. I myself am wedded to this garden, but, at the next full moon, you will feel me."

Abarōz didn't know what Māh had to do with it, but still managed a smile.

"Thank you, Şahmeran," she said, bowing her head. "Bükrek trusts you completely."

"As I do her." Her snakehead flicked out its tongue. "We will meet again, young Abarōz, that is a certainty. However . . ." Both her heads gave a sigh, ". . . the circumstances will not be pleasant."

Abarōz felt a deep chill.

"Is there anything I can do?"

"Win the war. As for me, you must show no mercy." Abarōz opened her mouth to protest.

"Heed the words I have spoken. And remember: Perfection lies only in nature."

Abarōz lowered her head. She feared to ask for another favor, but felt she had to.

"Great Şahmeran," she said, "I–I do not wish to seem ungrateful, but there is something else." The queen's human head raised a brow. "The–the Tree of Life, I assume that's part of nature?"

Şahmeran gave a close-lipped smile.

"More than anything."

"Well . . . I don't have time to climb. I was . . . curious . . . Could you summon Manuchehr and ask him to find me?"

Şahmeran remained still.

"Very well," she said, "I will grant this favor since you seek to free Dardan. But please understand I do not command the Perils."

"Thank you, Queen!" Abarōz cried, bowing as low as she could in her plate. "I only wish you could rule Dardan."

"Ah." Şahmeran gave her two smiles. "Perhaps I will someday, though not in my present form." Abarōz felt confused, but in light of her second favor, she decided to put this aside. "Go now," said Şahmeran, "back to Bükrek and the Aswārs. My Maran will show you out." She unspooled her coils, her yellow snake eyes intent. "Yes," she sighed, "we will meet again. For now, have a safe journey."

One of the snakes by her throne raised up and hissed at Abarōz. Taking the hint, she followed him past all the others. It was hard for her not to gape as more beauty unfolded before her: a flower-strewn meadow fed by a rushing brook; a mossy wood with slants of light between trees. She barely noticed her guide until he hissed out a spell, conjuring those silver runes. As before, a small door appeared which the Maran opened.

"Thank you," Abarōz told him, stepping through. "I suppose you'll be getting back."

He turned, and in a whirl of silver, the runic door disappeared. Moving away from the wall, Abarōz blinked in Mihr's natural light.

She heard her name shouted before Shāhpuhr ran up.

"Thank Tengri," he cried, "that Şahmeran let you go!"

Abarōz smiled.

"She's good, remember? She wouldn't keep me against my will." Still, recalling the queen's final words, she felt a shadow descend.

"What happened?" Shāhpuhr asked.

"I'll tell you as we walk."

They started across the sands, creeping past the two cities' gates. When they were able to stand, she related Şahmeran's words . . . all except the last.

"Well, that's a relief," he said, "my mother will be pleased." He looked down. "No thanks to me."

Abarōz brushed his arm.

"That wasn't your fault. I think that Şahmeran doesn't wish to be seen."

"In any case, this mission's success is yours. I can claim no part of it."

"Nonsense!" Abarōz cried. "Do you see me, alone, finding my way in the desert?"

"Hmm. On second thought . . ."

Their mood remained light even though Mihr was now searing. Once they reached the edge of Razūr, Abarōz savored the coolness.

Once they burst into the clearing, they sprinted toward Bükrek. Rastag—who never seemed far these days—jogged over to join them. Abarōz happily burbled out the snake queen's offer.

"She was going to send a Maran, but I suppose we'll do."

"And more," smiled Bükrek. "This is very good news indeed. The Maran are no ordinary snakes—they are possessed of high intelligence. When the time comes, I know they will serve us well."

"Daughter," her father greeted her, holding her closer than last time. "Do you think you could stay in one place? For perhaps more than a day?"

"I'll try," Abarōz blushed, kissing his grizzly cheek. "For now, I suggest we eat. I'm starved from all that walking!"

Shāhpuhr snorted at the shortness of their journey. But he unveiled more bread and even an urn filled with wine!

"My son," Rastag asked, taking a seat beside them on the grass, "how did you procure this?"

Shāhpuhr winked.

"That I cannot reveal. Let's just say that Kavad bore more than mere gold."

The three of them laughed, their thick, crusty bread making the wine taste better.

"Careful, Daughter," warned Rastag, pointing in jest to the urn. "You must not overindulge. The S̃āh has so decreed."

Abarōz stuck out her tongue, expressing her view of the S̃āh. Shāhpuhr did likewise before taking a hearty swig. Abarōz leaned back onto sweet-smelling grass. How charmed this was, to be with the two she loved best in the world, no urgent task looming. Of course, she thought of one, and she rose with a sigh.

"Excuse me," she said, "I need to talk to Bükrek."

Shāhpuhr looked surprised, but made no attempt to stop her.

"Abarōz," said the green dragon from spot by the edge of the clearing. "Is all well?"

"For–for the most part. It's just that . . ."

She paused, trying to settle her mind.

"Please," Bükrek said, her yellow eyes kind. "I will never betray your trust."

"I know that."

It all came burbling out: Şahmeran's last haunting words.

"I see." Bükrek gathered her coils. "The snake queen knows her own end. I promise that when the time comes, I will tell you all."

Abarōz felt a bit hurt: Did Bükrek not trust *her?* She decided to switch tactics.

"Can you tell me this then," she asked. "What is next for our side?"

"Ah," said Bükrek, "That I can relate gladly. We wait until Sangal's ebrens have returned from Abaxtar. Determine the threat of his new allies. If they are strong, he is likely to strike again."

"But where?"

"He failed to take Dardan, which might drive a second attempt. We must keep our eyes on the city."

Abarōz nodded, going back to Shāhpuhr. Her father had wandered off to join a group of Aswār.

"Well?" Shāhpuhr asked, guzzling down the last of the wine.

"Two questions asked and one answered."

She related his mother's plan.

"Sounds practical," he said. "Why does that remind me of you?"

"Stop," she insisted as he rose to tickle her neck. "Not when I'm wearing plate."

"Yes, Nārig."

"Don't you dare call me that! I am not a lady and I don't have a house."

"I disagree with the first and to the last I say, 'Soon.'"

Abarōz turned away, blushing.

"Tengri willing," she said. "For now, we must think of nothing but war."

"Nothing?" he asked playfully, helping her out of her breastplate.

"Perhaps an occasional something. But that is all."

The Two Cities

Abarōz and Shāhpuhr spent the next two days training. They practiced stabbing, lance-throwing, and more until Abarōz lost sensation in her limbs. Bükrek too was preparing by planting Archura before Sangal's lair. In his form as a blade of grass, he made a formidable spy.

Bükrek did not tell them everything since Abarōz found her whispering to a dragon. After that, the purple ebren flew off. Where was he going? Was he the messenger to be sent to the Erbörü? The green dragon kept her own counsel, but Abarōz's curiosity flared even while she was training.

"Shāhpuhr?" Abarōz asked after one ferocious combat. "Do you think our next battle . . . will be our last?"

"Why do you ask?"

"I saw your mother dispatch an ebren north."

"Ah." Shāhpuhr removed his helmet, looking down thoughtfully. "You may well be right."

"Shāhpuhr." Abarōz didn't want to admit it, but if she couldn't tell him, then who? "I–I'm afraid."

"So am I," he said, touching her arm. "I imagine all warriors are."

"If they're not foolish."

Still, the fear of death took hold. She led him to the edge of the clearing, where they sat beneath a tree.

"Have you ever thought . . .?" she began.

"About what?"

"What happens next. After we die."

Shāhpuhr gave a shrug.

"Not really," he said. "As a boy of the forest, I hope to join the trees."

Abarōz nodded, thinking of Şahmeran.

"I'm not sure what I believe," she sighed. "Will my soul ascend to Tengri, or be condemned to fire?"

Shāhpuhr's eyes widened.

"Where does the fire come from?"

"The new god," said Abarōz, tearing off a handful of grass. "Either that, if you're good, you go to a place called Heaven."

"You are quite good," he said with a smile. "I'm sure this heaven awaits."

"And if it doesn't?"

"Then Tengri must accept you."

"But I'm afraid both gods will reject me."

Shāhpuhr looked puzzled.

"Why?"

"I haven't been a good Dardan. I've broken every rule. I abandoned my rightful place, escaped, and as far as a husband . . . no man will take me now. My mother is right: I am stained with shame."

Shāhpuhr gave a loud snort.

"Madness!" he cried. "When it is your time, the wind spirit will take you to rest at Tengri's side. All else is nonsense."

"I hope so," sighed Abarōz, lifting the grass to smell it. In that small bundle, there was dirt, and green, and life. "Otherwise, I am in trouble."

"I can assure you're not," he told her, reaching for her free hand. "Also, as for a husband . . . did I not mention I am at the head of the line?"

Abarōz sighed.

"A line of one."

"So much the better for me."

She wondered if he were serious.

"Really?" she asked softly.

"Of course! Who else in Gehān would have you?"

She spattered him with grass.

"Be careful what you promise. I just might hold you to it."

Shāhpuhr narrowed his eyes, glancing around the clearing. Convinced that no one was looking, he moved closer to place a soft kiss on her lips. When he pulled back, his eyes held a question which she was quick to answer: by raking her hands through his hair and delivering her own kiss.

"I am going to Hell," she moaned with a smile.

"Don't worry," said Shāhpuhr, "I will be right behind."

He proceeded to touch her all over: her face, her chin, her neck. Just as he moved lower, they heard a woody crash.

"What was that?" Abarōz asked, pushing against his chest.

"I—"

"Bükrek!" a voice called, *"I must speak to Bükrek!"*

Abarōz saw a tree wildly bouncing toward them. His branches were clasped together like worried hands. Archura.

"I take it," she said, "Sangal's flight has returned with friends."

"I fear so, but what manner of creatures are they?"

They both rose and ran toward Bükrek, where Archura was babbling.

"Unnatural!" he cried, "an insult to Tengri! *And* they are skilled archers!"

"Mother," asked Shāhpuhr, "who is the tree man referring to?"

Bükrek looked solemn.

"Yaryonds," she said. "They once roamed the land of the Hrōmāyīg but were thought to have died out."

"Except in Abaxtar," Abarōz groaned. "What are they?"

"Wild, untamed creatures, half-man and half-horse."

Abarōz closed her eyes, wishing to drift away.

"—used to answer to Chiron—" Bükrek was saying, "—but their new master is Sangal. What he offered them in return, I do not know, but they love to indulge in wine."

Abarōz opened her eyes. Great. These Yaryonds not only had hooves and teeth—and bows—but sounded debauched as well.

She watched Bükrek peer over their heads to the east, where Dardan and Šahr waited.

"Archura tells me," she said, "that they already gather outside the two cities. We must engage them at present, but save our true strength for night."

Abarōz raised a brow, looking to Shāhpuhr. His face told her that he too was puzzled. Still, Archura's report was alarming: the fate of two zands now depended on Aswārs of Ebrens.

"We must prepare to go," said Bükrek. "Tell all Aswārs to arm themselves, mount their dragons, and be ready to fly. Though I cannot fight, I will attend this battle."

Thanks to their recent training, Abarōz and Shāhpuhr still wore their plate. They trailed Bükrek down to the Rōd where she spoke in Dragon to the beasts lined up on both banks.

That's when it hit Abarōz: she no longer *had* an ebren!

Well, that could be remedied after the Aswārs mounted. Three dragons were riderless: a purple, a silver, and a grey. She chose the purple: hadn't Bükrek trusted his kind to wing off to Abaxter? With a nod, she strode to its side, then threw herself on its back.

"Is he trained?" she asked Shāhpuhr.

"Let me check." He threw a leg over Catanes before they traded roars. "Yes. He knows how to take a rider. And his name is Mihrab[1]."

"Thanks."

She flashed Shāhpuhr a tight grin as she bent to address her dragon.

"Well, Mihrab[2]," she said, "I would be appreciative if you don't let me fall."

The ebren shook his head violently, emitting two puffs of white smoke. Had he *understood* her? Though it was doubtful, she clung onto this hope.

Abarōz looked around. Their entire force was gathered. All was silent except for the river's eddy and the dull clash of plate. Every Aswār sat their ebren with pride, swords and lances in hand. There was an air of tension also cushioned by calm as if their task were expected. Abarōz nervously checked her weapons. Of course, they were flameproof, but would that be enough against wolf heads and men who were half-horse? Abarōz pursed her lips, yearning to fly but afraid. Her impasse—and her side's—was broken as Bükrek soared overhead.

"Let us begin!" she cried. "Aswārs, direct your ebrens to Dardan!"

Abarōz grabbed Mihrab's spike as he took off with power. She knew she'd made the right choice once they were up in the air: Mihrab was large, bigger than Az or Iotapa, with sturdy purple wings and a tail as sharp as a spear. He flew with such speed that they were soon in front: the second dot of their flight's "V." Too soon, Dardan came into sight, the city clearly in trouble. Two of Sangal's ebrens roared before the gate, their flames striking

1. https://www.behindthename.com/name/mihrab/submitted

2. https://www.behindthename.com/name/mihrab/submitted

the boulder like Shāhpuhr with his two rocks. *Thank Tengri!* Stone didn't burn, and the gate held fast. But, up in the sky, there was nothing but chaos.

Sangal's horde was everywhere; flaming, screaming, and roaring. Abarōz steered Mihrab to join Shāhpuhr when they were set on by two dragons—one with the temerity to *bite* Catanes' flank! The black dragon looked enraged as he twisted his coils and barraged his foe with fire. The assailant flipped upside down, thumping into the sand.

That left his friend to face Abarōz. As Mihrab soared, she hefted her gold lance, hurling it straight for the enemy's throat. Then, he too was falling, gray scales hanging down loosely before he crashed into rock.

"Good start!" Abarōz yelled, raising a fist to Shāhpuhr.

"Tengri is on our side!"

Abarōz nodded, though she had her doubts. Still, to whatever god favored them, she bowed her head in thanks. That's when she saw Šahr below, its peaked entrance surrounded by two sets of creatures: the wolf heads and the Yaryond. The vague thought crossed her mind that they were supposed to be foes, but now they worked together to fell that runic gate. The half-horses kicked at the stone while the wolf heads applied their sharp claws, but, so far, they were unsuccessful.

Good, she thought with a smile. *Perhaps Sangal needed help when it came to picking allies . . .*

Abarōz snapped back to the moment since the neighboring sky was thick with ebrens. Sangal's horde was stubborn, coming at them full-force, and her stomach sank as they lost Aswārs and ebrens. She watched flaming figures speed downward like so many falling stars. Still, she readied herself as three dragons headed toward her. At her side, Shāhpuhr battled two more.

"Come on, Mihrab!" she yelled, kicking his purple sides. He lunged in a burst of speed, permitting her to lean over and stab an enemy wing. She tried to ignore the shrieks as Mihrab outflew his two friends and soared back over Dardan.

What Abarōz saw below had worsened. Four dragons now clawed at the boulder which had split into quarters. The gate couldn't hold for long and the guards within would be scorched. She circled on Mihrab, wondering how she could help. But this was decided for her as the ebrens battered the stone, reworking it into shards. The Dardan gate was now open.

"Oh no," Abarōz whispered. The dragons who flew were too big to enter, but not so the wolf heads. They swarmed inside like a pestilence, and even from this distance, Abarōz thought she heard screaming. This was soon succeeded by the sight of Dardans, threadbare, stumbling for the first time out onto the Bērūn.

Now, Abarōz thought bitterly, *they would learn the truth about their enemy:* not an army of men, but dragons! Shrieks reached her ears as she saw citizens—many children or barely older—erupt into flame before rolling away in agony. Abarōz knew how it felt to be put to the fire. And, if she could help it, this torture stopped now.

"Shāhpuhr!" she called behind her. *"We have to go down!"*

Catanes was free, he and his rider watching as their two assailants winged north. Shāhpuhr nodded to Abarōz before directing his dragon straight down to the harried Dardans. Mihrab plummeted, leveling out his snout before it hit the sand.

"Help us!" one woman screamed as she frantically clutched her children. Mihrab knew what to do, sucking in his breath before aiming at three crawling ebrens. Their attention on the Dardans, they didn't see his flames coming until the air around them was scented by burning scales.

Abarōz raised a fist. Maybe these beasts would think twice before they unleashed their fire . . .

As Catanes and Mihrab gained height, she stared down at the pack of wolf heads. So *this* was why they were here: to rip and tear helpless humans as they poured out the gate. The Yaryonds had split their herd so that some remained outside while others thundered in. They joined forces to drive out the Dardans, then promptly shot them with arrows. Sangal had chosen these allies well.

Into the late afternoon, she and Shāhpuhr worked hard to try to protect their zand. They flew so hard and low, flames bouncing off their plate, that as Mihr angled west, Abarōz felt bone tired. Even Shāhpuhr looked weary, and Catanes, though experienced, still winced from his bite. As he and Mihrab swooped over two dragons targeting men on the ground, their combined stream of fire did damage to tails and claws. Like the others before them, they fled, while the Dardans looked up in gratitude.

"Aswārs!" called a voice and it seemed to come straight from Mihr. "Pull back! To the river. We must rest for tonight."

Abarōz recognized this order as coming straight from Bükrek. That didn't make her glad to comply.

"What?!" she asked Shāhpuhr with a glare. "We just abandon our zand?"

He gave a shrug of apology, but still turned Catanes west. As the others followed, Abarōz fought an inner battle. With every part of her being, she did not want to obey. She was the last to leave, her reward a few clumsy fireballs. *No more,* she thought. She couldn't linger alone. With a sigh, she steered Mihrab after their flight, the cries from below haunting.

As she flew over sand and then forest, Abarōz's mouth felt bitter, as if she'd just swallowed iron. Why had they bothered to fight only to abandon the cities? She couldn't understand it, and for the first time, she resented Bükrek.

She brought Mihrab down by the Rōd beside Catanes. Seeing Shāhpuhr's face, she could tell he was disappointed. But before they could talk, Bükrek flew down to her rock and addressed her flight.

"You may dismount," she said. Abarōz noticed were missing ten Aswārs and dragons—a useless sacrifice? "Do not go far," Bükrek continued, "for we must be ready for battle at the first sign of Māh."

Abarōz huffed, swinging to the ground along with Shāhpuhr.

"The moon!" she snorted, as if she believed it didn't exist. "What, in the new god's name, does Māh have to do with anything?!"

Shāhpuhr, wanting privacy, beckoned her toward the clearing.

"I can't say," he told her, his eyes filled with fear.

After all they'd been through, he picked *today* to be scared? Of what—her?

"Calm yourself," she said. "I swear not to strike you . . . either with sword or fists."

He still looked wary.

"I'm glad. Understand, Abarōz . . . my mother has told me much. But not why we came back, or return with moonlight."

Abarōz turned away. It was wrong, she knew, to take out her frustration on him.

"What do you say to some bread?" she asked, trying to restore peace.

"I would say yes. I'm starving."

He retrieved two flat cakes from his private reserve. Abarōz didn't realize how hungry she was until he spread them with berry jam.

"Shāhpuhr," she said as they sat on the grass. "I can't help thinking . . ."

"What?"

"Well, it seems that Bükrek plans a surprise for Sangal. But why would she surprise *us?*"

"As a planner of war," he sighed, "I rank below a tree."

"I'm not much better."

He touched her forearm.

"You must learn to trust my mother. She is wise in the ways of battle and would not lead us astray." Abarōz nodded, releasing some of her anger. "Always remember that while Sangal seeks to destroy, my mother is a healer."

She patted his hand. Trusting Bükrek in this would take a leap of faith, but she was prepared to jump. Letting doubt gnaw at her mind was the surest way to defeat.

Abarōz looked up. Mihr was at the end of her descent, lighting only the treetops. For the first time in her life, she dreaded the rise of Māh. It had always seemed so serene, but tonight promised something different. She shook out her limbs, trying to empty her mind as she followed Shāhpuhr to the Rōd.

The dragons waited in lines at the edge of each bank. Abarōz walked to her mount, Shāhpuhr doing the same. Bükrek had told them they must be ready to fly. What would they find at Dardan? Corpses scattered on sand? She expected no human survivors—either from there or Šahr.

Battle of the Moon

Twilight was here, that brief punctuation between the light and the dark. Soon, dusk would fall.

By the river, there was silence from man and beast. The dragons surely realized that for some, this was the end. As for the Axwaš, it would be a second death. Abarōz gritted her teeth, not wanting to fly straight into her first.

"We go," Bükrek commanded from her usual post. "May Tengri be with you. I do believe he is watching."

Abarōz pressed her heels gently into Mihrab's flanks. He spread his long purple wings, and, from the corner of her eye, she saw Catanes' black ones. Once they took off, flying steadily east, Abarōz tried not to think of the future. The sky was opaque, flecked only with stars and the crown of Māh. It hung like a marble plate, solid, streaming a silver light over the soaring ebrens.

The sand beneath them was shrouded—it might as well be a sea. For the second time this day, Abarōz flew behind Bükrek, Shāhpuhr at her side.

Once they reached the Dardan gate, Abarōz steered Mihrab down. Her grisly prediction had come only partly true: yes, there were corpses, of ebrens, wolf heads, and Yaryond, but not as many as she'd feared from her zand. She could only assume they were sheltering in the zarr, the stairways leading to it proving too steep for beasts. In any case, they were safe.

At the first glimpse of their flight, Sangal's horde rose to meet them from the desert floor. As she and Shāhpuhr staved off several ebrens, Abarōz felt as if she'd never left. And what was all this nonsense about the power of moonlight? As far as she could tell, it helped them no more than Mihr's.

That's when a new herd of Yaryond came crashing toward the gate. Abarōz looked down in contempt as she saw them breach the cracked boulder. A lot of good that would do considering all those stairs! But alarm overtook her as she spotted a pack of wolf heads. What did *they* intend to do? Slither down to the zarr?

Abarōz saw Bükrek wing toward Dardan's mountain. She supposed the dragon would perch on top to watch. Again, Bükrek could not help. But when would Māh—or Şahmeran—provide them with their aid?

Her answer came within minutes. Bükrek unspooled her green wings, calling out a resounding, "NOW!" Loping over the sand came a pack of creatures which put the others to shame. Abarōz turned to Shāhpuhr but found she could not speak.

"Our journey to Abaxtar was not in vain!" he crowed.

"You mean—?"

"Those are the Erbörü. When Māh is full, they turn into *that*."

"Sweet Tengri."

Abarōz looked upon beasts three times the size of a man. Though they walked on two legs, their forms were heavy with fur, their faces distinct: they were those of bloodthirsty wolves.

They let loose a mournful howl which seemed to reach Māh herself. Moving toward the Yaryond, they set upon them in a tight pack, splitting their two halves apart. The wolf heads, cowed by these eerie creatures, set off at a slither faster than any serpent's. Still, they could not evade the Erbörü who loped after them swiftly, tearing them to pieces.

Even though they were the enemy, it was still hard to watch.

Sangal's horde didn't sit idle as they attacked the Erbörü from the air and the ground. Spitting flames from both mouth and tail, they attempted to halt the pack, but might as well have worked to fell that mountain. The wolf men, unafraid, treated the fire as a minor inconvenience. When some of their number fell, they didn't break stride as they loped over the bodies. To Abarōz, they seemed spectral, beasts not of this world but on it. After she and Shāhpuhr chased several airborne dragons, bringing them down one by one, Abarōz took a quick look at to the ground. She cried out, spotting new creatures: Marans flashing white under Māh, so many it seemed like the sand itself crawled.

"She kept her promise!" Abarōz cried, raising a fist as Mihrab rained fire.

"Of course," said Shāhpuhr. "Nature can never be stopped!"

Abarōz felt good—even great—as the snakes below inspired her. Her swords thrusts had extra force, her rider's seat never wavered, and her calm in the face of the horde was completely unexpected. She fought with the vigor of one who expected to win, and saw that Shāhpuhr did the same. All around them, Aswārs on their ebrens seemed energized, and she suspected it wouldn't be long before they could all go home.

But . . . she hadn't reckoned on the master. Something dark stirred the air, obscuring from her vision first Māh and then Dardan.

"Bükrek!" Sangal roared and the desert went silent. Even the wolf men looked up from their trails of blood.

"Sangal," Bükrek answered from her mountain perch. Her form was as still as a tree planted atop the crest. "To what do we owe your presence?"

"You know well enough." The red dragon arced his way toward her. "It is time again, once again. To renew our nine-year war."

Bükrek thrust out her wings.

"Perhaps you forget the result. Do you wish for a second defeat?"

As he winged upward, Sangal let out a deep rumble.

"Oh no. This time, I will prevail." He pointed a claw at Dardan. "And finish what I began."

"All for gold?" asked Bükrek.

"No. I mean to rule Gehān."

"Woe then to its creatures."

"Beginning with *you.*"

Abarōz watched as Sangal achieved a speed she had never thought possible. His wings flapped as rapidly as an insect's until he was over Bükrek, extending his neck to flame. But the green dragon evaded him by spiraling into the air.

Sangal set after her, the dragons now circling each other against the backdrop of Māh. Abarōz felt a growing despair: Could Bükrek, restorer of Gehān, defeat the dragon of chaos—again?

Light and Chaos

Sangal, of course, struck first, dropping like an arrow while blasting Bükrek with fire. Abarōz watched her plunge in one swift motion to barely avoid disaster. Then, it was Bükrek's turn: She bunched up her coils and hurtled at her foe's tail. He had no time to react as she struck him with her spiked one, drawing blood from one back claw. Sangal roared, retracting the claw, then soared to land on top of her. Bükrek writhed, attempting to free herself, finally breaking free with a double burst of flames. Sangal, far swifter than an Erbörü and more cunning than his wolf heads, twisted away from sure death while giving his own return blast.

From Mihrab's back, Abarōz sucked in her breath. She wondered how Shāhpuhr felt as he sat stiffly on Catanes. Knowing him, he'd want to rush in and help, but this fight, like the previous one, was for these two combatants alone.

Sangal gave a blood-chilling screech which seemed to echo through Abarōz. Then, for reasons of his own, he wheeled and darted east. Bükrek streaked off in pursuit, trailed by her son and Abarōz, though they could not keep up. But shortly into their flight, their ebrens had no need to flap, able to coast on winds stirred by the dragons before them. Abarōz grasped Mihrab's spike, too tense even to speak. She felt air batter her cheeks as they rode out the current like creatures of the sea.

Suddenly, Sangal halted, causing Bükrek to do the same. Then he did something strange: He plunged into a hole roiling with bright orange liquid.

His lake of fire.

This didn't stop Bükrek, who soared down like a rootless tree before being swallowed by flame. Abarōz felt her throat tighten. What, she wondered, was happening beneath that violent surface? She knew the lake was Sangal's real home, giving him a decided advantage.

Abarōz held her breath as the surface told her nothing, revealing no hint of the struggle below. Could Bükrek withstand fire? She snuck a look at Shāhpuhr who sat still as a gold idol. If Abarōz didn't do *something,* she thought she would go mad. She decided to count. One . . . molten liquid splashing; Two . . . Mihrab trembling beneath her; Three . . . stopping herself from plunging in; and Four, Bükrek rising from the depths, orange falling from her body until she was once again green!

"Di-did she win?" Abarōz asked.

Shāhpuhr spoke as if from a daze.

"I–I don't know. She never told me—"

He stopped as Sangal burst from his lake, the orange dripping from him scales accentuating the red.

"Oh no," Abarōz whispered.

She tried not to shiver as the two dragons clashed anew.

This time, they each formed half of a circle which hung high in the air. Nose-to-nose and tail-to-tail, they drifted over the lake. Abarōz felt as if she were watching something elemental: Good versus evil . . . chaos versus the light.

Then, the circle was broken as the two foes came apart. Sangal climbed above Bükrek, screeching down in a red fireball. Bükrek stayed eerily still, only her wings flapping. As Sangal bore down, she simply raised her head, closed her eyes, and emitted a flame. But this one was different: it was bright yellow with a blue streak down the center. As it struck Sangal, it grew to engulf him, trapping him inside a bubble which floated down to the lake.

Abarōz saw the trapped dragon careening over its surface before fiery waves took him. Then, the lake stilled, as calm as the waters of the Rōd. Chaos versus Light. And Light had won again.

An Unholy Bargain

Bükrek, now alone, wheeled over to her son and Abarōz. She looked tired but triumphant, Māh reflected in her yellow eyes. With a jerk of her head, she bid the two of them to follow. Their dragons obeyed, heading west back to Dardan.

What Abarōz saw by the gate startled her. Lit by hand-held torches, the sand revealed not one of Sangal's horde: and, above, they did not clutter the sky. They must have sensed the defeat of their master, left to pout in his lake for (Abarōz hoped) a thousand more years. The Dardans below could move freely as they tended to their wounded. The Erbörü feasted on wolf heads, joined by Marans who had clearly done their work by blocking the Dardan entrance.

Abarōz felt relief as she steered Mihrab to a landing. It seemed odd to get off: to not be an Aswār of Ebrens. Shāhpuhr dismounted as well to stand among the Dardans. Abarōz saw with happiness that they mingled with people from Šahr. *Finally.* That had taken millennia.

Once Bükrek slithered over, she thanked all their allies. The Marans went sliding off, but the Erbörü remained. To Abarōz's surprise, one turned into the human Berislav! She ran over to meet him.

"Thank you so much," she said. "You did indeed keep your word."

He smiled.

"Hard to believe, but we Erbörü always do."

"Where will you go now? Not to Abaxtar, surely."

He shuddered.

"We are through with the north. The great dragon Bükrek has promised us land in the south."

"I'm so glad. You know . . . you're not so bad after all."

"Tell that," he said, "to the Yaronds we ate for supper."

He threw back a wink before rejoining his pack.

With all the excitement—the many strange creatures; the battles; the fall of Sangal himself—Abarōz had been riding a ceaseless wave of energy. But now that it was over, she collapsed like the Dardan gate.

"Here," Shāhpuhr called, plopping down on the sand.

Abarōz gladly did the same.

"It seems so strange we won," she said, lying back in the moonlight. "I mean, I *hoped* we would, but it seemed like a silly girl's dream."

"Well," said Shāhpuhr, "that silly girl's quest for freedom has led to this." He swept a hand over the no-longer-separate zands. "You saved two cities. You, nearly as much as my mother, helped bring Sangal down." Abarōz flushed, glad that those candles weren't close. "Also," he said, "I think you just gained a husband."

Fatigue forgotten, Abarōz sprang up.

"Really?" she asked. "Even though I'm a terrible Dardan?"

"Me too." Shāhpuhr rose to stand beside her. "We'll have to live in the forest."

"I don't know," said Abarōz, "after we saved the city, maybe they'll let us stay."

"Maybe."

They both shook off their helmets to enjoy the night air.

"Dardan is free," Abarōz whispered. "No more tyranny . . ."

They turned to look at each other.

"The Šāh!" they both cried.

"Where is my god of a father?" Shāhpuhr hissed.

Walking toward the shattered gate, he and Abarōz found Al-razi in a circle of minions and family. Naturally, piles of gold glinted at his side.

"It figures," Abarōz mumbled. "Selfish people seldom die."

Shāhpuhr peered closely at his father.

"It seems," he said, "the little man's health is poor."

Noticing the two of them, a vizier Abarōz knew as Husrav broke away from his master.

"Nice work," he growled at Abarōz. "The city is in ruins, gold scattered, and our holy Šāh has been bitten by a wolf man."

Abarōz shuddered. Even though she loathed Al-razi, this was a cruel fate.

"You must heal him," Husrav choked.

"What?"

"You are the only one. *Someone* from the cities summoned Şahmeran's snakes. That means this person knows where she dwells."

"And?" Abarōz asked, trying to keep her face blank.

"And," cried Husrav, "it had to be you! Who else would break our rules? Lead us to the Şahmeran, and she in turn heals the Šāh. See? Simple."

Abarōz let out a snort. Why would *she* help this man, the one who killed her father and tried to burn her alive?

"You are mistaken," she finally told Husrav. "Who or what is this Şahmeran? Have all the Šāh's viziers taken leave of their senses?"

Husrav stomped closer, his face nearly pressed against hers.

"Do not lie to me, girl. No one else would attempt this foolishness."

Abarōz rolled her eyes . . . she hoped convincingly.

"I have a city to mend, and you are wasting my time."

"Is that so?"

Husrav turned to the Šāh's circle, motioning forward four guards.

Abarōz huffed: Did he really think he could seize her when she was surrounded by dragons? But her scorn turned to fear when she saw what the guards were dragging: the bound form of her father!

"Oh no," she breathed as Shāhpuhr unsheathed his sword.

"Put that away, boy," growled Husrav. "Or these men test their pikes on your whore's precious Rastag."

Shāhpuhr put up a hand, relinquishing his weapons. Abarōz's eyes grew moist, but she blinked back the tears. In front of these men, she would show no sign of weakness.

"Let him go," she said, meeting her father's gaze. "You can take me."

"Excellent!" Husrav cried, "I knew you could be persuaded." He gave his guards the order to exchange prisoners.

The men moved quickly, cutting away Rastag's bonds.

"Please," he begged. "I'll give you whatever you want!"

"And what do you have, Axwaš? From nothing comes nothing. If you were strong, you wouldn't have let yourself be taken."

"Four against one," said Rastag. "Not exactly fair odds."

"We do not rule by fairness."

"That is evident," said Abarōz, her hands now bound before her. Her sword and lance had become the Šāh's property.

Shāhpuhr confronted Husrav.

"Since you are cruel," he said, "you should take me as well. How do you know that *I* didn't see Şahmeran too?"

Abarōz could have sworn she saw Husrav's mind at work.

"Agreed," he said finally. "Bind the boy as well."

After this was done, he signaled his guards to march back to the Šāh. With a bow, Husrav addressed him.

"I have the girl, my god king, and the boy for good measure. But before they can heal you, they must be put to the ordeal."

Abarōz boldly stared at the man she'd despised for so long. He looked weak, pale, and held a cloth streaked with blood to one side of his throat. *Bitten.* What did it mean? Would he die or turn into a wolf man?

"We don't have much time," growled Husrav. "Our god's health worsens. Follow me."

He stepped over shards of the boulder, trailed by his party of six. Once they entered Dardan, Abarōz saw its state: Hamwar One was a shambles, its rope ladder cut, its livestock pens broken, its few surviving animals lowing and baaing sadly.

"To the first aqueduct," Husrav ordered.

Abarōz stiffened between two guards. What did this near-empty pool have to do with healing? What were they expecting: for her to make water flow?

She and Shāhpuhr were marched to a small door opposite the pens. Once Husrav unlocked it, his men pushed their captives through, Abarōz shook in the suddenly chill air. The reason lay before her: an enormous basin carved from rock, still bearing its high waterline to taunt them with what had been. Right now, the level was so low it couldn't be seen from the top.

How had her zand endured this? Abarōz wondered. Choking as their throats dried out while the Šāh enjoyed his fountain . . .

"Throw them in," Husrav ordered, causing Abarōz's head to jerk.

"Wha—?"

She wasn't able to finish as her guards grabbed her arms, the others seizing Shāhpuhr's. Before she knew what had happened, she was floating toward the yawning basin.

"Ow!" she yelled as her back struck rock. She must have fallen thirty feet, but her plate had saved her again. She looked at Shāhpuhr, his elbows and knees bleeding. What was this all about?

Abarōz dragged herself up to stand, her back drenched from the shallow water. She crossed her arms, glaring up at Husrav.

"And this accomplishes what? If we drown, the Š̄āh is healed?"

Even from this distance, she saw him smirk.

"Not familiar with the legend?" he asked. "You are about to learn."

Shāhpuhr got up to stand beside her.

"This is completely—" she started before spreading pain in her spine struck like a dragon's fire. She groaned and fell to her knees as her breastplate expanded. *"No!"* she cried. Silver dots blocked her vision. She heard her breastplate crack, its pieces now floating. But as Abarōz put her hands to her mouth, Shāhpuhr's opened in horror. He splashed back with a gasp.

"What is it?" she asked, the fire no longer licking at her. Shāhpuhr only stared. Abarōz took one arm, bent it behind her, and carefully felt her back. What her fingers met was not plate; not fabric or flesh: her touch told her there were *scales* running the length of her spine. *"What have you done to me?"* she shouted, too angry even to cry.

"Nothing," Husrav called down, motioning for the guards to take seize heavy ropes. These they affixed to an iron ring and then dropped to the prisoners. Stepping into knotted loops, Abarōz and Shāhpuhr tightened them before being hauled back up.

Abarōz glowered at Husrav, clutching the front of her breastplate close. She wanted to strike his grey head.

"I did nothing," he said again, crossing his pale arms. "It was *you*—you who did this to yourself."

Abarōz rolled her eyes.

"What nonsense is this?" she growled. "Tell me the truth!"

"Of course. According to legend, all who view the Şahmeran—" he laughed, "and S̄ah knows there haven't been many—are marked in a special way. When cast into pure water, snake scales appear on their back."

Abarōz didn't want to believe this. After all, she'd bathed often enough in the Rōd . . . but perhaps it wasn't as pure as water meant for drinking.

"So." She tried to calm her mind. "Now you know I am the one. And I suppose you wish me to lead you to Şahmeran's cave."

"Precisely," said Husrav. "Though you're a blasphemer and a whore, you certainly aren't stupid." He gave her a cold smile. "Shall we?"

The Šāh and the Şahmeran

After the six of them marched out the gate, Husrav returned to the Šāh, prostrating himself on the sand. He returned with his master, who looked much worse than before, his bloody throat now joined by knuckles tufted with fur. The four guards lifted him up, leaving Husrav to watch his prisoners.

Damn him, Abarōz thought, feeling the tip of the vizier's sword poking her scaled back. Of course, he'd still be groveling even when his side lost. What was he hoping to earn? More dēnārs? The Šāh's favor? Or did he truly believe that the man was a living god?

Whatever his motive, Abarōz felt like a traitor as she led him, the Šāh, and his men to the rear wall of Šahr. The sky had lightened and she supposed it was close to dawn. Clenching her teeth, Abarōz tried to think of a way for her not to betray Şahmeran. *We shall meet again,* the snake queen had said . . . *the circumstances will not be pleasant.* Had the snake queen actually foretold this?

With a sigh, Abarōz found herself pushed against the rock's carved runes until she stood at the spot where the door had appeared.

"How do we—?" she asked Shāhpuhr, but the silver rain descended and the dots became one, forming those floating runes. Once the door etched itself into rock, Husrav was more than happy to shove everyone inside.

Abarōz didn't look at the garden burdened as she was by guilt. Though the others gasped and exclaimed, she secretly wished for the scales to cover all of her. She was too ashamed to meet Şahmeran and be recognized for what she was. *Traitor.*

The others continued to wonder at this perfect garden. They were so engrossed they didn't notice the Tree of Life and its guardian dragon. But Abarōz cried out when she saw the queen on her throne.

"I'm sorry!" Abarōz sobbed. "They have my father! I'm here against my will."

Surprisingly, Şahmeran gave her two warm smiles.

"Do not grieve," she said. "All was meant to be."

Abarōz wanted to argue: to alter the spinning of time. But she knew she could not.

"Can we move on to healing?" asked Husrav, nodding to the increasingly fur-covered S̄āh. "Right now, he won't last, *but* if he lives, he'll make me his head vizier."

So that was it.

"Of course," Şahmeran agreed. "Since you have exposed my friend, you clearly know my entire legend."

"Not fully," said Husrav, backing away from her snakehead.

"You must kill me," Şahmeran said calmly, "then blanch my body in a bowl made wholly from soil. Whoever tears off flesh from my tail and consumes it will be healed and gain all my wisdom. But . . . whoever eats from my head will die immediately and in great pain."

"Why, this is all very simple!" cried Husrav. "I'll even do the deed myself."

Abarōz wished she could take Shāhpuhr's hand. She could hardly see through tears as Şahmeran welcomed death: her coils relaxed, her two faces tranquil, her pairs of eyes closed as if she waited for peace.

Abarōz shut her eyes too as Husrav raised his sword. She heard something roll to the ground before he struck again, and what rolled now were pieces. From the snake-covered floor, there came a rising hiss.

"Bring me soil!" Husrav ordered, followed by the scamper of boots. When the guard returned, Abarōz still refused to look. "Have the girl form the bowl!" Husrav barked, shaking Abarōz roughly until she opened her eyes. Shāhpuhr gave her a pitying look as bile rose in her throat: On the floor was the gracious queen, hacked into sections, her two heads severed. Abarōz turned and was sick, but Husrav had no patience. *"Get on with it!"* he shouted, slashing off her bonds.

Abarōz knelt, tears still flowing as she touched the soil, so rich it could nurture crops. Using both hands, she molded a bowl of mud, taking comfort from its rough texture. She worked the round shape to be worthy of her friend—a slice of the nature she'd loved. Abarōz smoothed the edges, making them even, as Shāhpuhr nodded his approval. When she was done, she rose, wiping the dirt from her hands.

"There," she whispered as Shāhpuhr's shoulder touched hers.

"Now for our feast!" cried Husrav. "You dogs, find me some branches. And make sure they're dry!"

Again, a guard ran to the garden, coming back with a handful sticks. Husrav crouched, laying them out close to his victim. From his cloak, he removed a rock and flint, creating a spark which he touched to the wood. Abarōz felt the heat as her bowl was placed over the fire. Though it should have melted, somehow it held its shape. Husrav poured in some water, causing a low hiss.

"Now," he said, "we wait for the boil."

As they gathered around the fire, Abarōz thought of the past. She remembered the living Şahmeran, majestic on her white throne as she ruled her Marans. And then there was her kindness as she helped them twice against Sangal. What would nature do now without a queen to rule it? Would temblors shake Gehān, bringing down mountains? Would all the rivers run dry? Abarōz—and the world—had no idea since there'd always been a Şahmeran.

"It's ready," Husrav said, and, as she looked down, Abarōz saw water leaping. Her feeling of sickness returned. "Both of you," Husrav told her and the Šāh, "will feast at the same time. Our god, of course, will partake of the head; while the girl will eat the tail."

"NO!" Shāhpuhr cried, straining against his ties. "Put me in her place!"

"Noble as always, Axwaš, but this task belongs to her. She's a rebel and a heretic who has plagued us for far too long. Her death will please Al-razi."

Abarōz glanced over. The Šāh didn't look very pleased since his arms were covered with fur.

"Let's get to it!" Husrav yelled, picking up pieces of Şahmeran and hurling them into the bowl.

Abarōz felt such a wash of disgust that she, like Şahmeran, almost welcomed death. But what did it matter now? Welcome or not, she would die and lose all those she cared for: her father, Bükrek, but most of all, Shāhpuhr. She wanted to let him know that she loved him, but refused to say the words before the S̄āh and his brutes.

Instead, her eyes met Shāhpuhr's and she gave him a look which she hoped conveyed all her feelings: that he was precious to her; that without him, she would already be dead; that he should, if possible, work to bring down the S̄āh.

"Looks quite tender," Husrav said, fishing two pieces out of the bowl. He offered the first to the S̄āh. "My revered god," he said, bringing a part of the woman's head up to his ruler's mouth. "And you." He thrust the snakehead at Abarōz. She was so numb it wasn't until she looked down that she noticed her palms were burning. Husrav lifted his sword in a command to for her to bite down as the S̄āh did the same.

Abarōz waited: for instant death; for pain. At least she wouldn't suffer long. Then she heard a guttural noise and whipped round to face the S̄āh. He was in worse shape than ever, his face flushed to the color of Sangal, his furry hands clutching his throat. Abarōz had to step back as his portly form pitched forward, unmoving on the floor, dead.

She could only stare for a moment before feeling her own effects. At first, she was tranquil, floating out of the garden and into the evening air. She felt the power of nature, both soft and harsh, as it filled her mind, offering secret knowledge older than the trees. When she drifted back, she was felt at one with the garden; the essence of Shāhpuhr; and the snakes at her feet.

Without knowing how, she gave them a silent signal, causing those by the throne to slither. They coiled up Husrav's legs, reaching his torso, until they covered his arms and head. His yell was muffled as he fell beside his master.

"You," Abarōz faced the guards with an air of authority. "Get out while you can."

They ran back through the garden, and, for assurance, were trailed by hissing Marans.

That left just her and Shāhpuhr. Abarōz quickly freed him using Husrav's sword. He seemed to emerge from a fog as he looked around blinked.

"Wh-what happened?" he asked, staring down at the two bodies.

"I will tell you," said Abarōz, "but not now."

He shook off the last of his shock before taking her in his arms. And, to both their amazement, his fingers grazed human skin!

"You feel different," Shāhpuhr said.

"I don't have scales."

"Not that. You seem stronger. Calmer."

He put his lips to hers and kept them there. They just held each other and kissed until Abarōz caught some movement—by the Tree of Life.

"I think," she said, stepping back, "we are going to have a guest."

Shāhpuhr raised a brow, then stiffened as Manuchehr dropped from the Tree. Though the Peril frowned at her lack of a breastplate, he seemed happy to see her.

"Ah," he said, coming close, and with a snap, snuffed out the fire. "So the legend is true. I will miss Şahmeran, but . . ." he looked over and winked at Abarōz, "I know her throne is safe."

Shāhpuhr didn't move as his eyes met hers.

"Whatever you are," he said, "whatever you want, I will always be with you."

Abarōz nodded, wiping away new tears. She would really have to control that—being a queen and all.

"Manuchehr," she said to the Peril, "I have so much to do. I trust that you will help me as much as you can."

He bowed.

"Paristan is proud to serve you."

Abarōz felt lightheaded as she thought of the tasks awaiting her: the restoration of Dardan; the source of its water; appointing someone to rule who was *nothing* like S̃āh. She wanted to decide which god she would follow: Tengri, Jesus, or perhaps a bit of both. *And* she had to ensure the Axwaš were welcomed back . . . but not Kavad or Adrina.

More than anything, she wanted Shāhpuhr as her husband and king. They would work together until Dardan and Šahr soared upward, free to enjoy Mihr's light and the trees of Razūr.

Yes, she thought, *there is so much to do, but for now I can only give thanks.* To Şahmeran, who passed on her legacy, and shown Abarōz that sometimes, a tail can be a head.

BOOKS BY AMY WOLF

The Misses Brontës' Establishment

The Cavernis Trilogy

Book 1: A School for Dragons

Book 2: A War for Dragons

Book 3: A Hero for Dragons // Dragons vs. Djinn

The Honest Thieves Series

Book I: A Woman of the Road

Book 2: A Woman of the Road and Sea

The Mythos Series

The Twelve Labors of Nick

The Further Labors of Nick

The Starry Labors of Nick

Upcoming:

The Spinners of Time – Book 2

ABOUT THE AUTHOR

Amy Wolf is currently working on a new series of dragon books.

She is an Amazon Kindle Scout winner for her novel *The Misses Brontës' Establishment*. Her dragon fantasy books, THE CAVERNIS TRILOGY, were released by Red Empress Press.

Amy has published 38 short stories in the SF/Fantasy press, including *Realms of Fantasy* (2) and *Interzone* (U.K.). She is a graduate of the Clarion West Writer's program and has an honors English degree from the University of London.

She started her career working for the major Hollywood studios, including 20th Century Fox and Warner Bros., and was a Script Reader for MGM.

One of three natives out of 10 million, Amy was forced from L.A. and now lives in Seattle, where it rains. She has an imported English husband and a future small, barky dog.

To learn more: https://amy-wolf.com

Don't miss out!

Visit the website below and you can sign up to receive emails whenever AMY WOLF publishes a new book. There's no charge and no obligation.

https://books2read.com/r/B-A-FGFK-GIDXB

BOOKS 2 READ

Connecting independent readers to independent writers.

CPSIA information can be obtained
at www.ICGtesting.com
Printed in the USA
BVHW040255120422
634012BV00015B/186

9 798201 321154